# The Mysterious Treasure
## of
## Blackberry Cove

# The Mysterious Treasure
## of
## Blackberry Cove

Written and Illustrated by
Richard D. Burkett

Foreword by
Lt. Denson Walker
World War II Pilot Navigator

Trafford Publishing
Indianapolis, Indiana

Reference to the flooding of the Hart Dam quoted for accuracy from "The Flooding of '86". *Oceana Herald-Journal.* Hart and Shelby, Michigan. Based on stories written by Editor Lowell G. Rinker with narrative by News Editor Mark Christianson. (See story on page 92 in *The Mysterious Treasure of Blackberry Cove.*)

Character Qualities indexed in beginning of book and used in Appendix A as a resource in encouraging the character qualities developed in this book are from the following:
Copyright© 2004 by Steve D. Spacek. All Rights Reserved.
Used With Permission
229 Gerloff Road, Schwenksville, PA 19473
Phone: (610) 287-4250 – Help Ministries

Special WWII Pearl Harbor navy photo credit: Photograph courtesy of Naval History and Heritage Command. Photo # NH94378. Photo of sinking of Battleships West Virginia and Tennessee during Japanese bombing of Pearl Harbor in World War II.

Author photo credit:  Photo by Herb Meldahl

Cover graphic illustration and design by Jim Jacoby

Order this book online at www.trafford.com
or email orders@trafford.com

Most Trafford titles are also available at major online book retailers.

Printed in the United States of America.

ISBN: 978-1-4269-3236-6 (sc)
ISBN: 978-1-4269-3237-3 (hc)

Library of Congress Control Number: 2010906678

*Trafford rev. 01/29/2011*

 www.trafford.com

**North America & international**
toll-free: 1 888 232 4444 (USA & Canada)
phone: 250 383 6864 ♦ fax: 812 355 4082

This book is dedicated to

my very special granddaughter

and

"Readergirl"

Maggie Elizabeth

in honor of her

10th birthday

May 15, 2010

# Foreword

I was born in 1923 and have seen many things in these 86 years. I witnessed the rise of the automobile and the telephone. The Model T Ford was invented in 1908, just 15 years before my birth. Although some public buildings in my home state of Texas had air conditioning, most homes—including mine—didn't have air conditioning until 1948-49. I lived through the Great Depression of the 1930's. I had the privilege to be Sales Manager of WFAA Radio in Dallas and was at work when President John F. Kennedy was tragically shot downtown Dallas in 1963.

I was born just after the end of the First World War. We were told that war would be the last world war. It wasn't. I know that personally. The bombing of Pearl Harbor on December 7, 1941 was a life-changing event for me. I was 18 years old and playing football when we were told about Pearl Harbor. I volunteered the next week and joined the U.S. Army Air Corps. After going to pilot, navigation and bombardier schools, I ended up based in England. My life in the military lasted three years and seven months. During that period I flew 55 bombing missions in B-24's and B-17's.

I would like to add that we have a better educated America due to the GI Bill of Rights which gave our veterans a chance for a college education. Many of us who became students are among today's most productive citizens.

Denson F. Walker
Plano, Texas
November 2009

Author's note: Referring to the infamous day when Pearl Harbor was attacked by the Japanese, Tom Brokaw wrote, "When America heard the stunning news that Sunday afternoon on the radio, it electrified the nation and changed the lives of all who heard it. Marriages were postponed or accelerated. College was deferred. Plans of any kind were calibrated against the quickening pace of the march to war."[1] Denson Walker was one of those brave men who opted to defend his country rather than pursue immediate personal goals. He is not only a hero of mine but is also my daughter-in-law's (Lacey's) grandfather, who helped her greatly in her formative years. His life also embodies two main themes of this book—the strong Christian character traits the young Maggie and Dillon are trying to learn and the real-life personification of someone willing to give his life for his country.

In the "Acknowledgments" to his book, Brokaw further penned, "To the men and women whose stories I did not get to—." [2] He didn't get to interview Denson Walker, so I had the pleasure through my son to do so. I wish to say, "Thank you," to Denson Walker (also a member of the "Greatest Generation") whom, along with his great wife, Patricia, sacrificially paved the way for all of us to enjoy the freedom and prosperity we do today. In fact, I write this note on December 7, 2009—"Pearl Harbor Day"—and can think of no better tribute to thank Lt. Walker than to encourage everyone to "Remember Pearl Harbor" ourselves. Remember 9-1-1, yes! But do not forget our brave soldiers who sacrificed their lives for the great liberties we enjoy today.

CREDIT:
[1] "The Greatest Generation." Tom Brokaw. New York: Random House, 1988. pp. 9-10.
[2] Tom Brokaw, Op. Cit. p. ix

# Preface for Parents and Teachers

*The Mysterious Treasure of Blackberry Cove* is the first in the series of the *Reader Whiz Kids'* adventures featuring the ever-curious Maggie and Dillon Burch of Elgin, Illinois. The reader will fall in love with this inquisitive sister and brother detective duo who constantly find themselves involved in as many mysteries as they read books of mystery.

Born into a family of readers, Maggie and Dillon began devouring books at an early age. Maggie, who appears in this heart-warming mystery as the loveable and well-spoken nine year-old, could be observed curled up with most any book since she was but three years of age. She has been affectionately called "Maggie the Readergirl" by her grandparents who often found their reddish-blond "Mags" reading a book from their collection of 1920-50's children's mystery novels. Truth be known, the subject of the book doesn't matter to Maggie. Nancy Drew books. The Bobbsey Twins series. A book on dolphins. The Little House on the Prairie series. Lamplighter books. The Chronicles of Narnia. Bible stories. Anne of Green Gables series. The Box Car Kids. A book of jokes and riddles. Fact or fiction. If it has printed words, it is read by the "Readergirl."

Dillon, the always curious, always brave younger brother of Maggie, didn't begin reading as early as his sister. Why should he have? He had a built-in reader with the ever-willing Maggie when his parents were otherwise occupied. Then, like a dandelion in spring, dormant all winter, his reading took off. The contented seven year-old decided listening to books wasn't good enough and he became a voracious reader like his mentor almost overnight!

Dad and Mom Burch had no choice—go broke buying books or get library cards at Elgin's great Gail Borden Public Library. To be sure, this hard-to-separate brother and sister love the nearby playground as any active children. They love Chicago's Brookfield Zoo more than most. Give Maggie a ballerina shoe or Dillon a drum set and the siblings reveal their love for drama. But, mention to them, "We are going to the library today," and the ever-bright eyes of this girl and boy get even brighter!

No one knows for sure if their natural love for adventure led them to their interest in reading mystery adventure stories or if their insatiable appetite for reading books of mystery led them to their eager involvement in real-life dramas. One thing for sure is that every day is a potential adventure for the *Reader Whiz Kids*!

*The Mysterious Treasure of Blackberry Cove* is a thrilling and heart-warming story that was birthed from a much-anticipated August vacation that the Burch family was able to take to their great-grandmother's in a rural Michigan town located among the beautiful fruit groves along Lake Michigan. Amidst the mysteries of the stranger in the barn, the medals in the orchard, an old friend facing losing home and dignity, you will discover the themes of love, hope, friendship and redemption weaved into unlikely characters whose lives are all touched by the kindness and bravery of the Burch family. Encourage your children to carve out some quality time. Let them find a secret location and then join Maggie and Dillon in solving a mystery that began decades before they were even born!

Some of you recall reading the Hardy Boys or Nancy Drew mystery books as kids. Some might recall reading the Horatio Alger series or The Meadow-Brook Girls from your grandparent's old library. I particularly loved the X Bar X Boys and the Mercer Boys. Like these and many other of the great children's mystery books of the first half of the 20th century, the *Reader Whiz Kids* books can be trusted to more than entertain your children. They are meant to build their character not to tear it down. They are written to increase their vocabulary not to dumb it down. The story lines are formulated to stimulate and inspire creative minds not to mute or darken them. In short, parents will find these children's mysteries educational and trustworthy. Oh—by the way—adult "children" will enjoy reading this mystery and discover a theme or two that is very relevant to them!

Readers will also find helpful definitions of character traits displayed through the activities and dialogues of Maggie and Dillon and other characters of the books in *Appendix A*. These are intended for an interactive discussion by conscientious parents and/or teachers as they ask their children what he or she learned from these fun-loving and daring adventurers from Illinois. Most of us who have lived a while have learned that real character is carved-out not just by major events but even more by the decisions and choices made through everyday events and challenges. Building young men and women of character in these formative years and to have the joy of seeing them walking in the truth as young adults takes loving effort. Character doesn't happen by chance. You will love the challenging questions. Even more—you will love your child's responses!

The art pencil illustrations are based upon real-life photographs and memories of the very setting described in the book. My wife, Darleen—Maggie's and Dillon's grandmother—spent her entire childhood and adolescence in this scenic area of asparagus fields and fruit orchards. The mystery takes place mostly in her actual home on Elm Street and on the adjacent fruited landscape in the quaint rural village of New Era, Michigan, not far from the beautiful sandy shores of Lake Michigan.

Last, but not least, I want to supremely thank my friend, Sue Colbert, for her detailed and careful editing of the manuscript. Her understanding of journalism standards of which I didn't have a clue, and the gracious way she presented them to me in her page-by-page, line-by-line editing saved much time and, no doubt, much money. I also smile as I realized that when I had given my "paper" to a few teachers for potential endorsements, I was reminded that teachers will do what teachers do best: grade them! This is one student who is glad they did. I am greatly indebted to the careful and wise editing of long-time teachers Joan Kenworthy (Minnesota), Connie Faulkner (Oklahoma), Dawn Gessner (Virginia), and Kathy Akey (Wisconsin).

Also, I'm not sure what I would have done without my daughter, Carrie. Her expertise with  making sure the graphic illustrations were formatted correctly and her artistic adjustments to make them consistent, saved me much time and grief and expense. I also very indebted and thankful to  Colonel John Gessner who kindly pointed out subtle but vital adjustments needed in the military history given in the book. Most of all, I want to thank my wife and life journey mate, Darleen, for her patience while I slowly scratched off the story that involved so much of her personal history while she fought her new battle with cancer this past long year. God, You are good.

Dick Burkett
February 2010

Wisconsin

Hart
Shelby
Mears
New Era
Whitehall
Muskegon
Grand Haven
Holland

Michigan

Elgin

Illinois

Indiana

RDB

"Mapquest shows the trip should take 4 ½ hours
and is 252 miles. Let's get going!"

# Contents

# Index of Character Traits

# Chapter One

## A Vacation without Books?

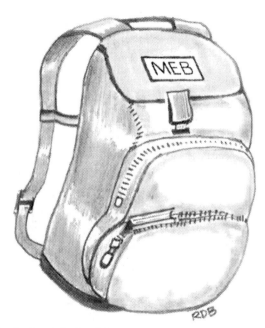

"Maggie, what's in this bag?" Maggie's mother was frustrated with the family's getting a later start for their vacation than she had hoped. Church let out right on time but they had bumped into friends from Rockford and saying, "Yes," to catching up at a restaurant set her game plan back considerably.

She was surprised when she quickly grabbed Maggie's book bag while heading out the front door to their already packed van. "It feels like a hundred pounds!"

"Mom, it's my book bag. What do you think is in it?" answered the excited nine year-old with a note of sarcasm.

"Watch your attitude, girl, or—."

"Sorry, Mom. I had a hard time just bringing only *these* books," apologized Maggie as she took the bag from her mother's over-loaded arms.

"You can't possibly read all these books—but never mind; if you can get the bag under your seat then you may bring them." Maggie Elizabeth Burch indeed loves to read! She had loved the written page since she cut her teeth on the classic "Golden Books" series as a three year-old. She had reasoned that a week's vacation at her great-grandmother's home in Michigan could be boring and she knew that the more than dozen books brought along might help put some adventure into it.

Pulling the side van door open with one arm, she saw her brother already belted in his seat. She rolled her eyes as only Maggie can and said to herself, " 'Course, with Dillon along, nothing will be boring!"

Watching his sister try to cram the bag under her seat, Dillon just couldn't resist, "What's in the bag, Mags, the entire library?"

"Dillon!"

Jesting with his only and older sister was always fair game for the fun-loving seven year-old son of Don and Carrie Burch, but then he quickly perceived this might not be a very good time for a wisecrack. "Don't worry. I brought five books of my own and—look—I'm taking this *I Spy* book I got from Grandma to read in the car."

"Good for you." Maggie knew it would be wise to counter Dillon's joking with her own best attempt at kindness. After all, she knew she would be sitting exactly 12 ¾ inches from her brother the whole trip. At that moment, Maggie spotted her father nearing the car with his highly-valued coffee containers, and asked, "Daddy, how long will it take us to get to Great-grandmother's?"

Placing the containers in their holders and making sure his fav five music CD's were cued and ready for the drive, Don answered Maggie's question, "Mom says maybe four hours. I'm not sure but I think it's about right."

Having double-checked the children's seat belts, Don was ready to get rolling. He, too, knew that a late start meant running into the thickest of Chicago's traffic, even for a Sunday. But a vacation is a vacation and he was looking forward to getting away regardless of what the interstates looked like. He had been ready to "get out of Dodge" all week.

"Carrie. We're ready. I got the coffees."

That's it. Her husband's mention of the coffees gave answer to the nagging question every mother has before such a trip, "What are we forgetting?" She reversed her exit out the front screen door and went back in. Air conditioning is off. Doors are locked. Lights are all out. Camera is in. "I think I put it in. Yes, I know I put it in." Just four minutes later she joins the rest in the van.

"What took you so long?" Don let slip a question he wished he could take back.

"I decided to take a nap before the trip."

"Touché. Sorry. I—."

"Don, you left the coffee maker on. I turned it off. Then I remembered our snacks for the trip. I put those in the cooler as you can see. I—."

"I said, 'I'm sorry.' You don't need to explain. I was just anxious of what **280/94** was going to look like in an hour."

"Me, too—but it's summer vacation at last! *Mapquest* shows the trip should take 4 ½ hours and is 252 miles. Let's get going," encouraged Carrie.

Although it would be dark when the exhausted family would arrive at their destination for the long-awaited vacation, they were all looking forward to getting away for a long week with no agenda. At least that is what they had thought would happen when they finally merged into traffic on the expressway. They had no idea the great adventure this week would bring to all of them—especially to the sister and brother detective duo innocently reading in the back seat.

They had no idea the great adventure this week would bring to all of them.

Nightfall was upon them when they finally saw the Holland (Michigan) signs. Don was in a zone singing along with the 4th CD he had carefully selected for the trip. Maggie was gallantly attempting to get through one more chapter in "Black Beauty" before darkness dictated she stop reading. Dillon, long bored with *I Spy*, peered out the window with his usual curiosity of the cool cars passing the van.

The hum of the engine. The hard-working air conditioning. The lyrics of Bono—or was it Don—singing? All these things and more competed for Mom's thoughts as she was now driving. Carrie was familiar with this portion of highway **31** as she and her parents and her brother, Derek, had lived in Michigan in the 1970's and early '80's and had visited Grandma Howard often. She had loved those trips. With grandpa's passing four years earlier, Carrie was glad she could visit with her grandmother but she wondered if she would be up for the four of them all week? 'Will she be awake when they arrive? Will the cherry trees still have fruit to pick? Will the luscious blackberries in the 'back 40' be ready to eat? Can't wait to show the kids my tree. Yes, I'm sure I brought my camera!" thought Carrie. Then she looked into her rearview mirror. "Don, look. They're zonked! Don. Don! Turn down the radio. Look at them. I wish I could take a picture of this."

"Carrie. Your camera. Did you bring the camera?"

Smiling, Carrie gave assurance, "Yes, it's in my suitcase and with a new SD card."

After Holland they drove past Grand Haven, Muskegon, Whitehall, and Rothbury.

They arrived in NEW ERA!

4477 Elm Street.

9:38 p.m..

"There's a light on. We made it," sighed Carrie as she turned off the engine.

# Chapter 2

## The Mysterious Light

"Grandma, I can't believe you are up. It's 9:30 at least!"

"Hi, Carrie. Hi, Don. Are the kids awake?" Grandma Howard didn't mean to by-pass her beloved granddaughter and her husband so quickly but she had anticipated the arrival of her two bright-eyed great-grandchildren since her morning coffee. She had killed the time as she always did—productively. She had prepared two pies from the fresh blackberries she had picked on Thursday. She wanted to bake them fresh in the morning. She had also canned 12 quart jars of the fresh vegetables she had maintained from the backyard garden. She had all the beds ready for the weary travelers.

"Grandma, give me a hug," smiled Carrie as she was glad to see the twinkle had returned to her eyes from the last visit they made almost two years ago.

"Sorry, Carrie. Yes, a hug would make my day."

"Don interrupted the love fest. "What am I, Grandma? Chopped liver?"

Another smile. Another hug. "I see they are sleeping," Grandma observed, looking around Don and toward the kids.

"Yes. They fell asleep somewhere between Holland and Grand Haven. Grandma, we are only going to bring the necessities in tonight. I don't think anyone will steal anything up here on the hill in New Era. You go ahead and wake the kids. It's okay. They have been looking forward to seeing you all week."

It was an unusually warm August evening even for New Era. The heat, however, was bearable because of the breeze coming from Lake Michigan, only a few miles to the west. Carrie could recall loving the

6

breeze through the screens of the bedroom she had slept in while a girl of Maggie's age in the 1970's. The air was so fresh. "Everything is so peaceful here," the relaxed Carrie commented to Don as they put the leftover perishable snacks in Grandmom's fridge.

Don smiled, "Can you believe we brought our own store-bought fruit up to God's own fruit country?" Carrie shook her head and both their heads turned when they heard—

"Wake up, sleepyheads!" Grandma shouted as if she were half her age.

"Great-Grandma! Yes! Yes! We made it!" Dillon was the first to awaken and get a hug unlike any other he had ever experienced. Maggie, on the other hand, simply turned her head slightly—even with the interior lights blazing against the dark night sky and Dillon's voice echoing loudly 12 ¾ inches away. "She could sleep through a tornado," her mother would always say.

Dillon was already chasing the lightning bugs flicking—as he would always say—their "flashlights off and on" in Great-grandma's front yard.

"What should I do?" Grandma inquired of Don when he came back out for the kid's bed buddies. "Should I wake Maggie, too?"

"No. Not sure if you could anyway. Let me pick her up and try to place her into bed in the house. If she wakes up, she wakes up. But my guess is she will remain in dreamland. She is probably riding Black Beauty through the English countryside right now, if you know what I mean." Grandma noticed the open book, barely resting on Maggie's lap and smiled with understanding.

"Dillon, come in now! Brush your teeth. You will get the top bunk tonight since Maggie is sleeping," Carrie reasoned with maternal wisdom to get the "motion machine" in bed since it was nearly two hours after his normal bedtime.

"Yes! Top bunk! Yes! I'm coming! Do I have to brush my teeth? I—."

"Yes! Young man," interrupted Grandma with a laugh, "You think I want your gobbledygook on the fresh pillow I have ready for you?"

Dillon laughed. "She is funny," were his delighted thoughts.

As anticipated, Maggie took her sleep from van to bed without a peep. "Only a sheet would be needed on this warm evening," deduced her Mom as she bent down to tuck in her little "Readergirl" in the lower bunk. Then she whispered to the oblivious Maggie, "We will all sleep tonight little girl and I will show you my old climbing tree tomorrow."

Dillon, to no one's surprise, had brushed his teeth in 20.5 seconds and was thrilled when he arrived on the top bunk that there was a window at one end. He saw that the moon was almost full and could see the shadows of the old orchard trees down the hill. "Man, it sure is dark here," said Dillon, thinking his parents had already left the bedroom after they had turned the light out.

"It sure is, Bud. Isn't it great though?"

"Mommy! You scared me."

"Sorry, honey, but I wanted to pray with you before you go to sleep."

"Sure. This is going to be a great week."

"Let's thank God for that then and thank Him for our safe trip." The fresh breeze lifted the cotton curtains while a mother's prayer seemed especially connecting tonight as she stroked the little adventurer's perspiring brow while she prayed.

"And, God, thank you that you put this window by my bed tonight. Amen." Dillon added to his Mom's gentle thanksgivings. Carrie grinned, shook her head, and got a promise from Dillon that he would get to sleep soon as she left the moon-drenched room. However, with Mom actually gone, promises to sleep became too difficult to keep as he peered out the window as if it were a 60-inch TV screen. The combination of the wind and the moonlight made the nearby apple tree branches appear to be moving creatures. To this brave seven year-old, the moving picture before his very eyes was exciting.

"Wait! What was that? There—what is that light moving between the trees?" Dillon pinched himself to make sure he was not dreaming. But this was real! "I can't quite make it out but it seems like a man. Is he holding a flashlight, maybe? Yikes! I'm going to bed. No one is going to believe me tomorrow," whispered Dillon, coming to grips with the fact that he wasn't as brave as people maybe thought he was.

"What is that light moving between the trees?"

# Chapter 3

## Daylight in the Swamps!

"Daylight in the swamps!" Grandma could wait no more. She, as usual, was up at daybreak and just had to wake up her precious great-grandchildren. "Daylight in the swamps!

"Great-grandma!" The two detectives were already wide awake, checking out the details of their temporary bedroom and the great out-of-doors decorated by long shadows by the bright early morning sunlight just beyond their window. They remembered well the admonitions of Dad and Mom that they were to wait in their bedroom and read and be quiet until they were told they could come out. For the *Reader Whiz Kids*, this instruction was a wise deterrent to keep them in their room. *Black Beauty* seemed even more interesting to Maggie this morning as she could smell the fresh country air breezing through the window. However, Dillon had laid down his Hardy Boy' chapter book entitled, *What Happened at Midnight*, and was peering out the window. This was a case of a mystery book being trumped by the real-life mystery just a few yards out the window. "Did I really see a man and a light in those trees last night?" Right now he kept those thoughts to himself, not sure if anyone would believe him.

"Daylight in the swamps?" What in the world does that mean, Great-grandma?" laughed Maggie, as she crawled off the lower bunk and ran to hug the beaming Deloris Howard.

Years of teaching children in Sunday School and backyard Five Day Clubs and rearing her own three daughters caused Dee to prefer the innocent laughter and comments of children to the safe, predictable chatter of adults. Besides, since her beloved Doug had died, it seemed the entirety of her conversations were with the 60 and over crowd.

This week was going to be joyous! "God, give me the strength to enjoy these days," was her inaudible prayer. "What? You mean your mother or father doesn't wake you up with that? It means: WAKE UP! The day has begun and time shouldn't be awastin'!" she answered, with each leg now straddled with a great-grandchild.

Like a pied piper, Dee led her special grandchildren to her "office"— the neat but crowded kitchen that reflected the tender loving care of cooking for kids, grandkids, and now great-grandkids for five decades plus. Their eyes followed their great-grandmother but their noses were tracing something else and it didn't take a detective's nose to recognize the immediate wonderful aroma of fresh blackberry pie already wafting throughout the house.

It didn't take a detective's nose to recognize the immediate wonderful aroma of fresh blackberry pie already wafting throughout the house.

"Why do you put the pies in the window, great—Can we call you Grandma? Great-grandma takes too long."

Dillon's comment confirmed Dee's love of children. "Which question shall I answer first, young man?"

"You *are* funny. This is not going to be a boring week. 'What should we call you?' Answer that question first." Dillon's mouth was smiling but his eyes were fixed on the glorious pie on the window ledge.

"Call me 'Grandma.' Great-grandma has too many syl-*la*-bles for me, too! Yes, call me 'Grandma.'" I would like that. Answer to question two: the pies come out of the oven very, very hot and need to cool. We don't have air conditioning like some folk do. The constant breeze coming though my window on this hill is my 'pie air conditioner'. What do you think of that?"

"Dillon's right, Greatgra—," Maggie quickly corrected herself, "Grandma, you *are* funny. We are so happy to be here. 'Pie air conditioner.' Now that's a new one on me," said the young wordsmith as if she were a peer to someone nearly seven decades older than she.

"Not as happy as I am that you are here! Now, where's your Mommy and Daddy? Tell them breakfast will be served in 20 minutes."

"Daylights in the swamps!" chimed in the bright-eyed duo as they leaped into their parent's bed. If they weren't awake yet, they were now. "C'mon, get out of bed. Grandma said, 'Breakfast is ready in 20 minutes'. "

"Daylight in the swamps!" Carrie had to smile. She hadn't heard that expression in years. Her mother had often shouted those words to roust her out of bed in her childhood. "20 minutes? Okay. Tell Grandma we'll be ready. Maggie, look at yourself. I think you might want to get out of those wrinkled clothes you slept in last night. Dillon, your Spiderman jams might not work too well if we pick blackberries today." Ever the mother, Carrie realized quickly how relaxed she was this morning. Maybe it was the country air or the fresh sheets or just the fact that an unscheduled week was ahead of her—maybe all three. Then she realized she should be helping Grandma with breakfast.

"Grandma! You should've called me to help. We usually just eat cereal or yogurt. You shouldn't—."

"I could, so I should. It gets tiresome to just cook for myself. Trust me; this is fun. How do you like your eggs, Carrie?"

"I like mine sunny side up," interrupted a voice in the kitchen doorway. "I also smell some coffee. Thank you!" Don, too, was well-rested and was drawn to the same window with the smell of the freshly-baked pie. Pouring the fresh coffee into one of the thick ceramic mugs by the coffee pot, he watched the kids laughing with Grandma and was glad now that Carrie had encouraged him to come up here for this precious week of vacation time.

"Okay, if you want to help, Carrie, throw some toast in the toaster. I've got some great strawberry jam like you used to love when you were your kids' age." the wise grandmother mused as she looked at Maggie and Dillon shooing flies away from the pie. Grandmom Howard was in her element in the kitchen. She found energy in this family setting. "God is good," was evident in her twinkling eyes.

"Grandma, you don't put toast in a toaster. You put bread in the toaster!" commented Maggie with a grin.

"Maggie! Don't tell Grandma what to say. Besides, she is not your grandma. She's your great-grandmother." Carrie wanted her children to give proper respect to Dee, and this comment—though she knew was not meant to be demeaning—was certainly in need of correction.

Before Maggie could respond, Dee chipped in, "Don't worry. While you two were still dreaming dreams, we three made a corporate decision. My name is to be 'Grandma.' not 'Great-grandma.' Life is short and we figured it would take too long to say, 'Great-grandma,' when I could just as easily respond to the two syllable title. Also, Maggie is absolutely right. One puts *bread* into a toaster, not toast."

The day started off with laughter and, as usual, the kids set the early agenda. It was a perfect day for exploring. Also, the already intriguing orchard beckoned them first, especially Dillon, who had hoped to discover some evidence to prove to Maggie that the mysterious light and visitor he saw the first night was real. The orchard was going to be a detective's playground for these two inquisitive investigators from Illinois!

# Chapter 4

## A Detective's Playground

"Maggie! Come here! Look! There's a barn over there! Hey, where are you going? Maggie!" Dillon's attention was in overdrive. He was the first to the backyard after breakfast and now saw in the daylight the entire setting of the dark, moon-drenched field he saw last night. What a difference! The view before him now said, "Come explore!" Last night's view of the same orchard said, "Come, but enter at your own risk." Explore he will—but what will he explore first? The distant barn? The rocky field full of Queen Anne's Lace and Cornflower Blue weeds just in front of him? The old orchard down the hill apparently not harvested for years and choked by tall bushes and weeds? The blackberry bushes somewhere down in a cove near old highway 31? Or—the area he believed to be where he sighted the mysterious light in the orchard last night? Whatever he would do, one thing is sure: he would not do it without his partner in discovery.

"Dillon, I'm coming. I had to go back in the house to change into my jeans. Dad said the field could get prickly. Besides, I had to get my book. Look, a barn! Want to investigate?"

Dillon quickly said, "Yes!"

"That settles it! The barn first. I'll race you!" Maggie responded just as quickly.

"That settles it! The barn first. I'll race you!"

Anticipating a challenge, Maggie got a head start on her speedy brother and she beat him—not to the barn—but to the thick underbrush where both had to stop in their tracks. The weeds at this part of the path to the barn had severely overgrown the past few years. What was once a soft dirt pathway to the barn was now impassable. Maggie's mother and her mother before her had enjoyed walking with Grandpa Howard to milk the lone cow and to get the mowing equipment and building supplies stored in the barn. Now—anyone less than a discerning detective could not navigate a trek to the barn.

"Dillon! Over here. Follow me." Maggie noticed that weeds and grasses under a nearby old apple tree were shorter than those on the overgrown path and looked like the best route to get through to the barn. Turning around and going back was *never* an option.

"Good idea. I'm right behind you. Mags, let's make walking sticks from these fallen branches. We could also use them as weed cutters like that story about *Last of the Mokegons* you read to me."

"Mohigans. Great idea, especially for you with those shorts," affirmed Maggie, always the protective sister.

Laughter and kidding helped them navigate their descent down the hill and through the ticking foliage. Maggie laughed to herself as she was reminded of those words in her grandpa's favorite poem, "Birches" by Robert Frost.

> And life is like a pathless wood
> Where your face burns and tickles with the cobwebs
> Broken against it, and one eye is weeping
> From a twig's having lashed across it open.

Soon they came across a clearing—then—"Watch out, Maggie! Wires!" came a warning shout from Dillon.

"Whew! Thanks, Bud! But this isn't just any wire; it's barbed wire. I just read about it in some book. I think it was the *X Bar X Boys*. Anyway, it can be dangerous. There must be a fence here or something. Now this could have ripped my face off!"

"Now what will we do? I don't want to turn back," challenged Dillon.

"Dillon! Never! Remember motto # 5: TO MOVE AHEAD, USE YOUR HEAD."

The cloudless August sky was beginning to make this farm country feel warm, but as of yet it did not deter these partners in adventure from keenly observing their limited routes for an escape. They remained as cool as the bent grass, still moist from the morning dew that encircled them from all sides.

Dillon offered the first suggestion. "Okay. I am using my head but I can't figure out what to do—unless—hmmm—unless we go back a ways and try to find another approach to the barn."

That brought a huge smile to the Readergirl. Then Maggie affirmed her younger brother,

" 'Approach.' Now there's a good word. Methinks your reading is paying off, Bud, but—."

Hardly acknowledging the compliment, Dillon interrupted, "Mags! I've got it! These walking sticks. Let's use them to prop up the barbed wire. Then we could crawl under the fence. You go first. I'll hold up the wire like this. Then you could do the same for me with your stick but from the other side."

"Again, brilliant! My good Watson. That is jolly brilliant." Maggie was now in her element. She was enjoying this adventure with her brother like few others. She couldn't help if her readings crossed over to her real-life adventures.

"Watson? I'm not Watson. You're crazy, Maggie. Just for that, 'Get your jolly bottom under the fence, Spiderwoman!'" They both laughed so hard that Dillon almost dropped his hold on the stick separating the barbed wire from his sister. Yet they found Dillon's scheme to work beautifully. They indeed got to the other side of the fence as they had hoped—but not without deep dirt and grass stains on both clothes and skin.

After this, it was easy to get to the other side of the barn and locate the large sliding door. But it was clearly not going to be easy to open this huge door. "Push, Dillon! We worked too hard to get here not to be able to get inside. Push! Let's do one–two-THREE!"

"One–two-THREE!" coached the oldest detective. Both fell to the ground with that shove but the heavy door yielded only a foot opening.

"Push, Dillon! We've worked too hard to get here not
to go inside. Let's do one–two–THREE!"

"Pfft! Dirt! Yuck!" spit out Maggie as she had fallen face first into the dirt and gravel. "Dillon, you should see your face. Is that blood?"

"Yeah—maybe—but I'm okay. A little blood never hurt anyone," responded Dillon. Besides, what little pain he had was trumped by his discovery that he could fit his slim frame into the doorway. Maggie took his lead and also slipped into the narrow opening with no problem.

"Cool! Look, Mags. It is huge inside here. Kind of dark but really cool."

Joining her brother in the assessment of the interior of this grand old barn, Maggie wisely advised that they both stand still until their eyes became adjusted to the dim and murky surroundings. The small windows at the top of the barn on the east side yielded the most light and slowly their awe was increasing to the degree that their eyes adjusted to the limited light.

"Look at this old car. Looks like a Chevy. Maggie, look—over here—an old tractor like the one we saw in Elisabeth, Illinois at Lilly's and H.D.'s farm. Except—this is no John Deere. What does it say on the grill? F–A–R–M–A–L-L. 'Farmall.' Never heard of that kind but it sure is cool."

"Dillon, watch out for the hole in the floor! Stay by me. Let's explore over here. Slowly. Slowly. I'm beginning to see some old saddles on the wall I think. Man, it is dark. Can you see them, Dillon?"

# Chapter 5

## Where are the Kids?

With the chores now done to assist Grandma, Dad and Mom Burch walked to the back yard. No Maggie or Dillon! "Where did the kids go, Carrie? I thought they were to wait for us before they went exploring." Don didn't conceal his concern to Carrie very well. There was a time and place to explore, but doing so in unfamiliar territory of the "back 40" was not a good idea.

"They were! They could be anyplace. Maggie! Dillon! Where are you?"

No response.

"Carrie. Look. Maggie's book. That's not like her to lay it down. She told me she was going to find her secret reading spot for this week. My guess is she went this way with Dillon—to—to—to that barn! If I were them, that's where I would go. Maggie! Dillon!" Don thought his voice might carry better but—still—no response. They began to follow the same path as it appeared the kids had taken. They raced quickly but not for the fun of it as was the case of Maggie and Dillon earlier. They had to find them soon. "I hope they didn't get into that old dangerous barn," they both thought to themselves. Carrie recalled her Grandpa Howard's cautions about the rotted flooring when she was Maggie's age.

The taller adults could get through the weeds and brush easier than the kids but had more difficulty with the low-lying old apple tree branches. Eventually, they came to the same ominous fence. "They couldn't have gone this way. Look, Carrie, a barbed-wire fence." Every blocked passage and passing minute brought more reason for concern. Time was of utmost importance now.

≈   ≈   ≈   ≈   ≈   ≈

Meanwhile—the wide-eyed adventurers walked slowly in the limited light of this mysterious barn. They used walking sticks now to brush aside the dirty hay on the wood floor ahead of their steps. Approaching what Maggie knew to be a horse stable, her excitement soon ebbed when she realized no horse could be kept here. "The saddles are really old and dry and no food or water dishes. I would guess that no horse has lived here in years, Dill. Sure would be great, though, if there was a real horse or pony here."

"Yeah, like grandpa's Kloppidity," offered Dillon. Both siblings laughed at that one as they recalled those bedtime stories about Johnny and his favorite horse named Kloppidity.

"Maggie, what's that by your foot?"

The inquiry brought Maggie to carefully bend over and she found, of all things, an empty McDonald's bag. The investigator in her discovered a receipt inside that clearly indicated an August 12 purchase. "Dillon, whoever had this bag bought this just two days ago. Today is the 14th, right? And look. That looks like a clean blanket. Somebody has been staying here!"

"Let's get out of here!" exclaimed both of them at the same time.

"Wait," said Maggie cautiously. "I hear someone coming." Following Dillon's lead, they hid behind the huge wheels of the old Farmall tractor and waited.

Maggie and Dillon could almost touch the
lengthy shadows on the barn floor!

The heavy barn door was now creaking open wider than the narrow crack for which they had managed to open earlier. Hiding in the shadows, the timid barn invaders waited, trying not to breathe too heavily. The bright daylight sun was shining through the dust in the air and looked like a morning haze. Then—two large and foreboding silhouettes appeared in the door way. Maggie and Dillon could almost touch the lengthy shadows on the barn floor.

"Dillon! Maggie! Are you in here?" shouted Carrie, as she stood still with Don, not content to wait until her eyes adjusted to the dark and murky interior of the barn.

"Mommy! Daddy!" screamed Dillon and Maggie in unison.

"We're so glad it's you!" a relieved Maggie echoed.

Finding the kids safe and witnessing the obvious expressions of gratitude from them both, Dad and Mom decided they would dish out the grounding for disobedience later. For now, all were relieved. At this moment, the brother and sister were simply the secure children of their father and mother. Fifteen minutes earlier, they were the brave barnstormers. Sometimes, it feels good just to be kids.

The foursome avoided the difficult path that led them to the barn in the first place. Not to return the original way was a no-brainer. Instead, they walked up the dirt driveway that led to Elm Street. The entire hike back to Dee's house was filled with a drama-enhanced, moment-by-moment recitation of the kids' strategy to get under the fence, the strength they needed to get into the barn, and, of course, their discovery of the McDonald's receipt and the mysterious barn guest. No one commented on the old, curtainless house that stood just opposite that driveway from the barn. The August sun now was giving an oasis look on the blacktopped street just ahead of them. The adults realized it was high noon and all were reminded how thirsty and hungry they now were from this morning's undertakings.

# Chapter 6

## Vagrant or Mystery Guest?

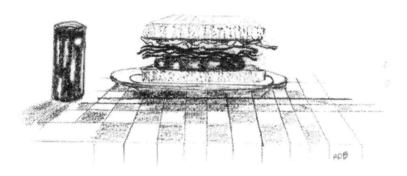

Lunch at Grandmas was never a snack.

Everyone was hungry after the events of the morning and Grandma didn't disappoint. What a layout! Delicious BLT's with fresh tomatoes and lettuce straight from the garden. Scrumptious potato salad as only Grandma could make. Crisp carrots and celery. Okay, straight from Vandermeer's grocery store. Lemonade made from real lemons. "How novel is that?" thought the Mags.

"And if you eat your entire meal—there's a dessert to be served on the picnic table in the front yard!" Even Grandma took her moments for dramatic flare. Then, not missing a beat with her eyes, she added, "Dillon! Do you want an upset stomach?"

"Ooops. Sorry, Grandma," said Dillon in a garbled response, exposing a mouth full of potato salad before a prayer of thanks was offered at the meal. "It just tastes so good—."

"Good try," Dee smiled. Don also smiled as he picked up on the quick savvy and wit of Carrie's grandmother. A smile from Carrie confirmed his observation.

"Let's pray. Dear Lord, thank you so much for this food you have given to us. Thank you for the joy you have given me to have Carrie and Don and Maggie and Dillon here this very special week. You are so good. Please bless this food to the nourishment of our bodies. In Jesus Name—."

"Amen!" finished Dillon unabashedly.

Although there was enough food to feed twice the Burch family, the supply was being devoured quickly. Still, it was amazing that Maggie and Dillon ate anything since they seemed to talk nonstop, retelling the adventure of the morning. Dee Howard's rapt attention and ready smile only fueled their storytelling—that is 'til they got to the part about the mysterious barn visitor. A look at Don and Carrie to determine the accuracy of her dramatic great-grandchildren's story let her know they were telling the truth.

"Vagrants. I was hoping not to have any vagrants in the barn before the new neighbors moved into your old great-grandmother's house, Carrie. It concerns me since I'm mostly isolated up here."

"Vagrants. Now that's new one on me, Grandma. What is a vagrant?"

"Sorry, Maggie. Let me try to tell you. A vagrant is not a welcome visitor. He is someone who comes—well—wanders about and doesn't have a permanent home. He will make his bed or home anyplace he chooses and doesn't tell you he is doing so."

"Like a hobo?" questioned Dillon, recalling this description of a person he had read about in his favorite book about railroads.

"Kind of. Yes, like a hobo or tramp or a rover. Anyway, we have had vagrants on our property before. They stole some of our vegetables even when your great-grandfather was here. I don't mind helping someone have a roof over his head when he needs it or give someone food if he is hungry, but I would rather that person ask permission. Being by myself, for the most part, I get kind of nervous when I hear there might be some unwelcome guest on my property."

"Sorry, Grandma. We didn't want to scare you with our discovery. Truth is, we didn't actually see someone. We only saw what we thought was some bedding," Maggie broke in with her best attempt at calming her beloved great-grandmother.

Noticing Dee's troubled face, Don told her he would go back to the barn and see if he could find the visitor and put an end to the worry and mystery. Carrie nodded approval and decided that the time he was gone would be a good time for Maggie and Dillon to stay in their room quietly for their grounding and think about their disobedience: taking off without clear permission as they had done this morning. "And—No, Maggie. That doesn't mean an opportunity for you to read or you either, Dillon. You will both go to different bedrooms for a full hour and think about what you did. No books for either of you. Understand?"

"A whole hour? The day will be half gone. What about watermelon? What about the plans to pick blackberries today?" bartered the Dillon, with Maggie agreeing with a sad look.

"Keep talking and it can be extended to two hours."

Smiling again, Dee echoed her granddaughter's wisdom as she talked to her grandkids, "I think you would be wise to go to your rooms now. I will keep the watermelon chilled for when you come out. Besides, the direct sun right now would not be a good time to go down into the hot field to pick the berries. Believe me. The bees and bugs are swarming right now."

Realizing they lost the debate on authority as well as logic, they did exactly as they were ordered: Maggie to Grandma's bedroom and Dillon to the guest bedroom. Both were glad for the floor fans, for the summer's heat was radiating into the entire house by now.

Don was more than willing to investigate the barn and its mysterious visitor. He didn't let on to the kids, but he was relieved that Maggie and Dillon didn't come upon this person on their own. He declined, however, Grandma's offer of taking one of Grandpa's old guns, still on the gun rack in the basement. "Thank you. I am familiar with guns and would like to see Doug's collection, but I think it might be overplay right now. My guess is that you are right in thinking whoever this vagrant or visitor is, it is someone who simply needed a temporary roof over his head. Let me just go down and check it out." Dee admonished him to be careful nonetheless.

"I will," promised Don.

Carrie helped Dee clean up and put the watermelon back in the refrigerator. The two parked themselves under the shade of the maple tree in the front yard. "Tall glasses of iced tea and relaxed conversation are what summertime ought to be about," thought Carrie with another smile as she looked up at the very branch from which she used to sit and hang when she was but Maggie's age.

Grandmother's words were warmer than the still and warm air on this side of the house. Carrie was particularly encouraged by her grandmother's strong commendations on how she saw the children were turning out. "Best of all, Carrie, I see you and Don are instilling in them godly character and respect. I see that less and less in children these days. I don't teach but I do assist once a month in Primary Sunday School and am saddened by the disrespect by children even at that age."

As Carrie shared her joys and challenges in being a mother, she thoroughly enjoyed hearing Grandma talk of her challenges in the 1950's and 1960's and into the 1970's of rearing her three daughters, Carrie's mother and two aunts. She couldn't wait to tell her mother of Grandma's particular fond memories of her, the oldest. She saw the twinkle in grandmother's eye in her mother.

$$\approx \quad \approx \quad \approx \quad \approx \quad \approx \quad \approx$$

"I didn't notice these tire tracks before. They have to be fairly fresh," Don observed as he walked the old driveway down to the barn. The heat waves were almost glowing off the dark barn roof as he approached its entrance. He purposely opened the door completely and left it open in hopes that some breeze would enter the stifling atmosphere inside and also provide more light. Once inside, it hit Don, "If anyone is inside and wants to do me in, they could do it without any trouble right now."

# Chapter 7

## A Mysterious Photo!

Don couldn't see a thing except the large murky shadow of the old Farmall tractor. Then—movement! "What was that?" an anxious Don reacted. "Who is there?" he blurted out without thinking. Silence. He waited. Don felt the dusty, almost sauna-like air more intensely than ever. "Who is that, I said?" He was hoping his strong voice would give the impression he was not frightened and had the ring of authority. His eyes began surveying the area in the horse stall from which he thought he had heard the noise originally. Then—the appearance of a dark figure! Then—some growling sounds!

A dog! "Whoa, doggy. I mean you no harm. Whoa! Good boy." However, the deep growling didn't subside until Don wisely bent down and put his hand out. He had learned this as a volunteer fireman in Traverse City during his college days. But this was no Dalmation. The growling finally stopped and, with his eyes now adjusted to the darkness (due, in part, to the light filtering through a nearby window), he saw that this dog was also no Doberman. He laughed now. The dog was probably a large Schnauzer or something. With a few pats under his chin and with the dog reciprocating with some licks on his hand, Don found the once ferocious enemy had become a friendly companion.

The dog's deep growling didn't subside until Don
wisely bent down and put his hand out.

Unnamed new furry friend in tow and his eyes fully acclimated to his surroundings, Don now saw the horse stall of which Maggie and Dillon had spoken. The blanket had no tag on it to indicate from where it had come. The McDonald's bag was still there and, "Sure enough, Maggie was right," Don observed, "the meal had to have been purchased only two days ago. Look, this receipt also reveals that whomever this visitor or vagrant is, he or she must have bought the hamburger from Whitehall. I wonder if that is where he or she is from. Also, the hay looks like it was slept in recently. If the indentation of the hay indicates the size of the unwelcomed guest then he has to be 6 foot plus." Don was in full detective mode now. He only wondered whether to tell Grandma or not, given her fears about a vagrant.

"What's that ol' boy? What are you finding?" The dog was sniffing near where the McDonald's bag had been and had unearthed something in the straw. "A Ziploc ® sandwich bag?" Further study revealed that it indeed was a plastic bag but with something in it. "Looks like an old photo. Yes, it is. An old black and white photo of a couple," he whispered, realizing that it was possible that the mystery guest was in earshot of him in the barn. He didn't want to wait to find out for sure. He had some very interesting evidence of some kind of a visitor and, after he got outside, he paused to get a better look at the photo. "Wow!" thought the would-be Sherlock Holmes, "This black and white photo had to have been taken back in the spring of 1941 if the writing is correct. I must show this to Grandma." He then closed the barn door and gazed once again at the empty old house across from the barn. Or was it empty?

A bark distracted him and reminded him of his new canine friend. Looking down, Don said, "Okay, come along for now, bloodhood." He knew the 'girls' would be getting nervous if he didn't get back soon so he kept the thought of the empty house to himself for the time being.

Grandma was relieved when she saw Don walking up the hill.

"There you are?" Grandma was relieved when she saw Don walking up the hill. He was okay and seemed excited about something. "Looks like you found a new friend," said Dee as she saw the barking dog at his heels. "C'mere, Ebony!"

"You know this mutt?" Don questioned with a boyish smile.

"Hey—he's no mutt. Ebony is the product of our old dog, Blackie. Surely, your mother told you about our old dog, Blackie, Carrie. He was a great dog and, well—Ebony was probably born in that old barn probably a few weeks before ol' Blackie died. Anyway, he belongs to a nephew in town and yet he finds his way up here on the hill quite a bit. He sure found you, Don!"

Mom was beaming as she and Carrie were enjoying this slow August afternoon, their sweating iced teas almost empty in Grandma's colored aluminum glasses.

"Yeah—well—your old Ebony almost scared me to death but he also helped me to find this." Holding up the photo in the bag, Don finished climbing up the front yard to get under the shade tree with Carrie and Dee.

"Well, just what did 'Detective Don' find out?" the relaxed Carrie inquired with humor.

"Not sure. It's an old photo of a guy and girl, maybe in their twenties with some writing on it that suggests it is from 1941."

Holding the photo closely, Dee exclaimed, "I know them!"

Holding the photo closely, Dee exclaimed, "I know them! That's— that girl is Claire. Claire deGroot and the man is her old boyfriend, Charles. Charles Hargrove! That photo is old, maybe 50-60 years old.

I went to school with them at Hart High. She was from New Era for awhile and he was from Hart. She used to go to my church. Charles died in the war. Where did you get this, Don?" asked the animated Dee Howard.

"The barn. I found it in the hay in this plastic bag near the bedding where our mysterious visitor—ah—vagrant is apparently staying. You really *do* know them, Dee. The names you just mentioned are written in long hand on the edges of the photo. Amazing!"

"Know her? We were pretty close friends in high school and because of her I got to know Doug. When I came to see Claire after she got out of work at the canning factory, she introduced me to Doug. This is amazing. I wouldn't be surprised even if Doug took this photo. He had a dark room for years as a teenager and took lots of pictures. I always thought that Carrie got her knack for photography from her grandpa." Looking more closely at the photograph, Dee then asked, "You found this in the barn? That is strange. This photo doesn't look any worse for wear. Look at the records and the record player. That's them. They loved their music."

With Carrie's interest now aroused, she asked, "Is this Claire still alive, Grandma?"

"Yes, she still lives in nearby Mears on a farm near the Barkleys. Remember them, Carrie?"

"Not sure, Grandma. Mears is near the Silver Lake sand dunes, isn't it? I vaguely remember lots of trees and going to a big farmhouse for a Thanksgiving."

"Good recall. Mears is also a small town—even smaller than New Era— and indeed near Silver Lake and Shelby, not far from Hart, and—yes— we were invited to a few Thanksgivings at Clyde and Pearl Barkley's home, including that one fall when you lived here. But that was years ago and their children now live on that property. Anyway, I ramble as always. Claire, the Claire in this picture, lives very close to the Barkley's. Her husband died only a year or so ago. I went to the funeral. Claire used to go to our church but I haven't seen her in some time. She seemed to stop coming a little while after Johanne's—that's her husband— funeral service. Truth be told, I should have called on her long ago." Still looking in amazement at the photo, she redirected the conversation to the photo itself. "This had to be taken just months before Pearl Harbor and is probably one of the last pictures of Charlie.

I think the inscription is accurate. It could very well be 1941. Yes, it must be and this picnic site must be at the State Park in Pentwater. This is indeed amazing. I can't imagine who has kept it and brought it back to—my goodness—our barn!"

"Can we come out? It's been more than an hour!" interrupted the well-rested and very antsy Maggie. The adults followed the direction of her voice and saw her and Dillon's heads appearing just above where the blackberry pie had been in the kitchen window. "Please," added Dillon. "We want some watermelon, too."

"Heavens yes!" Grandma answered, almost intuitively. Then she turned to Carrie and Don and apologized. "Ooops! I think that is your decision. Guess that was the mother in me. Is that okay with you?"

Don and Carrie answered her with affirming smiles but, before they could give agreement on the decision, the kids were out the front door running past their parents to another guest—a dog! Both members of this detective duo love animals almost as much as they love books.

"What's your name?" Maggie asked of the happy and excited dog. "Where do you come from? Is he yours, Grandmom?"

"Let your Dad tell you." She then got up and walked with a lightness in her step as she quickly remembered her role as hostess and went inside to get the watermelons.

A good hour went by with all enjoying the fresh seeded watermelons and the no-agenda summer afternoon. Ebony's name was heard often.

"Ebony, here!"

"C'mere, Ebony, to me."

"Ebony, look. Run after this!"

While Dee and Carrie watched and laughed at this busy scene in the shaded front yard, Don devoured his third slice of watermelon while his thoughts were still occupied with the mystery of the photo.

The ever-practical Grandma broke into this wonderful time warp. "I don't want to stop all of your fun but I think it might be a good time now for all of you to get the berry containers and try your luck with the blackberry harvest. As far as I know, no one has been down there yet to pick 'em. Every year the weeds around them get bigger and thicker and most people don't want to go to the trouble to pick these black jewels." Dee thought she would like to go with them but also realized this could become a cherished memory time for her grandkids and great-grandchildren. She declined Carrie's invitation to show them the path and go with them. Instead, Dee showed them where the berry cartons and carrying containers were in the garage. "No, I'd rather not go. I'm rather tired today but you go and pick to your heart's delight." Then she pointed to the orchard. "See where I'm pointing? Just go down the hill until you literally run into the blackberry bushes. Be sure to have on pants or jeans. Have fun and pick a few for me!" It's almost about 6:30 so you won't have a lot of time. Supper will be late but we *will* have supper!"

# Chapter 8

## Blackberries!

All Maggie and Dillon needed was to hear the word, "blackberries!" They ran from the yard, imploring Ebony to join them and went into the house to get on their blackberry-picking clothes as Mom and Dad had laid them out this morning. Then they rushed back outdoors for this long-awaited adventure. Time: 3 minutes, 22 seconds! They had been waiting for this time for weeks—ever since they were told they would be going to their great-grandmothers for their vacation. They had feasted on their grandmom's and great-grandmom's blackberry jam all winter and now they would be able to pick their own! More than that, of course, the curious siblings were wondering if this first-of-a-kind adventure would yield another discovery.

With their great-grandmother pointing the general way down the hill—toward the semblance of a path—the foursome plus their four-legged friend left at a leisurely hot summer pace. Well, that isn't exactly true. The energetic Ebony took off running as if he knew exactly where they were headed. He seemed very familiar with this overgrown terrain behind the Howard home and raced ahead of his new companions. Refraining from following the dog's pace, Dad and Mom began trekking their way through the old groves and thick brush—over some rocks— until they saw the huge blackberries just waiting to be picked. Great-grandmom was right; they had to be one of the first to pick this season of blackberries as the long branches of these Michigan-style berries were bent very low due to the weight of so many berries. Carrie passed on the "how to pick" wisdom of the maternal side of her family tree to her family. She dramatized the presentation so the kids would not see this as a Botany home school session:

1. To avoid the thorns, reach for the berry in the gaps.
2. A ripe blackberry is deep black with a plump, full feel.
3. It will pull free from the plant with but a slight tug.
4. If the berry is red or purple, it is not yet ripe.
5. Bend down and look up into the plant for "hidden" berries.
6. Don't drop them into the containers, lay them in.
7. Don't overfill the containers or pack the berries down and—
8. Don't put more into your mouth than into the container.

"Hey, you two, what's that on your mouth? Hmmm, I think you two came to eat blackberries, not pick them. They all laughed when Mom said, "Understand?" as she placed a large, ripe blackberry into her own mouth. "Seriously, if you get your container filled, put it carefully in one of these green-blue carrying flats. We will put these on this rock right here in the shade. Okay?" Before Carrie could finish the instructions, the competitive kids, including the oldest "kid," their Dad, were already picking berries.

Soon all four were engrossed in the fun of picking these "black golds." Truth be told, Dad and Mom also continued to perform a few "taste tests" and their lips also revealed the tell-tale signs of this irresistible practice.

No one realized a good hour and a half had come and gone, even in this summer evening heat where little air was flowing through this thick orchard grove. Maggie and Dillon were slowed down a bit when they realized that their canine companion was nowhere to be found. A few calls for Ebony had no result. "Where is Ebony? Where could he be?" the sad kids questioned.

In spite of their missing the four-legged friend—and maybe *because* of his absence—many berries were picked. It wasn't long when the two found themselves picking at one end of the bushes and their parents on the other. When Dillon saw this, he realized he and Maggie were out of earshot from their Dad and Mom. He saw this as the opportunity to tell his sister of his first night mysterious sighting—a man in this very cove with what seemed to be a flashlight.

"Dillon, you're pulling my leg! You're not serious."

"No! I *am* serious! I saw what I saw! Maggie, I'm telling you the truth. I really am!"

"You are. I can tell. I believe you. Why didn't you tell me before?"

"I don't know. Guess there was so much else going on. I wasn't sure anyone would believe me, even you. Then I began thinking that maybe there is a connection between the mystery guest in the barn and the man I saw that night. I don't know— but walking down the hill today just reminded me of it again."

"Dillon, sssh! Here comes Dad."

"How are you guys doing? Wow! Very good! Looks like we have no cartons left. Finish up the ones you are on and we'll head back. Good job, you two, but it looks like you put more in your stomachs than into your cartons."

"Ha! You should talk, Daddy. Look at your face!" Maggie retorted with a smile.

Laughter punctuated the walk back up the hill to Grandmother's. The setting sun was warm on their backs and the walk was slower with the blackberry bounty teetering with every movement. Also slowing them down were Maggie and Dillon who turned around often, hoping to find Ebony racing to catch up with them. He didn't but the contentment of an afternoon well spent was not lost on any of them.

It was difficult to believe it was past 8:30 p.m. when the sun seemed to be disappearing behind the orchard grove and the purple hills between them and Lake Michigan. Grandma took no apologies for her late-arriving berry-gatherers. In fact, she actually smiled as she recalled many summer nights when her Doug would need a late supper after working the second shift at the New Era Canning Factory because a production line was down. As with her husband, she complimented the foursome on their hard and productive efforts and then she took charge. "Hurry and scrub up. Supper will be ready in 10 minutes."

Fresh blackberries on vanilla ice cream capped another great homemade meal at Grandmas. No one complained when bedtime was suggested soon after dessert. All were tired from the very full day. Carrie and Don were particularly exhausted and they were more than thrilled and grateful at Dee's request to tuck the children into bed. They were also honored.

The warm westerly lake-borne breeze wafting through the bedroom windows at this home atop the highest hill in New Era seemed to accelerate everyone's fall into deep sleep. Everyone's except Maggie's and Dillon's. They had other plans. Their bedroom was dark except for the moonlight filtering its way through the sheer curtains. Dillon joined Maggie on the top bunk and carefully pointed out the spot in the orchard where he had spotted the mystery man and that moving light. They had to check it out—but how?

"Can you see anything, Maggie?"

"No, the air seems so hazy tonight. Maybe we could see better if we were outside in the back yard."

"What? Go outside? Let's go! Great idea!" That was all the more impulsive of the two siblings needed to hear.

"No! Stop! We can't just run out. We'd wake everybody and also if anyone was out there we could scare him off, too."

You're right. Sorry. What should we do then?"

"I'm thinking." Maggie began her game plan in a subdued detective-like tone that required a wise collection of facts before action would be taken. "I know Mom and Dad would not want us to go any further than the edge of the grass in the back yard. Remember the trouble we got into when we left the yard to go into the barn? Here it is: let's leave our jams on. It is certainly warm enough. Dillon, don't go yet! Let me lead this time. Let's carry our sandals 'til we get outside. Sssh! Listen. What's that noise?"

# Chapter 9

## Is That a Light?

Just two feet out the bedroom door, Maggie recognized the sound. Dillon did also. Their plan to go outside was almost foiled in its infancy. They had both begun laughing. Laughing so hard their eyes were watering. The "noise" they heard was Grandma snoring! Her bedroom was next to the one they were staying in and the snore was even louder now that they were just into the hallway. With their hands covering their mouths, they laid flat on the carpeted floor of the hallway until they could get a grip and be quiet. They couldn't believe their laughing didn't wake someone up. Cautiously, they tip-toed past Mom and Dad's room. They were relieved to see that their door was closed.

They knew the most difficult part was to get past the squeaky aluminum kitchen door without being noticed. Maggie began slowly turning the door handle while Dillon watched the rear. The kitchen was almost sheer darkness. Only the distant street light, struggling to shine its blue glare past "Carrie's tree" into the kitchen offered some help.

They proceeded slowly, their hearts racing as they crept through the partially-opened door. To open it fully wide would certainly make squeaks. The detectives recalled this fact the first full day they were here. The concrete step leading into the garage was surprisingly cool but the mystery-solvers were undaunted. They re-latched the kitchen door from outside. Maggie and Dillon then found themselves walking on a path of moonlight that beamed unhindered through the rear door window of the garage.

Once outside, they put their sandals on. The sight before them was both exciting and scary. They had never seen nor heard anything like this! "This is surreal!" said Maggie.

"What in the world does 'surreal' mean?" Dillon wondered out loud.

"I'm not exactly sure but I heard Daddy and Mommy use it a few times when they seemed to be amazed at something."

"Then next time say, 'This sight is amazing,'" said Dillon in a hushed tone.

Maggie couldn't help but respond with, "You're surreal, Dillon."

Dillon got back on point. "Sure isn't anything like this back in Elgin."

Maggie's moon-highlighted face smiled and pointed to the thousand "flashlights" going off and on created by the lightning bugs or, as Great-grandma calls them, "fireflies."

After a few, careful steps onto the grass, Dillon told Maggie, "I can hardly hear you. The crickets are so noisy."

"I think they are cicadas."

"There you go again. Crickets. Cicadas. Who cares? Those bugs sure are loud." said Dillon.

No laughs this time. The view before them made them both stand up straight, look up, and gaze in quiet awe. They weren't sure whether to proceed or go back inside. Finally, Maggie characterized what she saw. "This whole scene looks like what Daddy had once called a 'Twilight Zone.'"

Dillon remained in quiet awe but he said to himself, "This real-life TV screen before my eyes has like a thousand-inch screen."

Although it was warm and hazy, they could clearly see the almost full moon making scary shadows of the old fruit tree branches just beyond the lawn. The wind made things even creepier as it caused those same branches to sway like skinny arms reaching out to them.

Making things even more dramatic was the cacophony of the sounds—the crickets' or cicadas' eerie noises—the wind blowing the branches into each other—apples falling from the old trees— the distant sound of Lake Michigan waves, the—.

"What was that, Maggie?" exclaimed Dillon maybe a little too loudly about a clear and scary sound he heard.

"I don't know but I'm not moving another inch. Listen some more." she responded.

They both crouched down carefully and were ready to dart back into the sanctuary of the garage. Then—they heard the sound again.

"A hoot owl!" deduced the animal-lover and Readergirl. "Just a crazy hoot owl."

"Good. Let's think of him as that nice owl in Bambi," said Dillon in great relief and admittedly a little embarrassed.

The time of truth had come: Go ahead with the game plan or retreat now to the safety of the bedroom window. Neither would say it out loud but both wondered if the mysterious man with the flashlight was lurking nearby in the shadows of the field.

With the now yellow-blue lunar light making even their faces shadowy, the decision was obvious as they looked at each other: MOVE AHEAD! Their smiles were lit up and their youthful bravery triumphed. The detective duo stepped further onto the lawn—in fact, right to its edge, defined by the grass becoming weeds and the level lawn becoming slanted. They knelt at a good-sized rock. Committed to not going any farther, and as their eyes became more adjusted to the darkness, the two realized that this scene looked very little like the same one for which they had walked with their parents just a few hours before.

"Point to where you thought you saw the light."

Kneeling on the surprisingly dry grass, Maggie asked, "Dillon. Point to where you thought you saw the light—and that man."

"Maggie! Not 'thought.' I did!" Dillon indignantly clarified. "I *did* see it. Over there. Kind of half way down the hill by those apple trees."

"I see nothing but that doesn't mean anything. If—'scuse me— *since* there is a mysterious visitor here, he could be anywhere tonight." Maggie wisely figured.

Their eyes now completely accustomed to the night sky, the two knelt quietly, hoping to confirm Dillon's discovery of that first night in his bunk. They positioned their bodies squarely on the edge of the hill. The wind was picking up but that only added to their excitement of this mysterious evening lookout.

"What's that? Is that a light?" Maggie was sure she saw something.

"Where?"

"Over there," pointed the excited sister.

"I don't see any light." answered Dillon.

"Okay—well–I don't see it anymore."

The two focused on that area like great hunters of the north in the search for their source of food for a week. Nothing. They saw no movement whatsoever. They saw no beam of light. Just the moving shadows caused by the wind blowing the trees in the mood-drenched night. The continuing noise of the crickets and the distracting flashing lights of the lightning bugs occupied all their senses. You would never know it was midnight. Maggie and Dillon were wide awake.

"Dillon, look!" Maggie broke the silence with what seemed a serious sighting.

"What? Do you see a light again?"

"Kind of. Look up. The stars!" Maggie said with a huge teasing grin.

"Mags, you are star crazy," Dillon shook his head while allowing a laugh. The once very intense brother was tricked by his older sister. Yet, instead of responding in kind, he realized once more he was looking at the crisp dark night, unfiltered by a few street lights like he had in Elgin. Then—"Look yourself! Hey! Isn't that a falling star?"

"Yes. Good call, Bud."

The two mystery-solvers lost their original focus but couldn't help but take in the big sky picture above their heads. If the orchard was a thousand-inch TV screen, the galaxy created by God was a million-inch motion picture screen. Now lying on their backs, they tried to identify a few constellations they had learned from their mother's telescope. The detectives were transformed into astronomers and became temporarily oblivious to the possibility that a mystery man could be but yards away in the shadowy orchard. Looking at a dark sky they never see in the city, they were thrilled to be star-gazers at this very moment.

# Chapter 10

## What Happened at Midnight?

The stiff breeze from the big lake near midnight was intensifying and was enough to wake up Carrie as she heard the creaking of the aging windows Grandma had not been able to maintain. Her maternal instincts also now in gear, she decided to slip out of bed and see if the kids were covered.

"They're gone! Both bunks are empty! Where are they?" Carrie couldn't help but speak out loud. She checked other rooms in this small ranch home then ran to wake up Don. "Don, I can't find the kids. Wake up! They are not in their room or any room for that matter! I even looked in Grandma's room but they aren't there either."

"Maybe they are sleeping in the living room," Don said sleepily.

"Don! I looked there. I'm going to the basement."

As Carrie was about to go downstairs, she noticed that the garage door was open, blowing back and forth in the wind. "Could they be outside? No, they wouldn't do that. But, why is this door open? Must be the wind is stronger than I thought."

At this point, Don was already behind her and she pointed quietly to the open door. They walked quickly on the cool concrete to this door, highlighted at this hour by the bright moon light. They spotted the two imps.

"They are over there—look—they're laughing at something. Let's listen." Don and Carrie couldn't bring themselves to get on their case yet for leaving their bedrooms. Since they, too, were now wide awake and reassured that their children were safe, they watched the silhouettes of the adventurers. They only wished they had thought to bring their camcorder to capture this scene for posterity. This is a vacation moment they would not soon forget. They listened to the kids' every word. It also seemed that the crickets (Okay, cicadas, if you believe Maggie) lowered their volume to help these parents hear their children more clearly in this special moment of memory.

This is a vacation moment they would not soon forget.

"There's the Big Dipper, Dill. See the handle?"

"Yeah. And that must be the Little Dipper." added Dillon, his hand pointing upward at the heavens. They both paused talking as their clearly-focused eyes were acting like solarium's lenses, attempting to take in the magnificence of this evidence of God's creation. Their parents only watched and listened. They wanted desperately to run out and hug them but refrained only because they didn't want this to end.

Dillon broke the silence. "Look, over there. Isn't that Orion? You know, the Hunter? Maggie, isn't it?"

Maggie took her eyes off the night sky and looked at her brother. "You are something, Dillon. How did you remember that?" Then, to ensure she didn't give him a swelled head, she said, "You're an Oreo, Dillon!"

"What? You a little dipper."

"You a big dupper," countered Maggie.

Getting up laughing, to push his sister, Dillon thought he heard something and stopped immediately. "Hear that, Maggie?"

Maggie stopped shoving Dillon but asked, "You're trying to trick me so I don't beat you up. Aren't you?"

"No, listen," Dillon said in all seriousness.

Maggie again sensed he meant this and listened carefully now.

The two did hear something indeed. They did not realize their parents were but 20 feet away in the open "people" door to the garage. The sound was getting louder and coming from the orchard. Reacting instinctively as before, they ran for the door—right into the laughing arms of their Mom and Dad.

Arriving a minute later was a barking dog. "Ebony!" The secure sight of Mom and Dad and now the barking of Ebony quickly ended the frightened faces of the two pajama-clad children. Just as when they first saw Ebony, Maggie and Dillon began hugging him.

"Where did you come from, Ebony?" asked Maggie as if the dog could talk like Black Beauty could. At that very moment, Ebony leaped out of Maggie's grasp and barked and pointed as if he wanted the four of them to go with him. Maggie and Dillon got up quickly to oblige their canine friend. They were very curious. Then—a quick "No! Oh, no you're not!" from their Dad. Then a strong, "I think you two have had enough excitement for tonight and I believe you have a lot of explaining to do," from their mother, was enough to keep them from joining the lure of this mysterious dog.

As they watched Ebony race into the darkness down the path that led to the old barn, the siblings then turned and obeyed their parents. The dejected detectives knew very well they had to tell the whole truth to their parents. But would they believe them?

None of this activity or noise—not even the barking —woke up the sleeping Grandma Howard. Carrie and Don were very thankful for that. Since everyone else was very wide awake, the decision was made for Maggie and Dillon to clean up from this outdoor nocturnal adventure and to have them tell their parents what exactly was behind this potentially dangerous excursion to go outside near the orchard at midnight.

Maggie, and Dillon especially, were relieved to have their Mom and Dad finally and completely in the know about the mystery man and the moving light. Telling the truth, as they had found out so many times before, has a way of bringing peace. This was no exception.

All cleaned up and sitting on the bottom bunk, the two began telling the whole story. They also attempted to make the connections between the scene in the night orchard that first night and the barn mystery guest.

"You do believe us, Daddy and Mommy?" asked Maggie as she searched her parents serious faces in this small and dimly-lit bedroom.

"You know—on the surface—I would say, 'No.'" Dad was first to speak. He then added the hopeful, "But—but considering your sighting and the actual evidence I found of the mysterious barn visitor, it is hard for me *not* to believe your story."

"Did either of you see anything *tonight?*" Carrie was becoming curious herself. She was also concerned for Grandma if nothing is resolved concerning this mystery before they leave on Sunday.

"No, I thought I saw something for a moment—kinda by those trees down near the blackberry cove—but it was too far and too hazy to be sure," Maggie answered with a great appreciation for the fairness of the question. Her Mom assumed them that she felt they were telling the truth. That meant a lot to Maggie.

"Same with me. I mean I didn't see what Maggie saw tonight but—I promise you— I saw a man with a light, probably a flashlight, from my upper bunk window the night we arrived. Trust me. Please. I did!"

"Dillon, we do trust you. Mom and I believe you completely. It's just that it was not wise for either of you to solve this mystery on your own. Next time, tell us immediately and *we* will decide what to do. Do you not see that it was dangerous for you to go out there in the dark?"

"Yes. We sure do now. Don't we, Maggie?"

"Yes. We are sorry. I just thought if we just went to the edge of the grass and no further it would be okay. It was my idea, not Dillon's. I—we—both know now it was not wise."

Tucked into their individual bunks now, and finally tired as well as sleepy, it didn't take long for Maggie and Dillon to fall fast asleep.

The unresolved mystery, however, was the foremost thought in all their minds as they drifted off to sleep in their much cooler bedrooms.

# Chapter 11

## Real Horses!

"Daylight in the swamps!" "DAYLIGHT IN THE SWAMPS!" Grandma repeated her version of "reveille" as she had a difficult time this morning getting her sleepyhead great-grandchildren to rise. "Rise and shine!" she tried this time.

"Hey, you two! You'd think you had stayed up until midnight. Come and get breakfast. It's already 8:00 a.m.! You don't want to sleep on a beautiful day like today." Then came the grandmother tickles. If the two weren't awakened by Great-grandmother's voice, they certainly were now as they twisted and turned to avoid her fingers.

Now awake but with groggy smiles, Dillon and Maggie found their way into the bathroom and then into Grandma's "office". Her kitchen sure smelled good this morning.

"Do I smell pancakes, Grandma?" Dillon asked with great hope.

"Nope. Better yet. Waffles! Hope you will like them."

"We do!" said Maggie, overhearing the conversation. "We hardly ever get waffles but we love them! Thank you, Grandma!"

Dee didn't particularly mind that Don and Carrie were still sleeping. She had not seen Maggie and Dillon in almost a year and savored every moment of this morning. "Waffles never tasted so good," she thought to herself as she poured more maple syrup on Dillon's second waffle.

Dillon and Maggie looked at each other when Grandma inquired about why everyone was so sleepy this morning. The usually very verbal great-grandchildren were strangely silent until they decided it best to change the conversation into what today held for them. Grandma obliged, telling them that she was going to take all of them to a farm to meet some very good friends, the Barkley family.

"A farm! Did you say, 'a farm'? Yes!" Dillon, as always, did not hide his feelings.

"Do they have any animals on the farm, Grandma?" inquired the hopeful Maggie.

"Yes—and the Barkleys have two children I think you will enjoy meeting. I think they are about your ages. There is a girl and a boy. They might have some work to do today but they will be thrilled to meet you." Grandma was again in her sales mode and dodged the direct question about animals. She couldn't recall how many they had and didn't want to disappoint the kids.


With Carrie driving now and with Grandma in the front passenger seat, they all ventured north and then west toward Mears. Carrie grinned as she passed the *Mack Wood Dune Scooter*s sign as she was approaching the Silver Lake Resort area along Lake Michigan. Fun memories of her own childhood began to flood her mind. "Maybe I hadn't forgotten everything about my childhood. I just need more triggers like this to jog my mind I guess," Carrie mused to herself.

Don was squeezed in the unloaded back seat behind his curious kids. He was enjoying his morning coffee and reading the *Muskegon Chronicle*. His beloved Cubs were winning and doing so without him even in Chicago to watch them! He didn't notice Maggie motioning to Dillon to look out his side window. She had spotted a tall older man walking on the edge of the rural road they had turned onto and she wondered why he didn't have a car or a bike. Was he one of those vagrants or was he simply a man out just for a walk? She felt sorry for him and wished they had stopped to offer him a ride. She did note that he had a friendly face.

Carrie slowed down as she drove on the rural blacktop with trees on both sides. She surmised this has to be especially beautiful in the fall as the tree branches reached over the road to form a natural tunnel. Rolling her window down enabled the warm and scented country air to add to this almost perfect *Norman Rockwell* drawing all around her.

Grandma pointed out the Barkley farm on the right. She was right when she had told the kids that the two Barkley children would be working. They were in charge of the small wooden fruit stand along the road. Carrie granted Grandma's request and stopped the car so she could get out and introduce her Maggie and Dillon to the gregarious children of Bruce and Ruth Barkley.

Instant friends! Maggie greeted Ashley, and Dillon quickly sized up Jacob as one cool kid. With the Burch kids' offer of helping them at the fruit stand, the Barkley kids gave them a bonus for their help: all the blueberries they wished to eat! There were now four employees operating the fruit stand sales and the hint to their parents was not too subtle—no more help was needed in this crowded work space. The older folk got the hint, parked the car, and went inside to greet some new friends of their own.

"I remember you, Carrie. You probably don't remember me. We were in New Era Elementary together when you lived with the Howards for those few months. I grew up just outside New Era toward Rothbury. Mrs. Kinninikinnik taught us back then. It has been a few years."

Carrie didn't recall but she really liked her humor and her failure to mention it had been two decades, not a few years. "I can't recall a lot about that year but I do remember it took me most of the semester just to spell my teacher's name," Carrie countered with her own humor.

With the prospects of another no-agenda day, Don and Carrie and Dee were offered sweet iced tea and took the relaxed discussion to the cool and covered screened-in front porch. Besides, the four child laborers were in full view now.

Jacob and Ashley explained the different types of fruit and were surprised how much these city kids knew.

"We eat fruit a lot at home and love just about all kinds. When we shop with Mom at Meijers—that's our grocery store—she explains the different types. So we have tried just about all of them. I think my favorite apple is Honey Crisp. Dillon loves Jonathans best." Maggie didn't waste any time connecting with these new friends.

Dillon in the meantime was helping Jacob with transferring peaches from larger boxes into smaller containers. He learned that peaches are usually harvested from mid-July through September. That's why, he figured, that they had plenty to sell right now. Then his ever-roaming eyes saw a horse. "Is that horse yours, Jacob?"

"Clyde? The brown one? No. That's my father's. Mine is the barn now."

Overhearing the boys, Maggie asked Ashley if she, too, had a horse.

"Yes, my Ginger. She's only a two-year old and very gentle. I love her. Would you like to ride her, Maggie?"

"Yes! Would you let me, Ashley?"

"Of course. Have you ridden much?"

"I love horses. I—I—No, to tell the truth, I've been *on* a horse, but can't say that I've ever ridden one by myself. I've always wanted to though." Maggie responded with honesty.

While the fruit stand was more filled with conversation than fruit, a customer appeared at the counter. He surprised the youthful sales clerks because they had been occupied otherwise by lively talk of horses—and because they had not heard a car pull up. The customer must've walked up to the stand.

This tall, older man wanted to purchase just one peach. Jacob saw him first and asked if he had misspoken. "Just one peach? You mean, 'one peck'?"

"No, son. Just one peach. That's all I want right now. One peach. Thank you."

Maggie was intensely interested in this transaction, not because of the strange request but because of recognizing the man's face. Pulling her brother aside quietly, she asked, "Isn't that the man that was walking on the side of the road when we were almost here?"

"Yes. You're right. Why?"

"Never mind right now. I just wanted to be sure."

"That's all I want right now. One peach. Thank you."

As Jacob gave the man the peach, Maggie moved alongside him and kindly asked the older man if he were thirsty.

"Why I am rather thirsty. That's why I got this peach. Why would you ask, young lady?"

"Well, I was thinking you *must* be on a day like today, especially since you are walking. I'd like you to meet my Dad and Mom. They have some water in our van." Maggie offered further.

"You are too kind, ah—I—."

"Maggie. Maggie Burch is my name. I'm serious. And if I may say so, I can't imagine you are in a hurry right now. Besides, one peach won't carry you through to supper. Am I right?" Jacob and Ashley and Dillon, too, wondered what was in Maggie's mind to offer such help to a stranger of sorts.

"Well, I must say, you make it hard to say, 'No,' " the tall stranger responded.

"Then Mr.—ahhh—your name, Mr.—."

This old fruit stand customer was caught by surprise with this question by the youthful clerk. He had come across the fruit stand in his walk and only went up to it due to his thirst. He had not expected someone to ask him his name. "Ahhh—call me—call me—Mr. Hillsboro. Yes. Mr. Hillsboro. That will do."

"Well, Mr. Hillsboro. Follow me to yonder porch."

# Chapter 12

## The Fruit Stand Stranger

Ashley was too curious to stay at the fruit stand with the boys. Besides, it was a week day and it did not promise to be too busy. The boys could handle this without her help. She grabbed Maggie's hand and the two nine year-olds escorted Mr. Hillsboro to the coolness of the porch.

Ruth stood up first and let the three in the screen door. Seeing the confused look, Maggie took charge. "Dad, Mom, Grandmom, Mrs. Barkley, this is Mr. Hillsboro." Heads nodded with careful smiles from both sides of Maggie. Then Maggie broke through it all with the charm of Pollyanna. "Mr. Hillsboro was kind enough to take time in his long walk to purchase a peach from us. I only thought we could return the favor and give him some water for his trip. Could I get some from the van, Daddy?"

Smiling ear to ear—before Don could respond—Ruth quickly intervened and offered this fruit stand stranger a glass of iced tea instead and invited him to "join some country mice and some city mice on a slow August afternoon."

It was apparent to all that this visitor was becoming much more red in his face than what the walk in the sun probably put on his aging cheeks. He was overwhelmed with this generosity. He was also not a man of many words as Carrie found out when she asked him if he lived nearby.

"No. My truck broke down and I'm having someone fix it at a garage near here."

Noticing the awkward silence by all, Maggie once more took over. "Well, Mr. Hillsboro's problem has become our pleasure. She then proceeded to give a more detailed introduction of everyone in this small porch setting.

"Mr. Hillsboro, please sit here. Thank you. This is my new friend, Ashley Barkley. She has a horse named Ginger and guess what, Mom and Dad, she is going to teach me how to ride it. Have you ever ridden a horse, Sir?"

Laughter and talk of horses, past and present, and fruit farming and grandchildren and other such interchanges made the afternoon fly by. Jacob and Dillon joined the group after they closed up the stand. Grandma Howard didn't talk a lot but the glint in her eyes and constant smile spoke volumes. "This was what life is supposed to be about" she thought to herself. Most senior citizens talk about doctors and nursing homes and meds and aches and pains. She did wonder, though, about a few curious things she saw in this tall stranger. She just couldn't put her finger on it. "Was it his face? His graying curly hair? His straight stature for someone his age? She was a wise Christian lady and knew that it wasn't prudent at this time to pursue that line of questioning with this Mr. Hillsboro.

It was Mr. Hillsboro, though, who excused himself when he felt the line of questioning was indeed beginning to seem entirely directed at him. Dee had ventured to ask him his first name out of politeness. He never gave an answer but profusely thanked everyone and then asked permission to shake the hand of the gracious young lady, Miss Maggie Burch, who had "made his day—no—his year."

All smiled with this exchange but Maggie noticed a tear or two falling from the tanned, rugged face of this walk-up new friend.

Refusing an offer by Don to drive him to the shop where his truck was being worked on, Mr. Hillsboro walked off to the east under the shaded streets of this part of Mears. He was no doubt headed toward West Fox Road toward town where the only garage in Mears existed as far as Ruth or Dee knew. Don didn't press him to ride. He sensed the pride in this man was all he seemed to have right now. Still, Dee wondered, "He couldn't be walking all the way to Hart, could he?"

Maggie's sadness at seeing Mr. Hillsboro leave was quickly replaced by the joy of her first horse-riding lesson. She and Dillon were on cloud nine! Don and Carrie had not anticipated this great event for their children but were happy for one more wonderful vacation memory. They, in fact, were able to get photos of these riding lessons as Carrie and her Canon took many still shots from all angles. Don helped Dillon mount his pony—although the young rider told the story a little differently when he shared this highlight at supper later that evening.

"Ginger is a Missouri Fox Trotter. She has a willing and gentle disposition. It might be a good thing, Maggie, seeing that this is your first ride on a horse. Because this breed of horse has a four-beat motion rather than a two-beat trot like most horses. Most say that the four-beat gait makes it easier to ride. Anyway, you won't have to readjust to riding this horse differently like most people have to do since this is your first time to ride a horse. Let me show you how to get up on her first. Ginger is about 14 hands high so since you seem tall for your age, you should have no problem getting on her or riding her." As Maggie got up, Ashley complimented her and secretly wished she and Maggie lived near to each other.

"Since you seem tall for your age you should have no
problem getting up on her or riding her."

"Hands? You don't measure her by feet?" The best way to learn
something, Maggie had been taught by Mom and Dad, was to just ask.
Maggie did.

Ashley explained this measurement standard kindly and it wasn't
long that Maggie was riding the sandy-colored pinto all by herself.
Ashley mounted her mother's steed and the two soon caught up with
Jacob and Dillon who were riding slowly on the main orchard path.
Maybe because Dillon was a quick learner or because he was his usual
brave self, but the young bronco was up and riding Jacob's pony,
Rawhide, very quickly. When asked to share how it came to him so
easily, all he could offer was, "Can't 'splain but I love it.!"

The Barkleys and Howards had been friends for a couple generations
back. Doug Howard had worked the Barkley orchard for ol' Clyde
Barkley back in the late '40's and '50's. The two families had been active
members of the First Baptist Church of Hart for years and they simply
felt like family. Doug's three girls—Darleen (Maggie's grandmom),
Linda and Shirley—were taught to call Clyde and his wife, "Uncle

Clyde and Aunt Pearl." More than a few Thanksgivings were enjoyed together. Who could forget the unique taste of Aunt Pearl's baked beans? 'Course, her secret recipe is still a secret with the family.

It appeared a new tradition was taking shape as the next generation of these families was now getting to know each other. The meal they all had that evening after the kids' "ride of a lifetime" capped off what Maggie called, "the greatest fun day in her life." It didn't take Carrie long to entertain the thought that she wished she and Ruth lived near each other.

The food was indeed in the tradition of the Barkleys' best. The food for thought was also rich as Carrie and Ruth shared notes on their lives as mothers. Carrie realized Dee had been left out of the conversation and brought her into the mix with a question that she knew would tie her grandmother and Ruth into current events. "Grandmom, tell Ruth about the interesting photo Don found in your barn."

Ruth followed Carrie's lead, "Photo, Dee?"

Mission accomplished. An animated Dee shared, "Ruth, you won't believe this. Why Don found a photo of Claire deGroot in our old barn yesterday. It was probably taken back in 1941. It was in great shape and, even more amazing, it had to have been placed there in the last few days!"

"Claire deGroot? Our neighbor, Claire deGroot? How could that be?" said a puzzled Ruth, now looking at Don to confirm this strange discovery.

"Don't know who she is. Dee seemed to know her as you do. It had the names 'Claire and Charles' written in ink on the edge of the photo. 'Charles' is apparently an old boyfriend. They are at a picnic table in some park."

Dee confirmed that the Claire in the photo was indeed Claire deGroot, one of her old friends. She also shared her regrets that she hadn't visited Claire in some time.

Perhaps to soften Dee's guilt, Ruth brought her up to snuff on Claire's current state of affairs. "She is still living in the farm house by N. 48th and West Deer Road. Her husband's death has taken a bigger toll on her than I guess we all thought it would. We haven't seen her around much, even at church." Dee listened intently, nodding her head with that statement.

"I brought her a bushel of fruit for canning last weekend but she didn't seem like the old spunky Claire I knew. She seems depressed and distant. I can only pray for her and will keep bringing over fruit when I can. Do you have the photo with you?"

"No," Carrie jumped in to answer. "Wish now that we had. If we are able to come here on Sunday, we will bring it then." Then—

"Hey! Who let these strangers in? What is Dee Howard doing eating my food?" The gregarious and hungry Bruce Barkley burst through the door laughing and, after giving Dee a bear hug at the neck, sat down and started right in eating. Bruce Barkley was as outgoing as Ruth was kind. But it was the soft-spoken wife who pushed her husband out of his chair and said, "Try to convince these good people you weren't born in a cave and wash your hands first."

Bruce put up a fake fight, said, "Okay. You win" and accommodated her request by washing his hands in the large kitchen sink. "She's a tough one. Hey, Dee, just who did you bring in with you off the streets?"

Dee proudly did the introductions and the conversation took a turn in topic to Bruce's many trips to Illinois. He knew right where Elgin and Rockford were as he drove near both cities in route to the Quad Cities for his tractor parts when an emergency called for it. Don particularly enjoyed kicking back with the easy-going Bruce. Bruce was a hard worker like his father. He was both overseeing the busy fruit farm and working full-time with the Oceana County maintenance crew. The two men also connected when they learned that they had attended college together and got more than a few laughs about those crazy days. To boot, Bruce was a life-long Cubs' fan, to which Maggie rolled her eyes an added, "Oh, boy."

As all great things must come to an end, so did this wonderful evening of eating and relaxed sharing. Carrie noticed Dee was tiring and she and Don managed to pry Maggie and Dillon from their new "best friends". They headed back to New Era with both full stomachs and full hearts.

"You can't plan great days like that, Grandma. Thank you for inviting us. We all had a great time." Carrie couldn't remember being so relaxed as she drove home along old route 31. She was hoping she might see a beautiful sunset on Lake Michigan. "The low clouds were certain to make for a dramatic sky," she thought. It was exactly 8:44 p.m. on the car clock and, sure enough, Carrie was rewarded with a picturesque watercolor framed by her windshield.

Dee noticed the same but responded to Carrie's words first. "No. I thank *you*. That was the best day I've had in a long time. It was fun to watch all of you connect with each other. It was like time stood still. I remember many evenings when Doug and I—well—it was a great evening." Dee chose to leave it at that. Carrie looked over with a smile and put her hand on Dee's. Sometimes words are not needed.

She then noticed that their brief conversation was the only one going on. A quick look in the rearview mirror revealed that Dillon was fast asleep on Don's shoulder. Dad apparently took his son's lead to catch a few "zzz's" on the short trip home. A glance at Maggie disclosed a more pensive look. "Wish I could read that little girl's mind," Carrie thought to herself.

If one could "give a penny for one's thoughts," as the saying goes, then Maggie would have shared a thought for each side of the penny. HEADS: She had a great time with her new friend, Ashley, and made a promise to herself to be Ashley's pen pal. TAILS: Because the drive home was partly along the same tree-lined road that Mr. Hillsboro had walked, Maggie had hoped for a sighting of this other new friend. "Would she ever see this kind man again? Who was going to take care of him?" were her thoughts.

Sleep that night did not only come without complaint, it was a welcome event for all. Not only was it another wonderful and long day but no one wanted to be awakened tomorrow with another, "Daylight in the swamps" by Grandma!

# Chapter 13

## The Secret Reading Spot

Grandma tried a new recipe for getting the sleepyheads out of bed. She gently pushed the bedroom doors open and proceeded to bake two apple pies covered with heavy doses of cinnamon. A rare stiff breeze from the east this morning served as her partner in crime. With the kitchen window wide open and the wind pushing the cotton curtains inside like they were made of tissue paper, the wonderful wafting waves of wind carried the aroma of apple pie and cinnamon into every room of the house. The result: this game plan did in minutes what an hour of tickling and "Daylight in the Swamps" took to accomplish!

All four were up smiling and greeting Grandma with heartfelt gratitude. Plenty of hugs served to make Dee make a mental note of the effectiveness of this new pie therapy. All eight eyes were open and fixed on the window ledge where the pies were cooling off.

"Forget the eggs and cereal, Grandma. I think homemade apple pie would be best for our health this morning. Don't you?" asked Don, coffee cup already in hand.

"You do, do you? I had in mind these pies would be cooled off and ready for lunch before you all head off to the lake." Dee countered with a wry grin.

"Lake!" screamed Dillon.

"Yes!" shouted Maggie.

"Ooops. I think I let the cat out of the bag. Didn't I?" grimaced Grandmother sheepishly.

"It's all right. They would've figured it out sooner or later when they saw their bathing suits I laid out for them last night. Your pie therapy fogged their brains so much they passed by the dresser where the suits where shouting, 'Beach today!' Carrie reassured Dee.

With another great country breakfast sticking to everyone's ribs, Don announced that the morning was free and they would leave for the lake about 1:00 o'clock. "You can do what you wish but if you want to go beyond the yard—."

"I know, ask you or Mom first. We will," promised Maggie. "Won't we, Bud?"

"Yes, but don't keep calling me, 'Bud,' Maggie.—or I will call you—I will call you (now looking at the pie in the window)—'Magpie!'" Resisting looking at his sister's face, Dillon added, "Dad, can we take a hike this morning? There's got to be a lot of cool places to hike around New Era."

"Sure. First, though, let's go downstairs and borrow one of Grandpa Howard's old pocket knives and carve out a couple of personalized walking sticks. Is that okay, Grandma?"

"Of course. Though I must admit the knives haven't been sharpened in some time but you will see that. Use any of them you wish. I know Doug would have offered one to you if he were here," Dee said with measured melancholy. Then, looking at Maggie, she asked, "And what will you be doing this morning, Maggie? As if I couldn't guess."

"I'd like to find a special secret reading spot in the orchard, if Dad or Mom will let me. I brought quite a few books and have hardly made a dent in them."

"Maggie, you help me clean up from breakfast and I'll walk out with you. I think I will borrow that lawn chair in the garage and do some reading myself. Okay?" offered Carrie, giving great indication to the Readergirl that her hopes for the morning would be realized.

The morning was perfect. The threatening east winds wimped out and it appeared the scorching heat would take a day off. Dad and son were already on a mission to stroll down Elm Street to town and then to whatever path looks most interesting. Knowing Don used to be volunteer at a fire station up in Traverse City, Grandma thought the two "boys" would enjoy checking out the New Era Fire Station for which her husband used to volunteer. She also suggested they get an ice cream at the corner creamery, then follow the bike path north past the old feed mill. "It is a very nice trail that goes along where the old railroad tracks used to go."

With a little skill, they could trek their way a bit until they could find the direction back to the house. The prospects of this adventure excited Dillon to no end. The prospects of spending a whole free morning with Dillon confirmed once more to Don that going to Carrie's grandmother's for the entire vacation was not such a bad idea after all.

≈   ≈   ≈   ≈   ≈   ≈

"Thought you were going to read *A Secret Garden*," Carrie inquired as she set up her lawn chair and talked to Maggie about her boundaries in searching for a secret reading spot.

"I was but I got motivated to read this." She showed her Mom a copy of *Lassie Come Home*. "It became number one on my list when I met Ebony the other day. I sure wish he would come back."

"That's a good book. What's the other book you have in your arm?"

"Oh, this. It's that book of Michigan wildflowers I picked out of Grandma's collection in Rockford. You know, when she was sorting and tossing through her books after the flood in her basement. Thought it would be handy on this vacation—to—duh—Michigan. And it now seems like a perfect time to use it." Maggie was noticing that the sunrise was now at a perfect position in the sky to illuminate the vast array of plant life in the unattended field before her very eyes.

In seeking an ideal reading spot, she followed the same path the family took in picking blackberries. This time she walked slowly with her books, becoming more focused each step she took as she was going to find that ultimate location:

> Outdoors.
> Under a shade tree but with good light.
> Soft grass "seat"
> Yet—so hidden that people could walk by and not see her.

Maggie's thoughts were racing now with the excitement of finding this perfect location for which to read. "Maybe I could sit under that birch tree. It looks shady. No. Too rocky and not secret enough. That old apple tree would provide perfect cover. No. Not that spot. Too dark and spidery. Her keen observation caused her also to spot some beautiful wildflowers she would pick on the way back to give to her mother and grandmother.

The hunt for the ideal reading spot took Maggie eventually to the very thicket of Blackberry Cove. She noticed an old barb-wired fence that led to an aging and thick apple tree. "Perfect!" she said out loud. "The grass under the tree is dense and soft. No one could possibly see me under these low branches and the berry bushes that have grown thick and into the fence." There was also a perfect "skylight" for her reading, provided by a hole in the top of the tree that had been formed, no doubt, from a main branch being broken by one of those strong western Michigan storms. "And," smiled the newly-energized Readergirl, "plenty of blackberries to eat just in case I might need a snack."

The hunt for the perfect reading spot led Maggie all
the way to the thicket of Blackberry Cove.

Her back now leaning against the old gnarled tree and her bottom
on the soft grass, she was glued to the alarming words that began
Chapter Two of her copy of *Lassie Come Home*:

> The dog was not there! That was all Joe Carraclough knew. That
> day he had come out of school with the others, had gone racing
> across the yard in a rush of gladness that you see at all schools,
> all the world over, when lessons are over for the day. Almost
> automatically, by a habit ingrained through hundreds of days,
> Joe had gone to the gate where Lassie always waited. And she
> was not there!

Maggie was quickly into Chapter Six of the book and was so focused
on this sad story that she spoke Joe's words out loud when his mother
tried to encourage Joe that he will "get another dog" some day. "But I
don't want another dog. I only want Lassie!" Maggie startled herself and
looked around. She laughed when she realized no one could possibly
have heard her in this desolate location.

Taking this mental break, she felt this was a good time to pick
some blackberries within two feet of her reach. Standing up now, she
used her T-shirt to temporarily hold a few of the berries. She then
transported the berries back to the shady shelter of her chosen secret
tree. Then—she stopped dead in her tracks! Maggie thought she heard
something. She bent down and listened in the direction of the very
blackberry bushes she had just left.

She *did* hear something! It was a humming noise. Was she near the
old highway? Was the sound coming from cars? It sounded a lot like
the hum of distant lawn mowers back in Elgin when she would listen
out her upstairs bedroom window. What was it? "The sound is getting
close," she said to herself. "I hear weeds and branches breaking, too,"
a frightened Maggie thought to herself.

She dropped her blackberries. She crept further behind the safety
of the old thick tree. Her detective ears were heightened. She prayed
and hoped that this "secret spot" would prove to be just that—secret.
She didn't move an inch. She glanced back again at the blackberry

bushes—"YIKES! That's a huge hand picking some berries on the other side of the bushes and the barbed-wire fence! It looks like a man. God, help me. I can't yell to Mom. Whoever this is, I must be brave. What is that sound? It's that humming sound again." Maggie's heart was beating loudly but she remained coolly quiet. Then finally her prayers were answered—this man was moving away and the strange and yet familiar humming sound was becoming more distant.

Maggie's heart was beating wildly but she remained coolly quiet.

"HE DIDN'T SEE ME! I don't dare look now." Again, Maggie remained quiet but breathed a sigh of relief. She was still kneeling when she noticed her hands were almost attached to the tree trunk. She even allowed herself to laugh now.

When she couldn't hear that buzzing sound anymore, she ventured slowly out from the tree and looked carefully all around. "Nothing. I see nothing." Maggie decided to go back for her books she had left by the tree. When she stood up she noticed a light glistening from the elbow of the old tree trunk. "What could it possibly be in a tree that would reflect light?" This curiosity took over the fear she felt only a minute or two earlier. "Something is glistening in this tree. An old bottle? A bug? A bullet? What could this be?" questioned the now very curious Maggie.

Maggie looked back again to see if anyone else was around. No one. She felt more relaxed now and decided to try to touch this shiny object. The almost noon sun was beaming through the top of Maggie's special reading tree and it was very easy for her to see and now touch this—"It's some kind of coin or something. Seems golden." She now held the mostly-buried piece of metal between her thumb and pointer finger. It wouldn't budge. It's pretty thick. "Yes, it looks like a coin. Sure wish I had a knife or something. Even a screwdriver."

"I must tell Dad and Mom," Maggie thought. "Maybe I found a treasure in this blackberry cove. Maybe I will be rich. Maybe my discovery will be in the news. What could this be?" She then heard another noise in the field. "Maaaaybe I'd better get out of here!"

# Chapter 14

## Maggie's Big Discoveries!

Maggie raced out of the blackberry cove with her books, up the steep hill, jumped over a few rocks, and looked back. No one was following her so she decided it was safe to walk. Looking back up the hill, she could see her mother in the distance, still reading on that lawn chair as she had said. Seeing her reminded her of the wildflowers she had spotted that she wanted to pick and bring back to her mother and grandmother. She recalled their locations along the path and picked them carefully. Because of the pictures, the plants were easy to identify. Now within shouting distance and excited as ever to share her discovery, she started running again and yelled, "Mommy! Mommy!"

Finally reaching a standing and concerned Mother, Maggie shared her discoveries of sight and sound. She told of the mysterious large hand and strange sound by the blackberries as well as the "gold treasure in the tree." Grandmother heard Maggie's shriek and joined the girls outside. "What's going on? Are you okay?" Maggie's Great-grandmother was foremost a mother and all her motherly instincts coordinated with Carrie's to try find out what had happened to this adventurous nine year-old of theirs.

Still somewhat out of breath due to running and some to real fear, Maggie went into detail on both discoveries. She was in her CSI detective best as she caught her breath and spit out, "I—I—whew—I finally found a perfect reading spot and—you won't believe what I saw in the tree I had chosen for that spot. Mom, Grandmom. There is an unusual coin or something shining in the tree. It is really stuck into the trunk—kind of—you know—where the branches come out of the trunk. That area. You must come and see it!"

"Okay, Maggie, slow down. We will check out the tree. But what about this sound you heard that sent you running up the hill so quickly? What was it?" Carrie seemed much more concerned about Maggie's safety than her golden discovery.

"Mom, I don't know. It was a fairly loud humming sound coming from behind the fence where the blackberries are growing. Please don't think this is crazy but the sound was almost the same as the metal detector I heard at Lake Michigan. I also saw a shadow of a person and a large hand. I waited until this figure was out of sight. That's when I started running. I guess I should have stayed there to get more details. Sorry."

"Maggie. No. You did right! You saw what you saw and, knowing your eye for detail, there was most likely a person there in the orchard with you. Maybe he was simply picking blackberries. Maybe he was dangerous. It would not have been wise for you to find out which. You definitely should not have stayed around to check things out." Carrie clearly validated Maggie's wise, quick decision.

While Maggie wanted the "Moms" to ask more about the gold coin (or whatever it was), she was mostly interrogated about the humming noise and the mysterious person in the blackberry cove. Reassured that she was okay and getting her to agree not to go down there by herself again, Carrie and Dee asked about the beautiful wildflowers she still had in her hands.

"Oh, these are for both of you. It looks like I lost a few while I was running but these here are Queen Anne's Lace." Seeing her mother smile, Maggie then said, "Okay, I know you knew that but can you guess what this is?" challenged the young botanist.

"No, I can't. Can you Grandma?" Carrie answered honestly.

"No, but I have an idea you do, Maggie. Please tell us." Dee loved this tit-for-tat with her beloved great-granddaughter. She then sat in the other lawn chair next to Carrie.

"It is called *Butterfly Milkweed* or so it says in my book." Maggie proudly asserted.

"I like the bright orange color," added Dee. Then she surprised Maggie and her Mom when she recognized the other "flowers" to be *Sweet Clover* and *Sow Thistle*.

Their laughter was quickly drowned out by the crisp, strong voice of Dillon who was approaching from the side yard. "What are you guys laughing about?" The three "girls" only laughed harder.

Without waiting for their answer, Dillon proudly said, "Look what we found!" Dillon and Don obviously had the time of their lives and found "treasures" they both agreed had to be brought back with them to Elgin as mementos of their great hike. The "Show & Tell" session revealed:

Two Indian heads—"One looks like an arrow," Dillon reported.
One rusty old gun—"Looks like a 38 revolver." Don was sure of this.
One blue balloon—"Has this *'Come to Shelby Road Baptist Church'* attached to a card on it," Don showed.
One old jackknife—"This is really cool," said Dillon. "I think it is a *Case*," observed Don.
Ten beautiful wildflowers—"Well, they *were* beautiful, weren't they Daddy?"

The mutual sharing of this morning's discoveries by the two ardent adventurers carried over into the lunch table. It was served on this perfect day on the large picnic table under the front maple tree. Maggie, like the authors in her favorite books, dramatically waited to tell of the discovery of the treasure in the tree until the very end of lunch. Of course, the large hand that she saw picking the berries on the other side of the fence had grown to be at least a foot wide. The gold coin–or whatever it was–had to come from "maybe a rich immigrant who had come up to pick the blackberries and lost his coin—a coin that had probably been passed down for centuries from a Spanish galleon that had found its way through the Great Lakes to the New World."

"Maggie, methinks perhaps you read too many books," her Dad countered with a gentle smile. He didn't want to kill the obvious excitement of this unique find by the Mags. "I will check it out after we clean up from lunch. You can lead Dillon and me to this mysterious treasure of the blackberry cove then."

"Hey! I want to go, too! I think Maggie has found something very cool and, besides, I just might bring a blackberry container along. Want to join us, Grandma?" Carrie was excited and thought Dee would be, too.

To the surprise of the rest, Dee said, "Sure!"

"Maggie and I will help you walk down. Yes! Yes! Can't believe you are coming. Yes! You are one cool great-grandmother." For that comment from Dillon, Dee could endure muscle and back pain for a month!

The expedition down the hill went slower than the excited detective duo wanted but, at the same time, the Burch family got a walking history of the "back 40" property from the Matriarch of Blackberry Cove—Dee Howard. She spoke with surprising animation about how this very ground they were walking on was worked by Carrie's great-grandfather for the raising of cattle and for the growing of a fruit crop. Carrie and Don could tell Dee was also sad that the old farmhouse had to be sold to someone outside the family. "I only wish that someone—anyone—would move in soon." The discovery of the barn guest—"the vagrant"—caused her to become more anxious than before.

# Chapter 15

## Treasures in a Tree!

Dee's history lesson made the trek through the orchard to the what locals called "Blackberry Cove" seem to go quickly. Approaching the reading tree, Maggie raced ahead to show everyone her discovery.

"It is here somewhere—by the elbow of this tree limb. Hmmm—I know it's here somewhere. I saw it. I really did!" Maggie did her best to find the shiny piece of metal.

Carrie bent over to try to help her. Being taller, she was able to see a slight reflection that really shouldn't be there. The angle of the sunlight on the tree had changed since Maggie was there earlier and it was indeed hard to see. The shade of this aging apple tree was pervasive now but, placing her hand on the slight glint of light that she did see, Carrie then actually felt something. It seemed to be thick metal.

They all sighed when Carrie asked for a screwdriver to try to pry out this object. Then Don remembered the old jackknife Dillon had found. It was still in his pocket. It was difficult to open but, once opened, it was not too worse for wear. Noticing this, Dee chimed in, "'A Case is a Case, after all,' that's what Doug used to say," as she watched Don open this classic knife.

Carrie pried and pried and finally chipped deep into the tree. With Don and Carrie taking turns, the mysterious metal was finally pried loose!

"'A Case is a Case, after all,' that's what Doug
used to say," Dee proudly added.

"It's a MEDAL, Maggie!" Carrie quickly observed. It has a ribbon
attached to it, but barely so." Then, as if she couldn't resist, she seized
the chance to make a pun. "It's a medal that is metal."

Don groaned then, after looking back at the place from which the
medal was just extracted, exclaimed, "Look, there are actually TWO
MEDALS!" Having just taken out the medal that had the shape of a
cross, he uncovered a second medal below it. This one had a rounded
edge and looked like some material was attached to it also. "It's going
to be more difficult to get out. The tree has really grown around it. I
will need a saw or something. I don't want to cut this material." Don
now knew that Maggie had found something very special and didn't
want to damage this treasure just to get it out quickly.

The excitement had everyone asking questions and wanting to see
this discovery close up. Holding the cross-shaped medal in the sunlight
for all to see and adding a little spit to clean it off, Don was able to
make out the distinct shape of an eagle with what looked like a scroll
beneath it with an inscription of some sort.

Everyone watched as Don carefully cleaned this medal even more to
attempt to read the wording. "It says—just a second—it says, 'WORLD
WAR II'! Yes, that's it, 'WORLD WAR II'. Amazing." Don and Carrie

were so entranced in the discovery itself that they had to be asked the obvious from the Readergirl.

"Okay. What does that mean? What does 'valor' mean, daddy?"

"Sorry. It means 'bravery' or—or—'courage.' Yeah, whoever this medal belongs to must have been courageous. Wish I knew what war it was from. It is clearly a military medal from some war," said Don as he handed it over to the equally curious Carrie.

"Look," said Carrie as she thought to turn it over. "The reverse side also has an inscription on it."

As Carrie tried to clarify the wording on this side—also covered with sap— Maggie continued her own vocabulary treasure hunt. She asked, "All right. It's your turn, Mommy. What's does 'inscription' mean?"

"Sorry. An inscription means there is some kind of writing, usually with a dedication or message of some kind. This side has—check this out, Maggie and Dillon—has a person's name inside a wreath. It is C-H-A-R-L-E-S-J-H-A-R-G-R-O-V-E. Charles J. Hargrove. That must be the name of the soldier who earned this medal.

## CHARLES J. HARGROVE

There was a moment of silent awe from everyone. They were all asking themselves, "Who is CHARLES J. HARGROVE and why in the world would this medal with his name on it be in the middle of an apple orchard in New Era, Michigan?" Dillon broke the silence with, "Way to go, Maggie!" and gave her a "high five" to congratulate her.

"Great detective work, girl. Hug?" Carrie added to Maggie's admiration list. Not to be remiss, Don brought Maggie close to the medal in his hand and let her read the inscription on it herself. Then Dee, who had been silent up to now, broke into the conversation with alarm written all over her face.

"CHARLES HARGROVE? Charlie Hargrove? What in the world!"

The hearing of Charles Hargrove's name brought a spirited animation to Dee like no one could remember, even Carrie, who was now holding her grandmother to keep her from fainting. She then asked, "What is it, Grandmom? Do you know this man? Are you okay?"

Everyone was now looking at Dee. "Yes. Yes. I'm fine. Charlie. This Charles J. Hargrove was an old friend of mine. He was almost married to my long-time friend, Claire. Yes, the very Claire and the same Charlie in that photo that Don found! The same Claire that lives near Ruth Barkley. Claire deGroot." After these surprising revelations, Dee said, "Maybe I do need to sit down. This is too much."

The excitement of seeing that this was the medal of her old friend combined with the humid air in this protected part of the orchard was beginning to take its toll on Dee, who indeed felt like the great-grandmother she was. One could actually see the heat rise from the damp weedy soil.

Maggie knew just what to do. "Daddy, help me put Grandmom down by the tree. This is where I sat to read. It is very soft and she can lean against the tree trunk like I did."

Don, joined by the other "man" in the group, Dillon, did just that. Dee was escorted to Maggie's bent grass "chair."

Even though she was reluctant to bend that low, Dee knew she couldn't resist the good intentions of her beloved Maggie. She also found that the long branches and leaves of the old tree served as a large parasol, providing for some welcome shade from the unyielding sun. And now with a captive audience gathered around her, a refreshed Dee Howard began to fill in some amazing blanks to the story of this war hero.

"It was probably 1940—yes, the summer of 1940—when Claire started dating Charlie. Charlie was from Hart and Claire lived for awhile here in New Era. That was the opposite of Doug and me. I was from the Hart area and Doug, of course, lived for awhile on this farm in New Era. Charlie and Claire met in high school. I never knew why she didn't attend Shelby High School. Something to do with some farming clearance. I don't know. Anyway, I met Claire when I was only a freshmen and she was a junior. I will never forget how she was very kind to me in Home Ec and Typing class. The school was smaller then and they used to mix the grade levels. Oh, I'm sorry. I'm babbling again. Can't believe I still remember all that. Anyway, she and Charlie—this Charles Hargrove on the medal—went to a summer camp with the Christian Reformed Church and really hit it off after that.

Maggie, keyed on every word from her great-grandmother's lips, asked, "What do you mean, they 'hit it off after that', Grandmom?"

Whether Dee was loving this rare attention or the fact that someone actually cared about her past life or simply that she loved this inquiry from the honest Maggie, it didn't matter. It was probably all three and with a beaming smile, she reached up and grabbed her great-granddaughter's hand. "Great question, Maggie. That simply means that they really began to like each other a lot—like boyfriend and girlfriend." Dillon, hearing this, wrenched his face with disgust. It gave them all a big laugh but Grandma quickly continued.

"That was a great year for them. Charlie was a tall and handsome man with cute curly hair. He was a senior and also was on the basketball team. Claire was a cheerleader. I remembered I was proud just to know them as friends." Dee's joy on that reflection soon changed into a more somber look. "Then came the war. World War Two, Maggie and Dillon. The medal is from World War Two, Don and Carrie, as you have probably already guessed. Well—Charlie heard the news of Pearl Harbor. He was mad. It was December 7th—."

"1941."

"Thank you, Maggie. Most kids have never even heard of Pearl Harbor let alone know when it happened. You and Dillon, come sit by me."

It was a strange sight. Five people sitting under the shade of an old apple tree in the middle of a very humid day just talking. But Dee went on with her story. She told how Charles Hargrove was planning to graduate early due to needs on the farm and had the thought he might be drafted into the armed services. "His short basketball season was going well and he was even getting words of college scholarships. But he volunteered anyway to join the army. Doug's brother and half of the eligible men in Oceana County joined with Charlie. Your grandfather— my Doug—was upset he was too young to be drafted or able to enlist for the war," she continued.

Dee was beginning to slump some from the heat but completed what she felt she needed to say. "To stay on point, Claire was broken-hearted as you can imagine. She and Charlie had talked of marriage. They used to come to see Doug and hang out in this very orchard like we are doing now." Then—directing her attention directly to the kids—she said, "Who knows if they didn't sit in this very spot 60 plus years ago!"

Don and Carrie looked at each other at this point—not so much for Dee's last statement but for their observation that the sky was becoming overcast and the wind was picking up. From where they were seated, a storm was brewing from the west. They knew they were a good piece from the house and Grandma was in no condition to run for cover.

"Grandma?"

"Yes, Carrie. Am I babbling too much?"

"No, not at all. We see a squall or something coming in over the lake and thought it would be best to get to the house before we all get drenched. Could you pick up this story after supper? You are the only one who knows the real story behind these medals. I, for one, don't want to wait to hear the story but—."

"No. You are so right." Now looking at the darkening sky herself, she said, "We'd better go right now!"

With the parents promising to come back for the medal stuck in the tree—if indeed it is another medal—the five walked up the hill as quickly as they could. They didn't talk but Maggie and Dillon felt it was a very special time. They were beginning to solve another mystery and only five people in the whole world knew what they knew right now.

# Chapter 16

## Grandma's Amazing Story!

They arrived inside the house none too soon. The rain storm hit with a fury just as they entered the back garage door. The Howard house on the hill brought great views but it also took the brunt of many storms. This was no exception. As Grandpa Howard used to say, "This was a genuine Lake Michigan thunder clapper!" But Grandma was not frightened. In fact, this was when she took charge. She was in her "sergeant's role," as Carrie's Mom would always note.

"Don and Carrie, you get all the bedroom windows latched! Maggie and Dillon, see if you can crank up the front windows! I think you should be able to reach the handles without any problems." Dee closed the bathroom window and the kitchen window and brought in the pies which had cooled plenty anyway.

Windows closed and with all bunkered down to wait out the storm, a thought hit Don and Carrie both. The day they had planned to spend at Lake Michigan was not going to happen. The kids had yet to say anything about it. Maggie's discovery and the storm took care of those plans. Yet—with another great supper and a special evening of further mystery-solving ahead, no one seemed to mind. There would be storm stories and mystery stories talked about that the Weather Channel and Mystery Channel could not match on TV. Tomorrow will form its own agenda. The God who brought in the storm today will certainly order the affairs of tomorrow.

While Grandma was gingerly walking into the living room after supper to complete her story of Claire and her soldier boyfriend, Charles Hargrove, Maggie was sitting by the picture window watching the storm proceed east and fingering the war medal with fascination.

Carrie seized the moment and sat beside her. "Maggie, it *is* a treasure you found. It's a lost treasure. We must pray for God to match this discovery with this Mr. Hargrove, if he is still alive. If he is not, then it would be good to locate any of his relatives and give this medal to them. They would be as surprised of this amazing discovery as we are and very appreciative I am sure."

"I know, Mom, but I would sure like to keep this awhile. Can we find out what this medal is for besides 'valor?' I wonder if he saved someone's life or something." Maggie was in a reflective mood again.

The thunderstorm had passed and Grandma had the kids reopen the windows. She had always loved the fresh air after a storm and this early evening rain shower would not disappoint her. She seemed to sense that the storm symbolized this past year, and the coming of her Carrie and Don and children was like a wonderful breath of fresh lake air to her stifling life.

"Now where was I?" With Dee seated in her living room chair, her simple question brought the four Burches from the front window to gather near the storyteller. "Oh, yes. Charlie and Claire were planning to get married and he went and joined the army. He left after New Year's and Claire lost all track of him. I recall that like yesterday. We all heard he was sent—like he had wanted—to the Asian-Pacific theatre, and Claire's last communication—."

Seeing the frown on Dillon's face and even in the wordmeister's expression, Don interrupted. "No, Grandmom did not mean 'theater' like a movie theater. She is using theatre in this story of Charles Hargrove to mean a location. A field of operation. Like—like—Maggie's theatre today was the orchard and blackberry cove. Our home in Elgin is another theatre for her. Understand?"

"You mean our theatre right now is this living room and this afternoon's theatre was the orchard?" Dillon asked astutely, not realizing the slight spelling difference.

"Good guess, Bud." Maggie smiled with approval, not letting him know she didn't know what "theatre" meant either.

"Thank you, Don," said Dee, doing her best not to smile too much. "Like I was saying, Claire last heard from Charlie's parents that her Charlie was assigned in the battle to recapture the island of Guam after the Japanese took over occupation of this territory from the United States. It was in December, right after the Japanese had bombed Pearl Harbor. The next anyone heard anything about Charles was by way of the cold small print in the *Muskegon Chronicle* that he was captured as a POW (looking at Maggie and Dillon), a prisoner of war. Claire just couldn't get herself to believe the report and so she continued to wait for Charlie. She waited patiently and prayerfully for almost two years. She had many suitors—ah, would-be boyfriends—but she would always decline their interest."

"Now where was I?"

"Then the official word came to Charlie's parents that their only son was officially dead, though he was never found, 'IN THE SERVICE OF HIS COUNTRY.' Boy, do I remember Claire wept when she was told the news. We all wept, to be truthful. She and I went out to Stony Lake turnaround by Lake Michigan and cried and talked for what seemed half a day."

Grandma continued after a pause in which she caught herself wiping away tears. "Then it was like a light switch was turned on. Like King David when he learned that his son was actually dead. Claire stopped grieving instantly—or so it appeared. She started dating and married Joahnnes deGroot of Mears in May of 1944. She said she chose the date in honor of the apple blossom time in western Michigan. You won't understand that completely until you have chance to listen to the Andrews sisters sing the song, 'I'll Be with You in Apple Blossom Time'. It is all too sad to talk about now."

Although Dee had stopped, Carrie could tell she wasn't quite done. Don seized the moment to motion to the kids to join him to get the apple pie desserts while Carrie stayed with Dee.

It was what the doctor ordered. The pie ala mode brought a smile to Dee and she finished her story. "Joahnnes was a good, hard-working Christian man. I believe Claire learned to love him and they had a fine marriage and two children. I'm not sure why but our friendship seemed to change after a while. The farm work was hard and busy—yes—but there was just something different. I always thought that Doug and I reminded her too much of her Charlie and she wanted to put to rest that chapter of her life. Maybe. Maybe not. But it is difficult today to contact her. I know I should. I still feel badly I haven't gone over to see her."

Sensing Grandma wanting to change the story from herself back to Claire or Charlie, Carrie asked, "Did anyone ever hear any more official word about this Charlie?"

"No. Not that I know of. I was told his parents moved back to the Netherlands shortly after the war in Europe. No. If he had lived, I'm sure we would have known. That's why Maggie's discovering this medal (still in Maggie's hands) with Charlie's name on it was such a shock to me. A flood of memories, as you can see, just came rushing back."

With nightfall already here, Don and Carrie asked permission to pray for Grandma. Permission was not only granted but welcomed by the tearful grandmother. In the quiet of the evening at this home on the hill—as another cool breeze filled the room—they began asking God how—of even if—Dee should approach Claire and for the Lord to remind Dee of His presence and protection and provision for this coming Fall and Winter. Before an "amen" could be expressed, Maggie asked Jesus to help her know what to do with the treasure she found today.

To complete the Burch family circle of prayer for Dee, Dillon added, "And thank you, God, for giving us the best grandmother in the world, even if she really is our great-grandmother."

"Amen!" Don and Carrie concluded in unison. It was clear the request for His presence was already granted.

The promise of a rousing game of UNO—"if Maggie and Dillon got ready for bed"—was presented. Good call. This brought laughter back into the home and, as Grandma would often say, "It was one day they all had earned a good night's sleep." Sleep they did. More discoveries and mystery-solving could wait for eight hours.

# Chapter 17

## Squeaky Sand!

Yesterday's storm brought cooler air for today's trip to Lake Michigan. With everyone rising early, a full breakfast and the fun of filling coolers for a picnic lunch on the beach was accomplished before 9:00 a.m. Maggie and Dillon were out of their jams and into their swimsuits and flip flops before breakfast. The little time spent in lathering them up for sun protection allowed the excited Burch family plus one to be on the road by 9:30 a.m.

With windows rolled down, the van followed the winding old Route 20 from New Era to what Carrie recalled as the Stony Lake turnaround. It was so named because one would pass by the scenic Stony Lake with its small, quaint cottages, turn directly west and head to the big lake. When you could go no further—right at Lake Michigan—all vehicles would have to "turnaround" to retreat back from wherever they had come. Most summer evenings will find cars parked at this turnaround, facing west and waiting for the sun to make a colorful dip into Lake Michigan's far horizon.

"It's only eight miles to the beach so it won't be long," answered Dee to Dillon's anxiety about when they would get to the lake. He had been excited about this day since he located New Era on the Rand McNally map back in Elgin and realized it was very close to Lake Michigan. Only eight miles—but plenty of time to fire off a litany of questions from the curious quiz kids.

"Are those cherry trees?" Maggie began.

"Yes. It is past harvest but it appears some farmers are late in picking their cherries. The trees you are looking at produce tart cherries," Grandma answered.

"Tart cherries?"

"Sorry. There are two types of cherries. Tart and sweet cherries. Sweet cherries are grown primarily for fresh eating. I'll try to get you some before you leave. Tart cherries are used for making jams and pies. Did you know that cherry pie filling is the number one pie filling in the United States?" Grandma loved history, especially if it boosted the stature of her beloved western Michigan.

"No. But I do know now," smiled Maggie.

"That sign says, 'OCEANA COUNTY.' I didn't think Lake Michigan was an ocean." Dillon quizzically challenged his great-grandmother.

Loving every minute of doing her part in the regional home schooling of Maggie and Dillon, Dee answered this very serious and logical question. "It isn't, Dillon, though many people say it looks like an ocean. Actually, it *is* one of the largest fresh water lakes in the world."

"Wow! This is hilly! Go faster, Dad!" Dillon yelled, moving his attention from history lesson to this roller coaster of a road.

"Better not, Bud. This is an unfamiliar two-lane road. I can't be sure what's on the other side of a hill or curve."

"See Daddy calls you, 'Bud.' It must be okay." Maggie challenged her younger brother.

But something distracted Dillon from responding to his sister. "Look, Maggie. Is that Ebony?"

"Looks kind of like—no—Ebony has more white on his face and I think he is bigger." Maggie responded with detective-like analysis.

They had gone almost 8 miles and the road approaching Stony Lake was narrowing and mostly hidden from the sun, not unlike the same road leading into Mears. Driving slowly under a walking bridge that led to an array of well-crafted canoes and kayaks on Stony Lake allowed another question. This time it was from Don to Dee. "What's the bridge above this road for, Dee?"

"Carrie, you can tell your husband."

"Okay. If I remember right, it belongs to this international youth camp called Miniwanca. I think anyway. It borders on Lake Michigan. Apparently, the camp has bought rights to be able to use the adjacent Stony Lake for teaching canoeing and kayaking and swimming. I think it is a private camp for kids from all across the United States. You can see part of it from where we will be in a few minutes." Carrie again recalled a memory she thought had been lost long ago.

"Wow! This sure is steep!" Maggie and Dillon chimed in together. The narrow concrete road approach just before the full view of Lake Michigan at the turnaround does indeed have a sharp, steep incline. Don wanted to dramatize this steep ride up the hill so he drove even more slowly. At the top of this hill, now finally facing the blue waters of Lake Michigan, came two animated voices.

"Wow! It *is* like an ocean!" Dillon commented as he agreed with his great-grandmother. "This is so cool! Let's get out!"

Parking the car on the blacktop before the expansive natural beach, Don paused to take in the sight. He didn't say it but Carrie knew the boy in him was gearing up for a fun day at the beach. Yet—when he saw Maggie and Dillon racing to get to the water first, the father in him quickly took over.

"Dillon! Maggie! STOP! Don't get in the water!" yelled their father as his voice penetrated the strong westerly breezes coming off the lake.

Puzzled but obedient, the two sprinters stopped in their tracks. They said nothing but stared at the whitecaps on the waves and at the unending horizon beyond them.

When Dad caught up to them, Dillon asked, "Why did we have to stop? There are other kids already out in the water."

"The reason is," Don said slowly, "because—I WANT TO GET IN THE WATER FIRST!" He raced to the water, ran a bit in the shallows, then dove head first into the first decent wave. "OHHH! MAN, this is freezing!"

Maggie and Dillon laughed at the sight. They were glad their Dad learned first that even in August the "big lake" can seem cool at first. Then, with some hesitation, they waded until the water was up to their knees. But it still seemed cold and they joined their Dad who had run back to the shore.

Carrie, in the meantime, helped Grandma commandeer the one table by the sand dune. A flip of the red and white checkered table cloth on the weathered wooden table signaled what planned to be another great day of vacation. The overcast sky was already beginning to break up as the sun was attracted to this large body of water before them.

Two lawn chairs and a make-shift beach umbrella provided protected front row seats for Dee and Carrie. From this loft on the sand dune Dee noticed three little girls attempting to keep a sand castle together against the relentless waves. Her memory jogged back to a half century earlier when she would take her three girls to the lake when Doug got off work. She was in this zone of memory when Carrie asked if she wanted some sun protection lotion. Carrie traced her grandmother's stare and smiled as she knew exactly where Dee's mind was.

It didn't take two detectives long to make a discovery that all children have made since recorded time on this sandy coastline of western Michigan. "DAD! MOM! GRANDMOM! Listen! This sand is squeaky!" Dillon joined his sister as he, too, rubbed the bottom of his feet against this unique, nearly white, sand. No one knows why. Okay, the Creator does…but this phenomenon—this special occurrence— has marveled and entertained generations of children and adults alike. Carrie smiled and ran over to the kids and showed them how they could make the squeaks even louder. She then ran back to get her camcorder and—presto—a video memory was captured!

Maggie and Dillon discover squeaky sand at Lake Michigan!

And yet another discovery helped the family to enjoy the water of Lake Michigan without stepping directly into the cool lake itself. With Dee's encouragement, the Burch family decided to take a brief hike along the extensive shoreline to warm up a bit. Going north a bit they came across a narrow inlet of water coming directly off the lake.

"The channel!" Carrie remarked. "I forgot. My Dad and brother, your Uncle D, Mom and I used to love to swim and float in this channel. Follow me!" The suddenly brave Mom then led by example and waded into the shallow waterway. "Told you. It's warm. It really is."

It didn't take Dillon long to trust his Mom and wade into the channel himself. "It *is* warm! Come in, Maggie. Dad, it really *is* warm."

Before long they all dove in and enjoyed yet another discovery. They would be sure to point this out to their Uncle Derek and Aunt Kat in Texas when they see them next.

While Carrie was floating on her back, she remarked to Don, "What do you hear?"

Listening carefully, Don said, "Besides the wind and the waves—nothing."

"Precisely." They both smiled.

Not exactly enjoying the pulling sensation of the channel flow, Maggie walked out to the nearby shore of the channel. She became quickly absorbed in watching a teen boy walking slowly on a sand bar only a few feet away. He was holding something that looked like her neighbor's weed whacker. There was a sound coming from this thing that sounded like the sound she had heard in the orchard only yesterday morning. Every once in a while she would also hear the humming speed up. True to her inquisitive nature—and knowing she was within a few feet of her Dad—she finally asked, "S'cuse me. S'cuse me." She secured the somewhat perturbed attention of this tall youth. "Hi. My name is Maggie. What are you doing? What is that thing you have in your hand that's making that noise?"

"It's a metal detector," was his only response as he turned to ignore this "little girl."

Maggie was not just a Readergirl of books. She was also becoming—maybe *because* of her reading—a Peoplereader. She knew it would be a waste of time to pry more information from that boy. But her curiosity about this thing was not yet satisfied. She waded back into the channel and asked her Dad about the metal detector by pointing to the boy, now further up the shoreline.

"What is that thing you have in your hand that's making that noise?"

"He's was telling you the truth, Maggie. That *is* a metal detector. You turn it on, hold it over a piece of medal or coin, and it will make a buzzing or humming noise. It's actually pretty cool."

The information side of her curiosity was met but the mystery side of it was not. She was sure *that* was the same sound she had heard when she spotted that big hand picking blackberries yesterday morning. Her mind began some deductive reasoning. "Hmmm—metal detector. That barbed wire fence was metal. The sound she heard was the same buzzing, humming sound." Maggie was in full CSI mode at present. The mystery of yesterday's sound was more interesting than the mystery of today's warm channel from the Lake Michigan. At least it was to her.

"Earth to Maggie. Maggie to Earth." Carrie saw Maggie was preoccupied as she continued to watch the boy with that detector walk away into the haze of the sun now glistening brightly on the shoreline. Only an occasional sea gull would distract her thoughts.

"Maggie! Do you hear me? Come! It's lunch time and Grandma is waiting."

It seemed time stood still this warm August afternoon. All enjoyed Dee's unique egg salad sandwiches and lemonade and potato salad. Watching others enjoying this "best kept secret" location along Lake Michigan made the memory-building even more enjoyable. Once more, Grandma put some drama into a simple meal. "Close your eyes, everyone. You, too, Don and Carrie. SURPRISE!" All opened their eyes to see a huge red watermelon.

"How'd she sneak that into the car," Carrie thought as she her shook head in amazement at this surprising 80-plus year-old lady. Somehow, eating a watermelon—yes, one *with* seeds—was the perfect finish to a great picnic at the beach. In case anyone wants to know, Carrie won the seed-spitting contest by a full foot.

Whether it was the direct sunlight, the eventual running in and out of the powerful waves in the lake, the tossing and chasing the Frisbee, or the building of four sand castles in the wet sand along the shore—no one was too proud to admit they were exhausted after this, the most active day of their vacation yet. They knew it would be at least three more hours until sunset and, although they wanted to stay to see it, they knew they would be burnt to a crisp if they did.

The ride home had one burning question that even this very special day didn't erase from Maggie's mind. "Dad, will you and Mom be getting that other medal out of my reading tree?"

After affirming they would, Don and Carrie found her question generating a few questions of their own.

"Why would a man leave his war medals in that field?"

"How were they preserved so well after being in that tree so long?"

"Was the mystery berry picker using a metal detector as Maggie was suggesting?"

"Who was that mystery man?"

"Will Ebony come back before they leave?" And—

"Will we ever get all this sand out of the van?"

# Chapter 18

## War Medal Found!

After all was unloaded from the full day at the beach, Don and Carrie changed clothes and set out for the orchard to attempt to pry out this mysterious object out of "Maggie's tree." This time Don and Carrie came equipped. They brought an old tree saw Carrie's grandpa had in the garage. One of his crow bars, found in the ceiling, was also brought along just in case. Carrie carried a hatchet, an old towel, a screw driver, and a plastic container of water. Grandma got the job of caring for Dillon and Maggie for the duration of the medal extraction. They sat in the shade of the back yard tree watching their parents descend down into the warm orchard. They smiled when they also saw their Mom carrying a large Cool Whip container.

With full permission to cut into the old tree, Don still was conservative with the "V" pattern he cut to free up the second mysterious medal.

It took less effort that they had expected. Still, they lifted the newly-freed medal carefully. Success! They were especially glad that the heavy decorative ribbon attached to this strange-looking medal was left intact.

"Let me look at it, Don." Carrie asked with excitement. "It is too covered with sap to see what the inscriptions are on either side, but it *is* clear that it is basically round." She also noted that it, too, was gold.

As Don took his turn to hold this sticky medal, he agreed with Carrie. "You're right. Can't make out anything. It must be another war medal though since it was found with the other one."

"Think so?" said Carrie wryly. "You should apply to be a CSI agent in Chicago."

Don was too occupied trying to get the sap off with his finger nails that he didn't respond in kind. Instead, he turned to Carrie to suggest they had better get going. But he didn't see her.

"Carrie? Carrie? Where are you?"

"HERE. Over by the blackberries. Just wanted to 'kill two birds with one stone,' " she garbled with her mouth full of blackberries.

Knowing the kids and Dee were eager to see what the discovery really was, the two headed back up the hill. The very warm sun was now on their backs, their long shadows revealing the two were holding hands. Not bad, considering all the equipment they had to bring back up the hill.

Maggie and Dillon saw them first and raced to see the discovery. All marveled at the condition of this medal. More amazing to them was the heavy denim-like material attached to it. "Only thing I can figure out is that the sap functioned like a preservative for the medals all these years," Don deduced. "Amazing!"

"Preservative? What's that, Daddy?" It was Dillon's turn for a vocabulary lesson.

"Sorry, bro'. The word means 'something that protects things from decay or makes them at least last longer'— like—well—like the cooler with ice we took to the beach. It kept the egg salad cool so we could eat it later without it spoiling. My guess is that the thick sap from the tree served to keep or preserve the medal and the material through all these years. Because of the sap and the tree growing around the medal, the storms, the heat and cold, even the insects couldn't destroy them. Even so, Dillon, it's amazing they remain in such good condition."

Carrie and Grandma used a few cleaning products to further clean the ribbon, and some *WD-40* did the job of thinning the sap from the medal itself. This medal did not have a name inscribed on it but had very cool designs on both sides.

On the one side was the figure of a Roman solder with what looked like a broken sword. The embossed letters clearly read, World War II. The reverse side recalls the "Four Freedoms," speech by President Roosevelt. It is surrounded by the words, "United States of America" and had the dates of this war, "1941-1945". Maggie particularly liked this new medal.

The medal was lightly rinsed, dried by Grandma's old pink hairdryer, and was placed in an old but beautiful leather watch case. Grandma had found this case and the well-kept ring case for the other medal. "Glad I didn't just rush and toss all of Doug's things away."

Victory Medal (front)  Victory Medal (back)  Distinguished Service Cross

At supper, the girl detective decided to share her theory about the metal detector she had heard and seen at the beach and its connection to the sound she heard by her reading tree. "The sound was exactly the same. That boy must have been looking for some metal—something valuable. Medals are made of metal. Daddy, you said some detectors are made for finding gold. We found a gold medal in the tree. The man by the blackberries—let's say he had a metal detector—was looking for those gold medals we found. Am I crazy? I DON'T THINK SO!"

"Good critical thinking, Maggie." Her Dad confirmed with a proud smile. You get your critical thinking from your mother. Problem is, we just don't know for sure. It would seem to me a stretch in logic that someone would know those medals were in Grandmom's orchard after all these years. Also, if I were to use a metal detector, I think I would use it where a lot of people have been, not where very few people have been. I'm not saying it isn't possible. Could be that what you heard by your tree was indeed a metal detector. I have no other logical answer to offer you myself."

Grandma was smiling and had to speak up. "You are so right, Don. Maggie is just like her mother in that way. And, Carrie is just like her mother in the same way."

"Must be a female trait that came from you, Grandmom," Don just had to conclude.

"I think the air is getting as thick as that sap in the tree." Dee said to diffuse Don's compliment.

Suddenly—

Carrie got up from the table and, while putting her sandals back on, asked with utmost seriousness, "Grandma, what time is it? Is it 6:00 p.m. yet?"

"No, not yet. The factory's 6:00 p.m. siren has not gone off yet." Then, looking back at the clock over the serving window to the dining room, "It is 5:10 p.m. to be exact."

"Don, I'm taking the van downtown. Next to that little framing store I love, I noticed a community computer room sign on the window. Right, Grandmom? I'm going to see if I can get more information about those medals online."

All Don heard was, "Yes!" when he saw her back the van out of the drive after he questioned whether she would remember the shape and color of the two medals. He realized that was not a very smart question to ask of Carrie, the artist and color czar.

Maggie wanted to go along and was sad that her mother left without her. That's when the magic of her great-grandmother pulled the perfect question out of her maternal hat. "Maggie, would there be any chance you would like to help me eat a few of these?" She brought from behind her back two pint containers of fresh sweet cherries which she had promised during the trip to the beach. Dee had found them early in the morning on her front porch. She wasn't sure who would put them there from time to time but she was always thankful. She loved her sweet cherries almost as much as she loved the smile she now saw on Maggie's face.

Carrie felt somewhat ill at ease all alone in this empty hallway that doubled for a community WiFi room. Telling herself that nothing would happen to her in the Village of New Era didn't help a lot—but that concern soon passed when she got specific information from an Army website as to the name and purpose of the medals. A click of the mouse and 30 cents later, the info was now on paper. Five minutes and 30 seconds later and she was back at Dee's home.

"This Charles J. Hargrove was indeed in World War II! It has him listed as a POW. Remember that means a 'prisoner of war.' He must have been quite a soldier. Maggie, this is a bigger treasure than you can imagine! The round medal that has the Greek figure with what looks like a broken sword in his hands—is called a WORLD WAR II VICTORY MEDAL! Here's the colored print-out Isn't it cool? Each side of this medal has a symbolic message about World War II and how our victory preserved some important freedoms we hold dearly."

"The medal that has the American eagle on top of the cross with ribbon still attached—catch this—is THE DISTINGUISHED SERVICE CROSS."

"What does that stand for, Carrie?" Dee knew that Charlie had to be about 20 years old when he was taken captive by the Japanese on Guam and all this peaked her interest.

Carrie was stoked. "Well, Grandmom, I will tell you what it means, but you will have to bribe me first with some of those cherries."

Deal accomplished, Carrie said, "Maybe it would be best if I read it to you.

> The Distinguished Service Cross was established by order of the President in 02 January 1918 and confirmed by congress in 09 July 1918 for EXTRAORDINARY HEROISM IN CONNECTION WITH MILITARY OPERATIONS AGAINST AN OPPOSING FORCE."

"Extraordinary Heroism" stuck out to all of them. They wondered what heroic deed he had done. None of them could quite process all of this information nor what it was going to require of them to  bring these special war treasures to the proper person. And who is this "proper person?"

A whole hour was left to read before "lights out" this evening. The prayer tonight included this Charles Hargrove and how they could honor his heroism by giving his medals to a family member or someone close.

This was one of those rare nights that Dee could not sleep. She felt that these precious medals should go to Claire. "After all," she thought in the stillness of her bedroom, "she suffered so from his death. She is now single and I just know she would love to have the connection to her Charlie now. Oh, Lord. I don't know. Help me to sleep. I turn this decision over to You."

Back on the top bunk, Dillon thought it would be appropriate to re-open his Hardy Boys book, *What Happened at Midnight*. But it wasn't long before the real-life mystery outside the window lured him away from his chapter book again.

Maggie smiled when she read the last paragraph of *Black Beauty*.

> And so my story ends, My troubles are all over, and I
> am finally home. Sometimes, before I am fully awake,
> I imagine myself to be back in the orchard at Birtwick,
> standing with my old friends under the apple trees.

She thought of her new friend, Ashley, her horse, Ginger, and the orchard of apple trees.

Her mind was racing. "Was it the yet unsolved mysteries or just too many sweet cherries that was keeping her awake?"

Mom entered the room later to check on them. As she so often does, she lifted the book from Maggie's grasp, tucked her in and reached up to Dillon's upper berth to pull up the covers he had kicked off. Both were sound asleep.

# Chapter 19

## Pieces of the Puzzle

"Daylight in the swamps!" This time it was Mom and Dad who got the upper hand and burst into the kids' room to wake them up. One was asleep still but one was awake.

"You scared me," said Maggie, already awake but engrossed in wrapping up the fourth chapter of *Heidi*. "I was thinking about Grandma and—BOOM—you guys rush in."

"Well, if you remember, today is the day Daddy and I are going off together for the morning and afternoon. Your great-grandmother has a special day planned for you and Dillon. So we wanted to say, 'Good-bye' for now and we'll see you about 5:00. Please help Dillon get ready. We hope you both do your best to cooperate with Great-grandmom. She has to be fairly tired today. Today is already Thursday. We will keep our cell phones with us. Do you have any questions?"

"No—Yes—are you going to give me a hug first?" as if she had to ask. Then, beaming, she added, "Oh, another question. Where you are two *kids* going for your big date?"

"We aren't sure. That might be the best part of it. We are going to have a big breakfast someplace. Other than that, we are looking forward to having a no-agenda day," her Dad replied.

A no agenda day. Sure sounded nice to both of them. They were beginning to wonder what that was. They were glad they waited until Thursday to do this since they were both so relaxed. Their schedule back in Illinois was jam-packed with activities. With the kid's schooling agenda, Don's job—always peaking in the summer—, church activities, their own family needs, and the kids' many social activities, they found themselves depleted of quality time spent with each other. Carrie

98

recalled from somewhere the old phase, "Beware of the barrenness of a busy life." They both were beginning to feel barren. With shorts, T-shirts, sandals, a few beach items, a full tank of gas, and the prospects of perfect weather ahead of them, they drove out the driveway. Maggie and Dillon, still in their pajamas with grandmother behind them, were waving and smiling.

Their parents were about to turn and head north onto old 31, which also served as Main Street for New Era, when Don looked to his left and saw the sign, "*The Trailside Inn.*" He asked Carrie, "What about that restaurant. I kind of doubt if it is a chain."

"I've heard it has good breakfasts. Looks like a few cars in front. That's always a good sign. Sure. Let's go there."

They parked across the street in front of the frame store that Carrie loved. Being in no hurry, Carrie pointed out an Ansel Adams photo print in the front window. They turned to head across the street and Don pointed to the bed of a new Ford pickup just in front of them. "Look, a metal detector. That's what Maggie saw at the lake and what she thought she heard in the orchard."

The village restaurant was indeed filled with patrons. More than a few turned their heads at this new couple entering their eating hole. Don's and Carrie's attire shouted "Visitors: These people aren't going to work today." They quickly found an empty table and didn't have to wait long before being asked, "Coffee?"

Both turned their mugs upright and smiled when the server gave them a menu. A hearty order of pancakes, eggs, bacon "cooked crisp," wheat toast, and some very tasty fried shredded potatoes was in front of them before they could scrounge up a newspaper. Just as well; they were both hungry and not needing to catch up with the "noise" of the news.

When Carrie looked up to take in the character of the restaurant, she wondered if Dee and Doug used to eat here, but she couldn't recall this place in her childhood visits to New Era. As she dropped her eyes from some historic black and white photos of New Era, she saw a person she seemed to recognize. "Don. Look. Isn't that Mr. Hillsboro, the man Maggie met at the fruit stand and invited us to meet us at the Barkley home?"

"Isn't that Mr. Hillsboro, the man Maggie met at the fruit stand...?"

"Yes, I didn't recognize him at first but, yes, that *is* Mr. Hillsboro. Should we ask him to join us?"

"He seems to be about finished with his breakfast. Yes—yes—see if he will."

When Don walked up he noticed Mr. Hillsboro seemed to be preoccupied with looking out the front window. When he called his name, he didn't respond. "Mr. Hillsboro?" Don asked a second time. The man looked up somewhat befuddled. Then, when Don said, "Hi! Remember me? I am known by most people as 'Maggie's father'. We met the day she brought you in from the fruit stand."

"Yes. Sorry. I was lost in my thoughts. I blame it on age. It's as good a reason as I have right now."

"Hey—I forget and can't blame it on age so—no problem." Then, pointing over to Carrie, he said, "Carrie and I just wondered if you would like to join us. We have one of those no-agenda days and would love for you to join us for an extended coffee."

Two more cups of the great black java later and Mr. Hillsboro blew their characterization of him as a quiet man. He seemed to welcome the opportunity to talk. In fact, he asked three questions before Don and Carrie had one of their own.

"What are you two doing down here in New Era?"

"How is that wonderful daughter of yours and that great son?"

"Are you headed back from your vacation?"

Don responded in kind. "Visiting Carrie's grandmother. Maggie and Dillon are great. No, we don't head back until Sunday."

Mr. Hillsboro laughed out loud. Then comprehending what Don just said and with a quizzical look at Carrie, he asked, "Visiting your grandmother? She lives here in New Era? I guess I didn't pick that up at the Barkleys'. Wasn't that her with you at their farm?"

"Yes. My grandmother is Dee Howard. She has lived here in New Era as long as I can remember. We decided to take up her request and spend our vacation with her."

This older gentleman's tanned face turned almost white. His talkativeness suddenly changed. His mind was racing ahead of his mouth. "Then—then—that was your mother on the porch. That was Dee Howard? Your mother is Dee Howard! I must not be getting just old; I must be getting senile, too. I knew your grandmother years ago, Carrie. Maybe 50 or, more likely, 60 years ago. This is embarrassing. I didn't recognize her at the farm. She must think I'm terrible."

"No. Not at all. If it helps any, I don't think Dee recognized you either. It *has* been a long time." Trying to direct the conversation to this unbelievable connection between Dee and her old friend, Don asked the obvious, "How did you know Dee, Mr. Hillsboro? Did you once live in the area?"

This tall gentlemen paused. Took another sip of his coffee. Took a deep sigh and hesitantly said, "I've—I've got a terrible confession to make, Don and Carrie." Now looking directly into their eyes, he said, "My name is not Mr. Hillsboro. I am so sorry. I lied to all of you on the porch that afternoon. When Maggie asked my name—well—she caught me off guard. I didn't want anyone in the area to know I was back in town. My real name is Charles Hargrove. Dee used to call me Charlie. I am so embarrassed, I don't really—."

"CHARLES HARGROVE? You are *the* Charles Hargrove?" Carrie asked with a huge smile, also realizing she was probably heard by the couple at the table next to theirs.

Charles looked at Carrie with equal surprise. "You sound like you have heard my name before. This is crazy. How can that be?"

"Crazy is right," Don agreed. "You simply won't believe how crazy and yet how happy this makes us." While Don was saying these words, he was looking into the face of someone who looked stunned. Charles didn't know what to make of this but he did break into Don's words when he blurted out, "Then you are Dee's granddaughter, Carrie! Of course. And your very special Maggie is Dee's great-granddaughter! I don't know what to make of all this."

Since Carrie was just addressed, she said, "Charles, you are right but that is only a small part of how crazy this is." They were all smiling now and were ready to dig in for full morning of revelations and sharing. The other customers had mostly left the restaurant when the server, who did not know any of these three visitors at this table, brought Charles and Don refills a third and fourth time.

Just as Dee said when she saw the photo of Charles two days earlier, Charles told them he grew up in Hart. "I was good friends with your grandfather, Carrie, and got to know Dee through Doug. He was a fine man." So far, Charles had become a truth-teller as his story matched Dee's perfectly.

"I know. I loved Grandpa. We used to take hikes together. He let me ride his snowmobile. My family actually lived with him and Dee for a few months when I was in 6th grade."

The abundance of coffee and the explosive discussion motivated this elderly Mr. Hargrove to talk about his past. Don and Carrie purposely and patiently withheld the most startling news of finding this man's war medals. They let him talk freely.

"I drove here this week all the way from my home in—," Charles lowered his head again,—in Hillsboro, Texas." Don and Carrie both broke into a laugh, recognizing now just how he came up with his false last name at the Barkleys'. This caused Charles to laugh also and brought freedom to move on. "I moved to Texas after years of working and living in the St. Louis area." He didn't say as such but Carrie and Don picked up that he had been very successful in commercial real estate in Missouri. He retired only six years ago and almost immediately his wife died of unknown causes. "I didn't do very well after that," this private man opened up. "We only had one child and—well—let's just say she and I have been alienated for too many years. I was too busy making money to be the father I needed to be. Anyway, bottom line is that I had little to do in my retirement. I wanted to move to a smaller town but that proved rather dumb. There was little for me to do in Hillsboro. Nice people there but I just didn't connect. Truth is, I chose not to connect. Didn't need a shrink to tell me I was depressed."

Realizing he was controlling the conversation and not used to talking about himself, Charles said, "To make a long story short, that's what brought me back to this area. I felt empty and all the money I had made didn't do anything to change that. Honestly, I didn't feel of much worth and, worse yet, didn't know of anyone who really cared either way."

"So you came back here to find that?" Don couldn't help but inquire. Both he and Carrie realized that their "no agenda day" was beginning to take on an agenda, one in which they never could have imagined, one that would never had taken place if Don had turned right and not left.

"Kind of. The only time I felt I ever contributed anything on planet earth was in my stint in the army. I volunteered in January of 1942, I finished high school a semester early. I had my basic training right in Hawaii before I could even spell 'Hagatna'."

"Hagaat—what?"

"Sorry. That's the capital city of Guam. HaGATna. That's where my battalion was shipped to—the island of Guam. The Japanese had captured Guam, as you might know (they didn't) from the United States only a few months after Pearl Harbor was bombed—so we tried to regain it." Then it struck Charles again that he was giving details that this young couple probably couldn't care less about and apologized. "I'm so sorry. I'm going off rambling like the old man I am. You must have a lot to do on this beautiful day."

Carrie interrupted him quickly, "No, not at all Charles. You have no idea how interesting this is to us and how you are beginning to solve a puzzle that no one less than our Maggie and Dillon have been working on. Don smiled and knew that Carrie, too, was putting some of the pieces to the mystery together that they had all been working on since they practically arrived in New Era. "Please go on," Carrie encouraged. "It's only 9:30 a.m. and we have a full day ahead of us. Besides, the coffee here is great."

"You two are rare young people. I will attempt to cut through the details though. The fighting was fierce. I still don't like to think, let alone talk, about it. A lot of brave men died. I should have. I was captured with about twelve other servicemen. Why we weren't killed I have no idea to this day." Charles paused when he saw Don take a quick glance at Carrie.

Pretending to be surprised by Charles' comment, Don asked, "Then you were a prisoner of war?"

"Yes. I have never really talked about it but—yes—I was there for three long years. That was when the American troops recaptured the island and found us." Charles paused again. It appeared he was now fighting back some tears. He realized once more that he had told no one, save his wife, about this all these years. But, for some reason, all of this memory of the horrific acts done against him while in that prison camp came flooding out in this August morning in a small village restaurant to two, for-the-most-part, strangers."

Charles gathered some more composure and went on. "Don and Carrie, thank you for listening to me this morning. I think the reason I am telling you all this is because—as I'm learning all too slowly—this is the *real* reason I've come back to this area. I've been in Oceana County for two weeks now. I've been walking through Doug's parents' orchard trying to find a couple of war medals I had left somewhere here in the orchard after the war. It's a long story. I will tell you later about that maybe."

"Suffice it to say, it was around Christmas in 1945, after I was released from rehab at Walter Reed Hospital, I was very confused. Part of me wanted to make a bee-line for home. The other part was afraid since I didn't want anybody to see me in the state I was in. A friend I had made in the hospital invited me to stay with him at his home in Missouri. I was confused but thankful so I took him up on that offer. But I was restless. After a while, though, I got healthy and wanted so badly to see my family.

Some time in the summer of '46, I finally went back to Michigan. I found out soon that my parents had moved back to the old country. It was tough to hear that from total strangers from the new owners of my Dad's farm. That was devastating. But, the main reason I had come home was to look up my old girlfriend. In fact, she was my fiancée. We never tied the knot though because we both knew there was a good chance I might not make it back."

When Charles paused again and dropped his head, Don guessed that he was thinking that he wished he had died like the other men at Guam.

"I had a lot of time to think in that stinking hell hole outside Hagatna. I had stopped entertaining the idea that I would ever see home again." Another reflective pause by Charles. Don and Carrie let him do so quietly, riveted to his every word and did not care a whit about the passing of time in what was now an almost empty *Trailside Inn*.

"In inquiring where my fiancée might be, I learned she had given up on my return and married a man named deGroot. I didn't have the heart to find her. I—." Charles could no longer keep his emotions in check. He began to cry. Don and Carrie both held each of his big hands.

# Chapter 20

## Two Friends Reunited!

"Grandma, where are we going?" Maggie and Dillon were excited as they buckled their seat belts in their great-grandmother's Chevy. Their curiosity was getting the most of them. They wondered why she made them put on jeans as opposed to shorts on this warm day.

Dee was just as excited and yet just as determined not to answer. "Somewhere. I think you will like it."

Not to be outwitted by their great-grandmother, they peppered Dee with the "hint method" of investigation. They actually thought they could manipulate or trick her to get answers from her.

"Give us a hint or two. Is it a picnic? Are we seeing someone we might know? Will it be by the lake or another farm?"

"No use. I won't fall for that trick. You do recall I had three kids of my own and they were the national champions of trying to pry answers from me. Your grandmother Darleen was especially good at asking for hints. So, some things don't change." She beamed from ear to ear as she heard Maggie and Dillon groan with smiles on their faces.

On this morning's mystery drive the ever-watchful eyes of Maggie soon uncovered Dee's game plan. "Ashley's and Jacob's! Dillon. Look! The trees covering over the road. Remember? This is the way to the Barkley farm!"

Maggie and Dillon weren't out of their seat belts yet when their two new "best friends" ran out to greet them. Another day of riding lessons filled the morning for these four pals in the saddle. Ashley and Jacob were surprised how Maggie and Dillon had picked up so quickly from where they had left off in their riding skills.

Another day of riding lessons filled the morning
for these four pals in the saddle.

The four were quickly trotting back into the orchard and found
their way to the creek running through the property. Dillon did his
best at reaching the stirrups on Rawhide. Jacob's gentle pony seemed
to know and accommodate his new rider and deserved well the Burch
boy's pat on the neck. Dillon was proud when he slid off the saddle and
joined the others along the creek bed. Having stopped to give the horses
the cool water from the creek, the four enjoyed their own snack packs
prepared by Ruth Barkley that morning. Also, dessert—apples—were
but a reach away. Maggie discovered that although she enjoyed fresh
apples from the grocery store, nothing could match an apple just picked
from a sun-drenched tree. No wonder Jacob calls them 'Honey Crisp',"
Maggie thought as she bit in to one that tasted as sweet as honey.

Meanwhile, with Ruth giving assurance that she would watch the
kids per Carrie's instructions of last night, Dee left out on a mystery of
her own. "Would Claire even be there when I come for a visit? Would she
want to talk with me? Should I even be doing this? Are her concerns any
concern of mine?" Even with these reservations, Dee knew she would
continue. She recalled she had not wanted many visitors herself after
Doug's death but was glad when a few good friends braved rejection to
encourage her in those tough months after the funeral. "I must do the
same for Claire. I am late in doing so but better late than never."

The large farm entrance off of West Deer Road was familiar to Dee. She had been there few times to visit her old friend in years past. But now the long, tree-covered driveway was filled with weeds and an assortment of wildflowers that were probably not supposed to be growing there. It was eerily quiet except for a seemingly harmless dog running up to greet her.

Seeing Claire on the front porch was at first disarming to Dee.

Seeing Claire on the front porch was at first disarming to Dee. Seeing Dee approaching the porch was equally so for Claire. Attempting to break the awkward silence with some light humor, Dee got to the top step and asked, "I was bored and been wanting to husk some corn, Claire. Could you use some help?"

Hardly missing a beat, Claire countered with, "Then what has taken you so long? The corn has been in the field for weeks waiting for you. Husk if you must!" Dee smiled when she realized the old Claire hasn't changed, at least in her sharp humor.

"Claire, I am so sorry, so sorry I haven't visited you after Johannes' death. I won't go into any sorry excuses. Please forgive me. I—."

"Dee, you needn't explain. No need for apologies. You are here. Let's get inside. It is getting pretty warm on the porch. I must have some lemonade in the fridge."

The bridge to openness between these two old friends was much less difficult to cross than Dee had imagined. She and Claire brought each other up to snuff on current events: their health, their kids, their church, their finances, and then—their loneliness.

When the conversation turned to their husbands, the two cried, their tears like summer showers on the dry sandy soil of western Michigan. The arrival of the needed rain is never questioned, just praised and appreciated. The God of parched hearts and parched soil is One in the same.

It was as if time stood still. Dee and Claire were one in spirit. For some four hours they shared 60 year-old memories and talked transparently of recent not-so-pleasant ones.

"Claire, I was over to visit with Ruth Barkley and brought my visiting grandkids and their children."

"Ruth. She's a wonderful person. For some reason, she keeps bringing me fruit and bread and asks nothing except how she can help further. To my shame, I've accepted her food but not her counsel."

"Well, I can relate. I was slow to open up my wounds back when Doug passed…but it was Ruth who reminded me of your needs. She really didn't have to. I hadn't seen you at church in a long time and should've inquired. I've not been the friend I should have been."

"Pish! Posh! There you go again. Remember, no need for apologies. You were and still are my friend, Dee. Let's face it; we have both lost out for not sharpening our friendship."

Nursing her sweating lemonade glass, Dee's eyes surveyed Claire's barren shelves. "Claire, we *are* indeed friends. That's why I have to ask you. How are you going to make it now that Johannes is gone? You don't have to tell me if you don't wish but I have to ask."

"Dee—Dee—I don't know what I'm going to do. I am so embarrassed. And I've been too proud to ask for help, but come November," Claire paused, "come November I will no longer be able to keep the farm. I haven't told anyone. Not even my boys. They have their own families to take care of and are real busy. Buddy calls once in a while and I give the 'church vestibule talk'—you know—'Oh, I'm fine and how are you?'"

Both ladies laughed at that one, but Dee was quick to ask what Claire would do if her fortune remained the same as it was now.

"I honestly do not know. I pray and pray but there doesn't seem to be any answers. Dee, it would take a miracle. I have farmed out some of the acreage but it isn't enough to keep the farm going and pay the mortgage. I would hate to think of a nursing home. I can't live with my children. That wouldn't be right. I would like to think I have some years left. I am lonely and fearful to be honest."

Dee and Claire compared common fears and futures. The afternoon flew by. They shared a small brunch together and Dee finally made Claire promise that she would come out to see her tomorrow. "I so want you to meet my great-grandkids. They are something else! Darleen's daughter, Carrie, and her husband are very special. We have had a great week together. Please come."

"I would be intruding. Maybe some other time, Dee."

"No, Claire. Please come tomorrow night. Be there by 5:30 p.m.. You must promise."

Smiling, Claire said, "I think our roles have changed over the years. I used to tell you what to do and now you are telling me! Okay, I will be there. I think I still know how to get to New Era." After a pause when they simply looked at each other, Claire concluded. "Dee, your coming today was an answer to prayer. I mean that. You know me too well that I would never make that up. You are a godsend—and I guess, if God wants me to listen to you, then I will gladly listen. Can I bring anything?"

Now on the porch, Dee hesitated then said, "Yes, please bring some of that sweet corn you shucked today. We could use a dozen of your best. See you Friday at 5:30 p.m. sharp!"

Two "irons" were sharpened today; the countenance of each had blessed the other. The two aging friends both waved like they were still school girls. It would be hard to discern who was happier. Suffice it to say, needs were met on both ends. A load of guilt and hurt was lifted from Dee. A kernel of hope was planted in Claire's once-empty heart. God is good.

# Chapter 21

## A Mystery Solved!

"Charles, Carrie and I have something to tell you but maybe we'd better take our conversation outside before Alice asks us what we want for lunch."

Charles once more apologized for "wasting" this young couple's day. Carrie once more corrected Charles' thinking. "Charles, on the contrary, you and your story have *made* our day."

Carrie continued the conversation in the restaurant to the
other side of the unhurried main street of New Era.

Carrie continued the conversation in the restaurant to the other side
of the unhurried main street of New Era. "Charles, the little private

112

investigators we call Maggie and Dillon have been trying to solve the mystery of a secret visitor to the blackberry cove from the night we arrived at Dee's. It's also a long story but I think we know now who this mysterious guest is." Carrie just beamed.

Charles couldn't hold back a huge smile of his own and proceeded to listen intently.

Looking and pointing at the truck on the curve next to them, Don continued Carrie's point with a question. "This is your truck, right? I wonder what that metal detector is for. Our nine year-old Maggie was probably but a few feet from you this past Tuesday when you were hunting for your medals with your detector. She was frightened out of her wits when she heard a strange sound followed by seeing a huge hand grabbing some blackberries."

Don and Carrie tag teamed this surreal story, including the beginning of it when Dillon sighted a man with a flashlight. They also told Charles that it was Dee's determination that the mysterious barn guest was a vagrant. That brought laughter from all three. The laughing was heard all the way down at Meyer's Chevrolet but these strangers were in a zone by themselves. In fact, Charles may have recalled the most amazing of these coincidences when he added that he couldn't believe that Maggie had invited all of them to meet at the Barkleys' fruit stand in Mears.

That's when he sighed, shook his head, and spoke of Maggie once again. "Don and Carrie, your daughter's rare kindness—if you think of it—is what brought you over to my table this morning. Unbelievable. That's right. If she hadn't done that, you would never have had any reason to come over to me as you did. We simply wouldn't have known each other. This mystery of which you are now speaking would have remained so. That girl is something."

"We know," said Carrie. "Since you brought her up, let me tell you something equally mind-blowing. I have something to tell you that makes this story even more amazing that involves our curious Maggie. Please sit down next to us."

Charles obliged, bent his long legs and moved back into eye level with them. "What more could there be? I'm all ears."

"Charles, the medals you have labored to find after all these years. The medal search that brought you back to New Era. Maggie found them."

The few townspeople who had reason to be in downtown in the village of New Era on a perfectly fine working day had to wonder about the identity of these three strangers sitting on the sidewalk. Why were they laughing? Why were they crying? What did it say on their license plates? Where were they from? Why were they sitting on the hot curb so long?

Charles was caught off guard with Carrie's comment. He was speechless. He was not too proud to cry. Yet—no words came from his open mouth.

"It is true," Carrie continued. "Maggie found them in an old apple tree by the very blackberries you were picking. She had gone into the orchard to find a secret reading spot—as she so often does on our vacations—and, yes—just happened upon something shining in the elbow of the main tree trunk. Your medals. Don and I unearthed them and couldn't believe how well-preserved they are. We would take you now to see them and give them to you but Dee and the kids are gone. Also, come to think of it," Carrie was now looking at Don, "we would rather that Maggie and Dillon give the medals to you personally."

"They are still in good condition?" an incredulous Charles asked.

"Yes, and one has your name inscribed on the back. We now know who CHARLES J. HARGROVE is!" said Don.

The three new adult "best friends" gave each other big hugs and reassurances that they would connect again Friday night. They also made promises to let Maggie and Dillon tell their stories. They all knew that none of this good news of Charles' treasure hunt would ever have been realized but for the vigilant work of these two young detectives.

Still shaking his head, with a smile, Charles called back to Don and Carrie, "Hey, I think I know how to get to Dee's house but what time do you want me to arrive?"

"Six o'clock would be perfect. Listen for the town's siren. See you at six. Dee will be thrilled to see you again." At least, that is what they hoped. They were surprised and relieved that Charles hadn't asked about his "missing" photo of Claire. Did he even think it was still there? Did he ever go back to look for it?

≈   ≈   ≈   ≈   ≈   ≈

Dee's arrival back at the Barkleys' could not have been timed more perfectly. Four very hot and happy "riders of the sage" trotted up to the barn at the same time she was pulling in.

"Grandma! Grandma! Look!" Her two very proud great-grandchildren wanted her to take a picture of the four of them on their steeds, but were satisfied that she at least saw them and took mental pictures of their achievement.

"We are so hot. We had such a good time!" Maggie and Dillon slid off of Ginger and Rawhide almost as smoothly as their teachers. They put the horses away in their stalls and gave them some well-earned water as taught by the responsible Barkley children. Dee watched with pride. A hug from Dee after this confirmed they weren't just perspiring; they were sweating like they had worked a full day picking apples in the orchard.

Ruth came out and was about to offer all some lemonade but Dee wanted to complete her "big day" as planned for the kids. Inviting Ruth and Ashley and Jacob to join her, the six drove toward the Silver Lake Sand Dunes to a trailer that served as a *House of Flavors* regional ice cream shop.

Ruth noticed Dee was especially elated and soon discovered that the "reunion" with Claire went more than well and that Claire even called it a "godsend." "The prayers and babysitting had brought 'fruit' no orchard could," she said to herself.

It was called "House of Flavors" for a reason. There were so many flavors to choose from. This was a major challenge of decision-making for all but Dee and Dillon. "Butter pecan, please," was Grandmom's quick order and it took but two minutes for Dillon to settle on "Bubblegum." The two were seated outside on a shaded table when Maggie and Ashley came back with huge cones of "Mackinaw Island Fudge." Ruth and Jacob went the predictable route and got "Pineapple Orange" and "Creamy Strawberry." All six made the most of the cones and because of the heat, the two mothers made note that more than one T-shirt was decorated from the *House of Flavors* color chart.

With promises to write and see each other again "as soon as possible," the four "best of friends" departed with tears and knuckle hand shakes. Not a lot was said on the drive home. Dee was in mental overdrive with joy, wondering even now how to encourage Claire tomorrow night. Maggie and Dillon eventually talked about their adventures on the farm until Maggie found the warm air coming in the open windows of her great-grandmother's car lulling her to sleep. It was five o'clock now and they would be meeting up with their parents soon—or so they thought.

Don and Carrie had indeed lost track of time during their surprise and rewarding visit with Charles. They lowered their expectations of driving all the way up to Ludington and found their way to a quiet spot on the beach by Little Point Sable Lighthouse. Picking up a take-out lunch at Silver Lake, they headed slowly south along a narrow blacktop, following the signs to the light house until they found a shaded and empty parking lot. They were thrilled that they seemed to be the only visitors by the lighthouse this Thursday afternoon. They were equally thrilled that they could sit there and talk or do nothing and had no mysteries to solve. They were not so thrilled they had but a couples hours or so. They both realized the lengthy conversation with Charles made them feel "worded out." They also both realized a good marriage is often defined by being able to enjoy one another without the need for verbal conversation. The wonderful lapping sound of the powerful Lake Michigan waves was all Don and Carrie needed to hear. God's "still small voice" at such times is about as good as it gets!

They found their way to a quiet spot on the
beach by Little Point Sable Lighthouse.

Dee met Don and Carrie outside as they pulled up to her home
at almost 6:10 p.m. "The kids are sleeping like babies. They had a
wonderful day with Ashley and Jacob. They are in their beds taking a
little nap and I've got fans going to cool them off and to drown out
any noise. We'll have supper at 6:30 if that is all right with you. So how
was your day to get away from it all?"

Fortunately, Dee was sitting down when Carrie and Don announced
they had spent most of the day talking with none other than the "dead"
and decorated Charles J. Hargrove. It was Dee's turn to be speechless,
yet she was glued to the revelations of their chance meeting at *The
Trailside Inn*, the war memoirs, and the story of Charles' imprisonment
at the hands of the Japanese. Dee said nothing, but did shed more than
a few tears when she heard all this new information of Charles' alleged
death and his seeking to find Claire after all. The leaving of his medals
in her apple orchard was the most difficult for Dee to comprehend.
"Why there?" was all she could get out of her mouth.

Carrie then shared why and when he came back to look for those
medals. This finally put Dee into mental and emotional overload. Maybe
it was due to the emotional day she already spent with Claire. Maybe it

was simply all these shocking and deliriously happy news about Charles. Yet Dee cried with every detail. She was so overwhelmed that she had yet to tell Carrie and Don about *her* visit with Claire, let alone begin the promised meal preparation. Because of time, she opted to give them the "Reader's Digest version" of her visit with her old friend.

"Claire!" Dee managed to shout. "Claire. How will she handle all this news? This is hard for *me* to comprehend. Think about *her*."

"We have, Grandmom," Carrie began. "That's why we have something to tell you. We took the chance to invite Charles over tomorrow night so that he might be given his medals by the actual finders, Maggie and Dillon. We hope it is all right with you. We told him to come at 6:00 p.m. We didn't say anything about dinner."

Dee was anything but upset and then proceeded to tell more of her story of seeing God heal her relationship with Claire and of Claire's financial stresses and her need to move out of her homestead. Then Dee announced with a smile about her invitation to Claire to also come over tomorrow evening. She was, however, to come for supper. "She is to come at 5:30 p.m. and wants to meet you guys and the kids. I hope I didn't violate your vacation plans."

Don and Carrie were quick to squelch such thinking. "We are just glad you were able to patch up hurts with Claire and to renew your friendship with her. You both have so much in common and, Grandmom, we would like to meet her, too. By the way, Charles told us it was Grandpa's camera and dark room that produced that old photo of Claire and him in that park. It sure has held up through all these years. You guessed correctly."

Few words were said at this point except those of getting the dinner prepared. There seemed to be a mutual understanding that God was doing something very special. Both Dee and Carrie knew that they weren't orchestrating a meeting of the former engaged couple. The request to come to Dee's home was made separately and with sincerity by both parties. But what would Charles think? How would Claire handle such an emotional discovery after all these years? Their minds were racing but without answers. But the mystery of Dillon's sighting of the midnight orchard visitor and Maggie's finding the war medals were simply too strange not to be resolved.

The leftover fried chicken did not taste like leftovers to the Burches. It always seemed that even leftover food tasted better at Grandmom's. Maybe it was the fresh apple pie for dessert that made it so good. "Maybe it was that someone else prepared it," reasoned Carrie with a smile to her thoughts.

The three adults had made a decision not to tell the kids anything about Charles this evening. The two Readerkids were wired enough at supper, having taken a good nap and telling their story of the horseback riding to Mom and Dad. Any news of finding Charles and hearing the story of his hunting for the medals would have kept the curious siblings up all night. No, with a respite from the day trips, Friday would now be perfect for Dee and the kids to set the stage for the biggest discovery yet. The mystery of how Charles and Claire would react once they saw each other—for better or worse—would make Friday night "an affair to remember".

Before she retired to her bedroom, Dee told Don and Carrie that she would be out early in the morning and that they would have the house to themselves.

# Chapter 22

## Preparing for the Big Evening!

Don found Carrie's grandmother true to her word. He found a note next to the coffee pot that was music to his ears.

> Good morning!
>
> You are on your own. I'm off to meet up with my friends, Harmon and Nancy Raga, for breakfast. Then I'm off to do some grocery shopping. Help yourself to anything, except the apple pie that is in the window cooling. That's for tonight for you know whom. Looks like another beautiful day. Hope to be back by noon.
>
> Grandmom

The morning sun was not shy in coming through the front picture windows and into the living room. Dee must have awakened early to open the curtains and bake that pie. The lower windows were also open, allowing the ever-present breeze on this hill to secretly drift into the living room. While Carrie remained in the bedroom catching some very rare 40 winks, Don also was enjoying a rare moment: a no-agenda weekday morning with his beloved coffee, his first penetration into one of the three books he brought, no phone nearby, and the kids—the kids. "How come the kids are not awake? This is too good to be true."

"No, I'm not going to get out of this La-Z-Boy. I'm not. Rats! I should have guessed," as Don followed his instincts and not his comfort. "They are not in their room. They had better not be back in the orchard." At this point, he peered out the kids' window. No sight of them.

Not willing to wake Carrie out of her well-deserved rest, Don ventured quietly through the kitchen door, out into the garage, and that is when he heard the laughter. They weren't in the back. Those voices were coming from the front yard!"

"We're just sitting under Mommy's tree and I'm reading to Dillon.

"Hi, Daddy! 'Bout time you are up. We're just sitting under Mommy's tree and I'm reading to Dillon."

Breathing a sigh of relief, Don asked what the laughing was all about.

"Oh, catch this." Dillon rolls his eyes as Maggie read from his Hardy Boys' book, *What Happened at Midnight.*

> "I'm sure I don't know," said Mrs. Hardy, no less mystified by Frank's extraordinary behavior. "Boys are strange creatures. You never know what they are going to do next."

Maggie laughs all the harder and Dad says, "Well, Dillon, I think Mrs. Hardy is more right than wrong. I know. I'm one of those boys. Sometimes we are 'strange.' " Don smiles at Dillon. "But I do know what *this* strange boy is going to do next. I'm going back to my chair and read. You two may stay here but come in for breakfast when I call you."

A leisurely morning and casual breakfast was perfect for all. Carrie did get her rare forty winks and settled for her barley green this morning for her breakfast. She joined Don in the living room but seated so as to see Maggie and Dillon reading. "I could get used to this," she thought. She reasoned that there was also some quality unplanned homeschooling going on this week.

> Geography: Fruited landscape, a Great Lake, thunderstorms, squeaky sand
> Biology/Astronomy: Horses, growing season, insects, gardens, star-filled skies
> Botany: Trees, orchards, wildflowers, blackberries, unique weeds, fruits galore
> History: WW II: a living, talking history of it; generations: primary source info
> Bible: I Peter 5:10—restored relationships; III John 4—children walking in truth

English: Reading, reading, reading; vocabulary lessons from Great-grandma
Sociology: Meeting new friends, communication between the ages
Math. "Carrie sums up sadly, "7 minus 5 equals 2. Only 2 days left of vacation!"

Time seemed to stand still on this perfect morning until Maggie and Dillon saw the mailman drive up. He handed them Dee's mail and they ran it inside with a message. "We're hungry! What can we eat?" Their normal Elgin morning meal of cereal and milk and fruit was all that was offered and, although it didn't draw smiles, hunger won over bickering.

With breakfast soon behind them and the realization that Grandmom would be home in an hour, the four divided up the tasks they thought should be accomplished and set out to surprise Dee by cleaning up the house. Don and Carrie, of course, knew that more than one guest would be coming over tonight and Dee would naturally want everything in order for them.

"Carrie," inquired Don, "where is Maggie? I thought she was going to do the breakfast dishes."

Carrie found Maggie in Grandmother's bedroom room sitting on the rocker, looking once more at the war medals. Carrie saw her daughter in a very pensive mood and, rather than chastising her immediately to get her back to her task of doing the dishes, she quietly asked, "Wha'cha thinking, Maggie?"

"I'm so sad for this man, this CHARLES HARGROVE. I've been thinking, Mommy. If he was captured in 1942 or so—as you found on the internet—then he would be about 85 or more today if he had lived. And if he joined the army at age 18 then—then—he sure missed a lot of years of living. It makes me sad that such a brave man had to die so young."

Sitting on the bed next to Maggie's chair, Carrie answered. "Yes. Good math, girl. He would have been pretty old if he had lived. He did a lot for our country. Also, to just imagine that he was a prisoner of war for a few years as Grandma told us! That had to take quite a toll on him." Now touching Maggie's shoulder, she says, "I think he would be very glad to know you are thinking of him, having not even met him. We'll have to read up on World War II and learn what it meant to America and the world. Would you like to?"

"Yes."

"Maggie, why don't you put those medals back in their cases for now? You could honor your great-grandmother by getting her dishes done before she gets back."

Dee arrived and Dillon was the first out the door to help her with the groceries. "Why Dillon, you sure are strong. That is my heaviest bag."

"Yeah, that's what everyone says. I think it is because of all the drumming I do." Placing a sack of groceries on the breakfast counter, the highly-esteemed seven year-old said, "I'll get the other bag, Grandmom."

Dee had Don grill some hotdogs outside. Seeing that the day was turning out to be very pleasant, she made an executive decision for all to eat outside on the picnic table. Maggie and Dillon cheered. She had plenty of potato salad left and had picked up some buns to go with the dogs. Dee also chose to tell Maggie and Dillon about Claire coming that night for supper. She wanted to set them up with an accurate appraisal of how Claire would appear so they wouldn't read her as just an old lady. They would no doubt see her somewhat depressed appearance as Dee herself had seen on Claire's porch. She spoke fondly of her teen years spent with Claire and of her strong Christian faith. She even mentioned Claire's love of blackberries and how she used to visit their great-grandfather as a girl since she had grown up in New Era.

The usually curious kids said little until Dee told of Claire's farm. "Does she have horses? Does she live near Ashley?" asked Maggie. "How old is she?"

"The last question addressed the very issue Dee wanted to bring up. "She is about 84. She is old and she has been through a lot but she is a wonderful lady. I hope you will be as kind to her as you are to me. And, yes, she has four horses I believe, and she lives about a mile from Ashley."

"Wow! 84. That is old," chimed in the not-too-subtle Dillon, not knowing or thinking that his great-grandmother would be 83 this very year.

Everyone smiled without comment except Maggie who remained in her detective mindset while hardly eating her hot dog. "Then this Claire would be about CHARLES HARGROVE'S age, Grandmom. I figured he would be about 85 today if he had lived, didn't I Mommy?"

This comment startled Dee for a moment until she glanced over at Carrie to silently connect that Maggie's comment was just an innocent observation and that she knew nothing of Claire's relationship with Charles or of Charles being alive.

"You are probably right, Maggie. Now, Claire is coming over at 5:30, so I have a few things to do to get ready. I say 'few' because it looks like some cleaning elves came in and straightened up my house. Thank you. It might allow me to even take a nap." Nevertheless, Dee was already up from the picnic table, surprisingly spry this afternoon.

"Can we help anymore, Grandmom?" The two great-children laughed when they almost spoke as one.

"Why, yes, there is something that you could do, if your parents will allow it. I told you that Claire loves blackberries. I don't have any left it appears. Could you two take the holder and four pint cartons or so and pick some blackberries? That would save your great—," Dee caught herself one more time, "your *grand*mother a lot of walking."

Don gave Maggie his cell phone and told the two to change into their jeans and be back by 3:30, no later. Knowing now who the mysterious visitor was, assured he and Carrie that they did not have to worry about the kids venturing down the hill to the blackberry cove.

"Yes! Let's go, Maggie!"

Maggie and Dillon re-entered their detective's playground. On the way down the hill, Dillon kept his eye on the old barn. He was just tall enough to look over the weeds in front of him to see the top of the barn. "Hey, Maggie. Do you think we could take a few minutes to check out the barn one more time? Maybe Ebony would be there?"

"No, I don't think it would be wise right now, Dill. It would be fun, but not wise. We have a task to do for Grandmom and it should be fun. I don't suppose she would mind if we ate a few blackberries while we were also picking some. Besides, maybe Ebony would find us down there."

Picking up a walking stick had to be expected. Throwing
some fallen apples at a wasp's nest as not.

The two somehow made it through the jungle of weeds and brush
and hidden rocks without stopping too often. Picking up a walking
stick had to be expected. Throwing some fallen apples at a wasp's nest
was not. Luckily for them, it was deserted.

Grandma had a two-fold task in sending the kids to pick blackberries.
Not only did she want to surprise Claire with her favorite fruit but she
felt uncertain as to how tonight ought to proceed and didn't want the
kids in earshot. She would be ready for Claire, but seeing Charles and

introducing him to Claire was clearly something she wanted Don and Carrie to weigh in on.

She found them outside. They were carrying the large picnic table Doug had built from the front yard to the side yard as she had casually talked about two days ago. "Thank you so much! I didn't mean for you to do that but thank you anyway. It will be fall soon and I'm not sure who I could've gotten to do that for me."

"No problem at all. Is there anything else we could do while we are here? Ask now or forever hold your peace. Carrie is the strongest woman I know so don't hold back asking. We are willing and able."

"No, I can't think of anything to move, but I do need some advice."

"We are probably stronger than we are wise, but we'll give it a shot," Don responded.

Carrie was glad that Dee wanted to go over a game plan and was willing for her and Don to suggest a few ideas. This would not be a normal evening of entertainment. They anticipated a potentially dramatic night and felt the need to be ready to have more than one plan of attack. The three had a good and open discussion with each involved in taking a role, depending on how Charles and Claire reacted. The two old friends, once engaged to be married, just might be angry at this uninvited intervention and the reunion could be explosive. On the other hand, they might be extremely happy. All three were pretty sure that—at the least—they would be overwhelmed and feel very awkward. This special event would require all three to do what they do best.

Don agreed to meet Charles and assist in his meeting with Claire. Carrie would involve Maggie and Dillon in the presentation of the medals and assist them when they realized that the "Mr. Hillsboro" at the fruit stand was the one and only CHARLES J. HARGROVE. Dee would naturally be the one to greet Claire and help her in any way needed with Carrie as a go-to substitute if she stumbled in that attempt.

Dee held Carrie's hand on the picnic table and said, "I never told you two this, but Charles has his name inscribed commemorating his service in the war at the VFW hall over on Wilson Road in Hart along with Doug's brother, Norman, and several others who died in World War II."

Reassuring Dee of their help, Carrie and Don felt led to pray with Dee for the evening. This was almost interrupted when they heard, "Daddy! Mommy! Grandma! We have the blackberries! We each picked two pints. Sorry we are late. Why did you move the picnic table?" the ever-observant Dillon asked, not missing a beat.

"Grandmom wanted it moved here before we left." Taking the berry holder from Maggie, Carrie was quick to encourage their diligent work. "Looks like you did a great job with picking the blackberries. Thank you for helping. Claire will love these. Hey, we were just going to pray for Grandmom. Want to join us? Let's all hold hands."

Don led and Carrie joined in, both knowing to pray generically so as not to reveal the actual plan for the evening. All knew such an evening would be best to leave in God's hands.

# Chapter 23

## Claire and Charles

"Claire!"

Dee did indeed greet Claire at the door but she was caught off guard when she saw the transformation from the Claire she saw shucking corn yesterday to the Claire she witnessed on *her* porch tonight.

Knowing exactly what Dee was thinking and attempting to ease her friend back from the shock, Claire cut to the chase, "Pish! Posh! Dee, this old gal doesn't look good in sad rags or glad rags but after you came over yesterday I realized I needed to get my act together and get back in the world of the living."

Dee regained her composure and said, "Well, Claire, you sure have done that! You look wonderful!" Dee noticed that it wasn't just the surprising visual change in Claire; her old spunk was back also. "Her light yellow summer cotton dress and putting her hair back made her look 20 years younger," Dee thought as she led Claire into the living room.

"Claire, this is my granddaughter, Carrie, her husband, Don, and—

"Hi! My name is Dillon. Hi, Mrs. Claire."

Rolling her eyes at her younger brother's interruption of the greetings, Maggie gave her own. "Hi, Claire, if it is okay to call you that. My name is Maggie."

"You certainly can call me Claire. I've been called worse. Dee you were right. I can tell this is a special family indeed. At least, my kind of family. Very nice to meet you all."

"Nice to meet you, Claire. We have heard a lot of good things about you. Sounds like you and my grandmother go way back," Carrie responded.

"We do. Back before we had indoor plumbing and TV."

They all laughed and Don tried to add to the humor when he asked Claire if she had a hard time finding New Era tonight.

"Don, that's your name, right?"

"Yes, I've been called worse."

Claire laughed heartily and asked, "Is your last name Skelton? You are sharper than Louis Postman's fish fillet knife! Don, I would guess that Dee told you I grew up here and I did. But truth be told, I haven't been back in New Era for some 25 years. I have driven through it a few times—going to Muskegon and back. But my family has either died or moved out. So, I must admit it was kind of eerie turning left onto Ray Road."

"I think Claire would like to sit down, you guys. Let me take you to the chair I picked out for you." Maggie grabbed Claire's frail hand, the one feature that did not belie her age. She then took her to grandmom's favorite chair by the fireplace. Carrie and Dee looked at each other with a grin as their plan to take care of Claire was taken over in the first 10 minutes by the youngest lady in the house.

Dee and Carrie had decided to hold off on supper since Charles was supposed to come only 30 minutes later, guessing that all the food could possibly go to waste with the "meeting".

Dillon joined Maggie, with both standing like guards at her side. Don and Carrie offered lemonade to all and brought them into the living room. Dee was beaming with pride for her daughter's family, who were honoring her in front of her newly-retrieved friend.

However, with Dee still at loss for words to carry the conversation further, Carrie took over. Noticing that most of the talking was between the kids and Claire, Carrie mentioned that they had developed friendships with Ashley and Jacob Barkley. That was all there was needed to ensure animated discussion for the next ten minutes. Horses and horsebackriding. Horsebackriding and horses. Oh, and some talk of ponies.

That is when Carrie began her game plan.

With Charles due to arrive in 5-10 minutes, Carrie began by telling Maggie and Dillon to show Claire the books they had brought along. Carrie had heard Dee mention that Claire had taught third grade a few years at the small schoolhouse in Mears. She had gone to Central Michigan Teacher's College for three years just after high school but couldn't complete her studies due to the needs of her parents' farmstead here in New Era. "Claire has always been a lover of books, Maggie. You ought to see her library—even today. Grandmom says it is very large."

"Pish! Posh! They are mostly full of dust. But I would like to see *your* books, Maggie and Dillon."

"Maggie, why don't you and Dillon take Mrs. Claire to your room. You help her, too, Dillon. We'll come get you when supper is ready. It won't be long." Telling Maggie to talk about her books is like asking her great-grandmother to talk about her pies. Books are like appendages at the end of Maggie's hands. And Dillon was catching Maggie's fever for most anything written. He was also convinced that a few pictures never hurt a book either.

Job One completed. Now for Charles to show up. He must. He will. Seeing Dee look more than once out the front windows for Charles, Don quietly assured her, "Grandmom, Charles has been searching for the medals for a long time. Believe me—for that reason alone—he will be here."

While Don's comments did indeed reassure Dee, it also confronted her with the stark realization that Charles Hargrove—Charlie—the high school basketball star who went off and joined the Army like so many other young men in 1941 and '42—the tall, good-looking man who was a sure thing to marry her good friend, Claire—the curly-haired hero who "died in the war"—the man who defied all odds and actually lived after being a POW—was about to walk into her living room!

Carrie noticed her grandmother's instability and held her elbow and led her to the La-Z-Boy. With lemonade quickly in her system, Dee sat and waited. Carrie then left to check on the status of Claire and the kids. Don stepped outside and sat on the small porch to get a heads-up view of Charles' arrival.

If ever a minute seemed like an hour, it was now. "Where is Charles?" Don thought to himself. The 6:00 p.m. factory whistle sounded and broke up the more subtle sound of the constant breeze coming off of Lake Michigan and of a far-off tractor doing plowing in a field somewhere. It was still light out and was an ideal 72 degrees in New Era. Then—

Like a movie played in slow motion, the blue truck revealed its windshield over the crest of the Elm Street hill. Then its grill and the familiar Ford symbol. Although Don couldn't make out Charles with the glare of the sun shining off the glass, the detective Don knew it was Charles by his unique Missouri *Show Me State* license plate.

Don knew it was Charles by his unique Missouri *Show Me State* license plate.

Dee saw Don leave the front porch to greet Charles as he promised. She couldn't get herself to look out the window. Carrie came back with the report that Claire was glued to the "book reports" Maggie and Dillon were giving. Except for the back door compliment that Dillon didn't think Claire looked 84, all was going well. Claire was seated deeply on the bottom bunk and not likely to leave her place of honor. The voices of Maggie and especially Dillon were plenty loud enough to drown out voices from the living room. Carrie had also subtly closed the bedroom door a few degrees just to be sure.

Dee became very anxious knowing she was about to meet–after all these years—her old friend whom she thought had been dead for decades, Charlie Hargove. She quickly called for reinforcements. "Carrie, will you help me up? I think Charles is here." With the two ladies standing in front of the stereo cabinet, Don walked up to Charles' truck. "Glad you made it."

Charles was still in his seat with the windows rolled down when he heard this comment from Don. "Wouldn't miss this for the world. Still can't believe you found the medals. How are you, Don?"

"I'm good. Well, I'm well." The two laughed as Charles went to the bed of his truck to show Don the metal detector. "I thought I would bring this along for your kids to see. I'll leave it here for now."

Charles was ready to see Maggie and Dillon and Carrie and Don again, but he knew to see Dee again after all these years was going to be tough. He knew she was still living on the Howard farmstead somewhere but resisted coming to the house to see her. He had heard from an earlier breakfast at *The Trailside Inn* that Doug had died of some kind of cancer. He wasn't sure he could talk to Dee about it. But, with the medals being found and the chance meeting of Dee's granddaughter and husband, and his not getting any younger, he knew the time had come for such a meeting.

Charles' eyes were not yet adjusted to the darker living room and Dee, now more steadied with Carrie at her side, broke the awkward silence of these long lost friends.

"Charlie!" Looking at his face as carefully as she could, "Yes, you *are* Charlie. I—I—I—." That was all Dee could muster. All her practiced scripts were now inoperative. She walked ahead two steps and the two hugged.

Proud a man as he was, he was no match for this moment. Who could fault either for not knowing what to say? They substituted deep crying and tears for words. Don and Carrie had planned a lot for tonight but had not prepared their own hearts for such a sight. They cried. All were tears of joy.

Charles still towered over Dee and when he pulled back and rested his large hands on her shoulders, he said, "You are still a half-pint." This attempt at humor still wasn't enough for Dee so Carrie jumped into Job 2: Help Grandma out, if needed. "Here, Grandmom. For some reason, I found a box of tissue. Here." Now looking at Charles, Carrie added, "So this is the Charlie you told us about. I can see why you said you looked *up* to him in high school."

Dee finally smiled. Then her expression changed dramatically. It was if a dark Lake Michigan storm had entered the room. Dee exploded with anger of the like that Carrie had never heard from her beloved grandmother.

"How could you, Charlie? You never came back! We all waited! The paper said you were dead. You never—you never—Doug would have given anything to have seen you! Why? Why?"

"Grandmom!" Carrie said firmly. She didn't know if she should interrupt. She hadn't counted on *this* being one of her "jobs." But she was watching her grandmother express grief she had closeted in for a half-century and more. There certainly was a need to do this but it didn't seem to Carrie like this was the time to vent right now. Carrie had heard of post-traumatic stress and guessed that Charles had suffered with it for years. "To find fault for his not returning home was a discussion for another day," were Carrie's thoughts. She also knew that Claire and the kids were but a few yards away and much more had to be done yet.

Carrie gently grabbed her grandmother's hand to console her but was soon relieved of this duty by none other than Charles himself. He looked kindly down at Carrie with an understanding look and with his long reach, he pulled Dee to himself with a hug and the two cried some more. The cries were certainly cries of joy. Also on display was wisdom. Wisdom that you won't learn in the pages of a psychology text book. Charles had been through a lot and displayed the fruit of those tough experiences at this very moment.

# Chapter 24

## The Reunion!

"Dee, I'm not getting any younger. I think I'd better sit down. Is that okay?"

Looking at the two old friends now seated and feeling like they had resolved the immediate storm of old wounds, Don tried to change the conversation back to Charles' spoken reason for coming. "Well, let's see, Charles. You came here for something tonight. Help me. What was it? I'm a couple years younger than you but I just can't remember. Guess I'll have Carrie go and ask Maggie. I think she will recall."

Charles and Dee remained silent but were now smiling, although Charles had no clue of the surprise in store for him. Carrie then left for the bedroom as Charles was reminded of the medals.

Job 4 (what was supposed to be only Job 3): Get Claire to come out and meet Charles. Carrie knew this might be her most difficult task—not just to get Claire out of the bedroom but to get her ever-curious Maggie and Dillon to remain in the bedroom while they would no doubt hear the commotion of this traumatic 60-year reunion.

"Well, how are you coming? Carrie asked casually as she entered the bedroom, now vibrant with the sharing of a common love of books. It suddenly hit her how rare a sight she was enjoying—two children and a woman separated by almost eight decades yet having fun and understanding each other as if they were peers!

Separated by eight decades and yet having fun!

"Mommy! Claire's favorite book when she was my age was *Rebecca of Sunnybrook Farm*! That is one of mine! She says that I read very well. She was helping me with a few words in my *Hans Brinker* book. Do we have to come to supper now?"

Although peppered with a shotgun of statements, Carrie chose to address the last one first to ensure they didn't all walk toward the living room. "No, you don't have to come to supper now but I have a huge favor to ask of you and Dillon. A huge one. Grandmom wants Claire to come out right now but when she does, I want you two to stay here for a little while." Her children's eyes told her that this request would be a difficult sell. Maggie's and Dillon's faces were easy to read now—their mother was going to keep them from something important and they wanted to be in on it. Carrie's dilemma fortunately found a solution from an unexpected source.

Claire's years as a public school teacher and Sunday School teacher—negotiating deals with children for years—and her own experience as a mother, kicked into gear at this interchange between this mother and these two children.

"Maggie and Dillon. I had the time of my life talking with you about your books. So much so that I'd like to make a deal with you. May I?"

Carrie smiled but knew intuitively to stay out of this negotiation about to be made between these three. Plus, she had a hunch this was the solution for which she had prayed.

Holding Maggie's and Dillon's hands and looking directly into their eyes, Claire further asked, "I understand you will be staying here through Sunday. Right?"

"Yes—."

"Well, with your parent's permission, I'd like you to come over to my house after church and pick out five books each from my library and honor me by reading them and then keeping them on your library shelf."

"Keep them!" both echoed in unbelief and in unison. Their eyes were as big as Carrie had recalled ever seeing them.

"Why, of course. They are only collecting dust and they are special to me so I wouldn't want to give them to someone who wouldn't read them—and it is obvious to me that you two are readers." Before Maggie and Dillon could respond, Claire added, "But there are two conditions. First, you must promise to take good care of them. Second, you must listen to your mother and stay in this room until she comes to get you as she just asked."

Pretending to be reluctant to allow this, Carrie said—with the most serious look she could muster—"Okay. We will allow this very kind offer from Claire but you cannot violate her conditions. Understand?"

Maggie looked at Dillon and the two of them looked back at Carrie and then at Claire. "Yes! We will stay here on the top bunk even." A hug of Claire for this kind gesture almost toppled her but, unknown to anyone, she knew that the books would someday have to go. It is just that these books were her friends and she wanted them to go to good homes if possible. The deal she just made was a perfect one for all parties, including whatever Carrie was trying to do. Plus, she was thrilled that her books, her treasures, would now be in good hands. Maggie and Dillon might not realize it for years, but these books would someday be *their* treasures.

When Charles decided not to "return insult for insult but with a blessing," Dee began to feel ashamed. "I'm so sorry, Charlie. I can't believe I reacted that way. You had to be hurting so much all these years. I am so ashamed—after all you have been through. I—I—."

"Dee, no need to apologize. We are still friends, after all these years." Charles had forgotten momentarily about the medals as he felt a huge load leave him by talking to Dee. The medals seemed not as significant as before. A restored friendship seemed much more valuable thing to treasure.

Dee smiled as she recalled hearing those very words—"No need to apologize"—from an old friend just yesterday.


With Carrie closing the door to the bedroom, Claire went ahead of her to see what Dee had wanted. She turned the corner from the brief hallway to the living room.

As one focuses on a printed page without his reading glasses, Claire and Charles looked at each other, trying to adjust their eyes and minds that the person each was looking at was whom they thought. There was a major mental disconnect. Their eyes said, "Yes." Their logical minds said, "No." After all, it had been 57 years. Only a 1941 photo served as a tangible reminder, an outdated view of a person each thought was before their eyes. A death notice stood between them—then—and—now. "This can't be. My mind and eyes are playing tricks on me." Whether these thoughts were Charles' or Claire's mattered little. Perception can often trump reality but this was not perception. This didn't seem real. This was surreal to them both.

Don and Carrie stood mum. Neither could have come up with anything to counter the hushed silence in the room. When once the air seemed breezy and refreshing, it now stood still and oppressive.

Dee's eyes were focused on Claire, her hands over her mouth. It was certain she would say nothing.

The man with the worn out photo spoke first. "Claire, is that you?" Charles was suddenly struck with the thought that this stately woman in the yellow cotton dress would react much like Dee. His face reflected this fearful apprehension.

"Claire? Is that you?"

"Charlie? It *is* you. Your voice. Can this all be true? What am I seeing?" She looked at Dee as if to get some kind of validation that this was indeed Charlie—the Charlie who had proposed to her nearly 60 years ago but went off and died on a forgotten island. The Charlie for whom she had given her heart and saw the same yanked away by a war that more than divided the world—it divided her personal world, the world she had envisioned would be hers for a lifetime.

Dee was seemingly frozen but managed a nod of her head.

It was fortunate for Dee, whose job was to assist Claire at such a moment, that Carrie moved quickly into what amounted to Job 5: Serve as Grandmom's failsafe in the event it would be needed. It was needed. Now.

"Claire. I am so sorry we have shocked you like this…but you are not hallucinating. This *is* Charles, or Charlie, as you and Grandmom call him. Don and I met him downtown at *The Trailside Inn* just yesterday. He—." Carrie stopped when she saw Charles move toward Claire.

The words that he had practiced for those 1,095 days in that hell hole in Guam spurted out like it had been rehearsed a hundred times.

It had. At least in his mind and in his heart. Never in words. Never face-to-face with the object of his rehearsals. Charles spoke simply and profoundly. "Claire. I am so sorry. I never wanted to leave you. I *did* come back but it was too late. I didn't have the heart to see you then. You were married. I have beat myself up for years. I am not sure what is going on right now. I came tonight to pick up some medals found by Dee's great-granddaughter, Maggie—and—I—I just don't know what to say."

Like the sudden effect of a squall on Lake Michigan, his words turned into an emotional floodgate of tears. He stopped short of hugging Claire as he sensed still an unworthiness to do so at this time.

The amazing strength of this 80-some-year-old was beginning to fail. Don saw this and played the counterpart of Carrie, and grabbed Charles' left arm to bring him some balance.

Then—

"Charlie! Charlie!" Claire, though lost for words, fought her disbelief and reached out to hug the still towering Charles. Maybe hope conquers disbelief more easily when one loses it, as Claire had found in recent months. Where else could she turn but to hope that a sovereign God could do the impossible? She had hoped to salvage her farmstead but instead her hope for a love once lost was salvaged. It appeared that way to her right now anyway.

The two held each other and cried until Dee finally found her voice. "You two are welcome to sit down. I *do* have chairs. It is almost 7:00 p.m. and I'd better get to that supper I promised you, Claire. And, by the way, Charlie—you are welcome, too—no, we *want* you to join us. Dee's simple words were just like the sudden burst of Lake Michigan air that seemed to always find its way into Dee's living room—always welcomed.

Don and Carrie led Charles and Claire to the corner sofa chairs so they might continue their conversation without an audience.

Well—that was their intent, anyway. Hearing Great-grandmother begin to make noises in the kitchen brought Maggie and Dillon to the bedroom hallway. Their strong promise to Claire was being severely challenged by their curious nature. "Mommy, can we come out now?"

# Chapter 25

## The Medal Presentation

"Stay in your room you guys! Mom will be right there," said their Dad quickly. Don then took over Carrie's task of helping Dee make final preparation for the dinner for the two special guests. Carrie then made a bee-line for the kids, knowing that their curiosity might just get the best of them and come running out. She wanted Charles and Claire to have some quality time to themselves to bridge the conversation from shock to understanding—at least what understanding could come from 15 short minutes.

"Maggie. Dillon. Let's go back into the room for a little bit. Yes! Now! Get back in and sit down on the bunk. I want to talk to you about a few things." She had no earthly idea what she was going to say, but she did know she had to stall them a little while longer. Maggie and Dillon obeyed—in bodies, at least.

"*First*, I want to thank you for staying in the room. Daddy and Great-grandmom and I really appreciated you doing that. *Second*, I'm also glad you entertained and encouraged Claire while she was with you. She seems to really like you guys. I'm proud of you. *Third*, I want you to follow me and walk directly back into Grandmom's bedroom. Don't turn left. Turn right. I want to talk to you about the medals you found."

"*Fourth*, we *will*, Mommy," interrupted Maggie. "Can we go now? We are really getting bored." Even Maggie was realizing something was going on even more exciting than reading another chapter of *Hans Brinker*.

Sensing that, Carrie said, "Listen, Maggie. You, too, Dillon. Follow me now to Great-grandmom's room. Shhh—be as quiet as mice and tip toe into her room."

"Claire, I'm not sure how I had imagined you would look if I were able to see you again. But, you look wonderful." Charles was sincere.

"Pish! Posh! Charlie, the war or something must've ruined your sight. You used to be able to see and hit a basket from half court. Now, you can't see an old woman from half a foot."

"Well—if I remember right—I still have a year on you in age."

"Then do the subtraction. 85 minus 1 equals 84. I believe by most people's deductions, that is still old."

Both smiled as they eased into more serious conversation. Charles could see that the spryness he used to love in Claire was still there. She commented on his mustache. He complimented her "pretty dress". She commended him for keeping his posture so well. Charlie finally broke through the small, "safe" talk when he shared his wife had passed away a few years ago. Claire took this lead and told of Johanne's death this past year. While they chose not to talk about the war and the years following, they did share about their families and where they lived. Claire heard the pain of Charles' estrangement from his daughter. They then made plans to see each other tomorrow morning at Claire's home.

"Dillon, close the door behind you." So far, Carrie's plan to stall the kids was working. The plan of what to say and do was getting much clearer as she had both Maggie and Dillon sit on Grandma's bed. She picked up the medals that were still in their cases on top of her dresser. Showing them once more to the kids, she said, "Maggie, remember when I saw you holding these earlier and you said that if this CHARLES J. HARGROVE were living today he would be about 85 or so?"

"Yes," Maggie answered with a 'where-are–we-going-with-this-look.'

"Well, Mr. Hargrove is 85 exactly—and he is still alive."

It was the kids' time to be shocked. The usual verbal brother and sister were both stunned in silence. Finally, Maggie managed a smile with this unbelievable information, and then Dillon asked the obvious, "Then where is he and can we give him his medals?"

"I will tell you *where* he is soon, but to answer your second question directly, Dillon—yes, your Dad and I felt that you two should be the ones to give him the medals." This brought smiles and excitement from them both. "But when that time comes, I want you to be sure to know the names of each medal and give exactly *that* name when you present them to him."

The stall was on but it turned out to be a very purposeful delay. Maggie, having already studied each medal thoroughly, pointed to the round medal with the ribbon attached, said, "That's easy, that one is the 'World War II Victory Medal'. The one in the shape of a cross is the 'Distinguished—something Cross'."

"*Service*. Distinguished *Service* Cross. That's good, Maggie. Now, because there are two medals and there are two of you. I'm going to have you each make the choice of which one you will present. Carrie realized this last suggestion might not have been a wise one. She was greatly relieved when they pointed quickly to different medals. "Good choices! Here, Maggie, you hold the 'World War II Victory Medal' just like it is in its case. You, Dillon, hold the 'Distinguished Service Cross' medal in its case."

She practiced the presenting of the medals to Charles with them in the bedroom, being careful not to disclose yet that the man they knew as Mr. Hillsboro is the real Charles Hargrove. She wanted them to know the names of each medal well and this practice was doing just that. Also, it was helping to delay their entry into the living room.

Then—because she knew she could delay no longee—Carrie told them  the reality that the one and only CHARLES J. HARGROVE was here in grandmother's house—in the living room.

The two jumped off the bed—almost losing the medals from their cases—when Carrie said, "Calm down. I want you to do your best at making this a very special presentation. You may tell Charles how you found them. By the way, he is sitting next to Mrs. Claire right now so be sure to let her see them also. Maggie and Dillon could hardly hold back their excitement when Carrie knew she had to be the one to let them know about Charles' not telling them the truth about his name.

She knew they would be very confused if they went out in the living room expecting an unseen Mr. Hargrove and then saw the man they knew as "Mr. Hillsboro" sitting there. She didn't want the taint of Charles' lie to them about his name putting a damper on what could be an emotionally uplifting evening.

"Maggie and Dillon. Please sit back down. Please. I need to tell you something very important." Seeing them smile in anticipation of some good news, Carrie found it difficult to let them know of this war hero's weak moment. But she knew she had to. "The man you are about to see—this Charles Hargrove—is the man you met at the Barkley's fruit stand as 'Mr. Hillsboro'." Smiles tuned into quizzical expressions. "It is true. I will let him tell you more himself. But, Maggie, when you asked him his name at the fruit stand, you caught him by surprise and he quickly made up that name because—well—because he was afraid it wouldn't be a good time to let people know he was alive and back in town after years of those same people thinking he was dead. That might not seem like a good reason to lie—and it isn't—but I wanted you to know he is very sorry and ashamed for making up that name to you. He thinks so much of you both and—."

"Mommy! I get it. Dillon gets it, I think." With Dillon nodding his head, Maggie continued, "Mommy, it kind of makes sense. Mr. Hillsboro—I mean—Mr. Hargrove was so sad that day. I knew something was wrong. That's why I wanted him to meet you guys and Mrs. Barkley. It wasn't just that he was thirsty. Anyway—in a funny sense—this all makes it even more exciting. WE KNOW HIM. WE KNOW 'MR. CHARLES J. HARGROVE!'" Looking down at the medal in her hand, she said, 'WE KNOW THE BRAVE MAN WHO EARNED THIS MEDAL FOR VALOR!"

Carrie wasn't sure they actually understood why Charles fabricated the story but one thing she did know was that Maggie and Dillon were not about to be upset about the face not matching the name of the man in Dee's living room. They were certainly ready for their part of the presentation. Realizing once more that she could stall them no longer, and seeing that some 15 minutes had already elapsed, she said, "Okay. Ready to go? Let's do as we practiced and march out s-l-o-w-l-y. S-L-O-W-L-Y. Hold the case flat in back of you. Yes. Backs straight."

Don and Dee were watching and waiting while they stood in the doorway of the kitchen. They smiled broadly when Maggie and Dillon, the distinguished detective duo—discoverers of the long lost WW II medals—were about to turn the corner into the living room. Maggie and Dillon looked as proud as the time they walked down the aisle together as flower girl and ring bearer for Uncle Derek's and Aunt Kat's wedding.

When Claire had turned the corner from the hallway to the living room just a half-hour earlier, she stood frozen when she saw Charles. Now—when *Maggie and Dillon* turned the same corner—they went ballistic! All attempts at decorum were out the window as they placed the medal cases on the floor and ran to greet the man they had known as Mr. Hillsboro. Maggie made the name/face association quickly. The man she met at the fruit stand was indeed the one and the same Mr. Charles Hargrove as her mother had informed her just minutes earlier.

"Charles! You *are* the CHARLES J. HARGROVE!" A few screams of delight and she and Dillon not only ran to him, but didn't hesitate to hug him. Claire beamed broadly. You'd think *she* was the kids' great-grandmother. Dee's eyes were typically squinting when she smiled with joy. If cameras were rolling, one could probably show her smile as the biggest of the evening. Don and Carrie couldn't have been prouder. None of this would be happening if Dillon had not been brave and informed everyone of the mysterious visitor he spotted in the orchard, nor if Maggie had not been so observant to notice the glistening gold in "her tree" in that same orchard.

As Carrie and Don watched the interchange between the unique friendship of four—separated by some 70 years of life—it struck them that the precious medals were yet to be presented. Don asked Carrie to whisper to the kids to step back, pick up the medal cases, and re-enter the room as planned. He then walked over to Dee's stereo console to see what kind of records Carrie's grandpa had. Besides a few *George Beverly Shea* albums, he noted that Doug had also a few patriotic albums. While everyone watched Don's actions, Don now knew exactly what he wanted to do.

Noticing that Carrie had Maggie and Dillon ready just around the corner, Don coughed to gain everyone's attention. He then emptied and utilized a black plastic flower vase as his makeshift microphone. Holding it to his mouth—standing upright in a serious military posture—he said in a dramatic voice, "May I please have your attention."

"Now that I have your attention."

"I would like the distinguished Maggie Elizabeth Burch and Dillon Ezekiel Burch to stand at attention." The drama queen and king did exactly that—although their bare feet made the visual presentation somewhat less than formal. "Now I would like the honored and revered veteran of World War II—Master Sergeant Charles J. Hargrove—to stand at attention." In any other setting, Charles might not wish to do this, but how could he refuse this request from such a wonderful family? He stood as straight as his 6' 4" and 85 year-old frame could.

Don then placed the needle on the old record, the first song playing, "God Bless America." Who the *Fred Waring Orchestra and the Pennsylvanians* were he had no idea but the musical presentation was perfect.

The musical prelude played while Don said, "For this presentation—high on this great hill in New Era—in the sovereign state of Michigan—this 15th day of August in the year of our Lord, 2009 (the choir began singing the lyrics)—

> God bless America
> Land that I love.
> Stand beside her, and guide her,
> Thru the night with a light from above.
> From the mountains, to the prairies,
> To the oceans, white with foam,
> God bless America.
> My home sweet home.

He didn't see Charles begin to tear up so he continued—"Now I would like the two representatives we have from the District of Oceana step forward and flank our honored veteran of World War II." Dee and Claire picked up the hint and played their roles perfectly. Carrie, not to let this moment be lost, put her hand up to Don for him to pause and to let the music play while she positioned the camcorder on the tri-pod.

Not missing a beat, Don thanked the news media for being here on this memorable occasion. Knowing the next song was, "The Caissons Go Rolling Along," with its famous drum taps beginning the song, Don again waited until these drum beats began—then—with all the military pomp and circumstance he could muster—

"Bearers of the medals of honor for our country, please march forward for their presentation to CHARLES J. HARGROVE."

Don could never have imagined the sight before him now. The towering figure of Charles—fighting fiercely to hold back his tears of joy—was looking down at the four foot statues of Maggie and Dillon, who were having their own battle of trying not to cry. Both were trying to be soldier-like but couldn't keep from displaying proud smiles with their tears.

Don then nodded at Dillon to begin. There was a little hesitation in going first, but Dillon didn't fail to deliver as he and his mother had planned. "I present to Mr. Charles J. Hargrove this medal, THE DISTINGUISEHD SERVICE CROSS!" Charles bent down to receive it and, on cue, all except Maggie (her hands occupied with a medal) began to clap loudly. Dillon then remembered his mother's last instructions, "And—oh yeah—this medal is for *Extraordinitary Heroism!*" Some smiled at the unique pronunciation but all clapped once more. Claire looked up at Charles' response and began to cry.

Maggie continued the medal presentation on cue. She stepped forward alongside Dillon and directly in front of Charles and said, "I present to Mr. Charles J. Hargrove the distinguished WORLD WAR TWO VICTORY MEDAL for his great valor (she loved this new word) and for the brave part he played in the victory of the United States in this war." Charles bent to receive this medal from the outstretched arms of Maggie—then he couldn't hold it in any longer. He picked up his friend Maggie and cried like he hadn't in years. It was like 1986 all over again when the Hart Dam burst and spilled onto everything in its path. Years of repressed feelings and grief erupted into Dee's living room and seemed to flood the entire room. But—like water so often does—the tears cleansed this hurting man from all his stuffed guilt and anger and regrets. Truly—God's presence filled the Howard home this evening!

All became silent in time. This live "picture" spoke a thousand words. The only sounds were those of the humming camcorder and the clear male voices on the record, singing—

> Was it high, was it low,
> Where heck did that one go?
> As those Caissons go rolling along.
> Was it left, was it right,
> Now we won't go home tonight—

For sure, neither Charles nor Claire wanted to go home tonight. No one wanted this special evening to end.

But the maternal instincts of a lifetime kicked in for Dee, the hostess. "I think the dinner is more than ready." Dee walked over to

Charles and calmly said, "Thank you, Charlie, for your service. God bless you." Then she retired to the kitchen. Don and Carrie followed this lead. "Charles, this has been quite an honor. You are indeed a hero. You are hero to more people than you probably think."

Charles was shaking his head in humility but Claire stopped him as she reached up with her fragile arms and grabbed his elbows. "Yes, Charlie, you are. You were a prisoner in another country. You were a prisoner in your mind for many years. But, Charlie, you are home now. You are free. You are home and free—at last!" Those who really knew the depth of this strong Christian lady would know she was referring to more than just his physical freedom as a prisoner of war.

Oh—Maggie and Dillon? They became smiling fixtures at each end of this man's long arms.

Dinner this night was an afterthought, which is quite a statement if one has ever eaten a meal at Dee Howard's. No one, however, had much of an appetite this evening. The only food offering much interest might have been the freshly-baked apple pie which seemed to have more comers than the special roast beef and asparagus that was to be the prime meal. The "dinner" most relished this evening was the food for thought—the joy of the occasion's surprises—and also the racing minds of the adults who wondered, "What was next?"

With Carrie in the room, one could be sure there would be the steady "click" of her Canon, taking more than a few photos of this memorable night of a memorable vacation. Maybe her favorite was of Charles kneeling, with his long arms around Dillon's and Maggie's shoulders, the medals being held in each hand. Draw your own illustration.

Then—

LIGHTNING! Followed by a loud THUNDER CLAP! The weather, as so often happens in western Michigan with its infamous "lake effect," broke into the home like an unwelcomed guest. They all knew rain was soon to follow. Reality concerning the evening now set in. It was time to go home.

Charles, who had owned up to being the mysterious barn guest, was now actually staying at the *Best Inn* in Hart and was the first to get up and acknowledge he should leave. He offered his deep gratitude to all, "Dee, Don and Carrie, Maggie and Dillon, thank you. This has been the best day and evening of my long life. Thank you. Claire, I will see you tomorrow. I think I can find the deGroot farm in Mears," he smiled but with the tell-tale signs of exhaustion.

He got to his truck and realized he had not shown the kids his metal detector. He looked back but decided he could do that Sunday before the Burches left for home.

Dee offered for Claire to stay at her home tonight, what with the rain coming and all. Claire declined the offer like most old troopers from the "greatest generation" and made it to her car before the rain let loose.

> The woods are lovely, dark, and deep
> But I have promises to keep,
> And miles to go before I sleep,
> And miles to go before I sleep.

quoted Claire of Robert Frost—then added her own line—"If I *can* sleep." She smiled all the way home.

# Chapter 26

## Worth More than Gold!

The effects of the all-night rain were displayed in the driveway of Claire deGroot. Puddles filled either side of the tire-trenched long dirt driveway leading to her house. Charles' hefty new Ford F350 truck had no trouble navigating the path but it did strike him that the driveway was in serious need of repair. It was also obvious that the out buildings were in disrepair. "A simple good coat of paint or two would help the house," he thought. Claire's love for flowers did bring some life to the front porch.

As he closed the door to his pickup, Charles paused to take in the cool, nitrogen-filled fresh air of the farm after the rain. Memories of his youth, growing up on a farm in nearby Hart, occupied his thoughts as he took in the sight of the tree-covered property. "So this is where Claire has lived all these years," Charles ruminated to himself.

"Charlie!"

Claire's presence on the front porch caught him off guard. He did come up with a smile as he had thought of this moment for years. Somehow, his mental rehearsal of how this might be was nothing like it was now. "Must be 'cause I saw her last night," he reasoned to himself. As he avoided a few puddles and approached the steps to the porch, he began with small talk, "Hi, Claire. You look nice. Sure was some storm last night. Did you have any trouble making it home?"

"No, except some trouble with night vision—you know, the lights reflecting off my windshield—but, no, had no problems. My faithful Chevy got me home."

That was another thing Charles noticed. He knew his automobiles and the car he saw at Dee's he now realized was Claire's. It had to be an old Impala from '84 or '85. It was indeed a metal monster but also spoke of her financial state or maybe her frugality.

"Come in Charlie. Got some coffee brewing. Did you have any trouble finding the place?" Claire noticed Charles was quieter than last night. "I must not read into this," she told herself, "this is indeed still a shock to both of us."

"No, it was actually easy to find. I realized I had walked this road for awhile the day I saw Maggie at the fruit stand while I was getting my truck repaired. But, thanks—I could use some good black coffee. Seems I smell something awfully good besides the coffee."

"I wasn't sure what to bake for you. I felt like a young girl again at the Oceana County Fair trying to decide what to make for my 4-H entry. It *has* been a few years."

Once in the kitchen, Charles saw the cinnamon rolls. He smiled his approval and picked up one as he surveyed the kitchen/dining room. It was like time stood still on this 1950's-style kitchen.

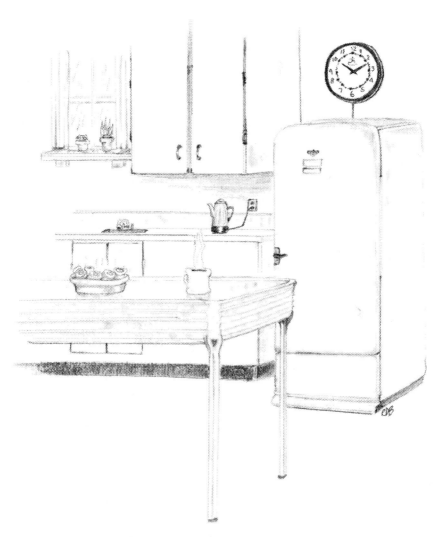

It was like time stood still on this 1950's-style kitchen.

The morning was slow in conversation but at the same time rich. Being 80 years-plus teaches you not to hurry and, at the same time, not to waste much time with just empty talk. Charles pointed out a panoramic photo of Claire's family on a bookcase and Claire took the cue to talk with pride of each of her kids and grandkids. It extended the sharing of family history that had begun last night at Dee's.

≈    ≈    ≈    ≈    ≈    ≈

"Grandmom, you sure are quiet this morning." As was his style, the direct statement by Dillon pointed out what everyone else was simply thinking.

Dee liked that in people, though such openness wasn't her nature. "Guess your old grandmother got all tuckered out last night. That sure was a wonderful evening. And how are you my special hero?"

"Grandmom! I'm not a hero. Charles is the hero."

"Well, you are half right. Charles is a hero, but without you and Maggie we might not have been able to tell him he is a hero. I think you two are heroes to him."

"I didn't do anything. I just saw him. I mean, I *thought* I saw him that night. I didn't know who he was. Maggie is the one who found the medals."

"Dillon. Mommy and Daddy are the heroes. They found Charles in that restaurant," corrected Maggie.

Helping put the breakfast dishes away, Carrie corrected both. "No. Truth is we all were used by God to help a man who has felt very lost for many years. Grandma is right. That *was* a wonderful evening last night—to see Charles finally be re-connected with the medals he earned. And most of all, for him to find something that was worth more than the two war medals. He found people who really cared for him. Maggie, your reaching out to him at the fruit stand before you knew anything about him told him somebody cared for him—not for his medals or his POW status or money he has earned—but just for him as a person. And Dillon, the way you bravely announced the first medal last night—well—you made us all proud. We are proud of you both."

"And," added Don, "Charles told us in the restaurant that the time and efforts he put into the war was the only thing for which he ever felt significance. He wanted to find the medals, he told us, so he could realize that he had some worth. I kind of think he sees how he was wrong with such thinking. I think he discovered that his worth is how God sees him."

Grandma Dee was listening intently to her "family" and was beaming that they would see things this way. She was feeling pretty low herself in the past few years since Doug died and her girls had all grown up and moved away. It was just this past spring, however—when she was all alone in the living room having her devotions—that she read something that lifted her heart and set her straight in her thinking. She had chosen as a New Year's Eve resolution to read through the book of Psalms, reading a chapter a day. She had been faithful in doing so and on April 18th—she recalls as if it were yesterday—she read Psalm 139. The words reminded her of how God sees her.

> O Lord, you have searched me and you know me. You know when I sit and when I rise; you perceive my thoughts from afar. You discern my going out and my lying down.

Dee particularly liked verse 5—

> You hem me in—behind and before; you have laid your hand upon me.

Dee had spent years sewing her daughters' clothes and mending Doug's shirts and pants, and knew better than most what a "hem" was. It was this thought and that of this Psalm as a whole that brought her a peace that her worth and value came from how God saw her and not from all her noble efforts in being a good wife and mother.

"Grandma, why are you smiling at me?" Maggie pulled a Dillon and asked exactly what was on her mind.

"Oh, nothing and then again, a lot. This has been a wonderful week and I was thinking how much I was going to miss you after you all leave tomorrow. I also realize how God is answering my prayers as I listen to all of you talk. And I was thinking that I want to make the most of this day. Unless you have a special plan, what would you say if we drive up to Mears to visit with Claire a bit so we can give her those blackberries you two picked yesterday that I forgot to give her last night?. Then—and only if you want to—we could stop by and see the Barkleys." That statement got Dee two big kisses of pancake syrup on her cheeks. And she didn't mind one bit.

This game plan was actually drawn by Dee with Don and Carrie last night. They all knew that seeing Ashley and Jacob again would end a "perfect week" for Maggie and Dillon—not that Carrie and Don didn't want to visit with Ruth and Bruce once more either. Truth be told, Dee was anxious as a teenager to see if Claire and Charles were "hitting it off" like they had in high school.

≈    ≈    ≈    ≈    ≈    ≈

The talk about families between Charles and Claire went well as long as it was about her family. Charles was still uneasy talking about his relationship with his estranged daughter. As a result, Claire steered the conversation to reminiscing about the "good ol' days". This brought some laughs, especially after Claire resurrected her old class of '42 yearbook. It had included many shots of the three-sport athlete, Charlie Hargrove. They had a lot of laughs, especially when they saw the short shorts he and other basketball players wore in those days.

Then came the picture of them at homecoming. Neither Charlie nor Claire had expected this line of school days talk to turn to a reminder of their once strong love for one another, a love that almost took them to the altar—an altar altered by a war and separated by an ocean. The wrinkled crow's feet around their eyes watered up at this recollection. They wanted to avoid the emotional discomfort this brought—but, then again—they didn't really want to avoid talking of it either. They both had strong senses that God was rekindling this love since they saw each other last night at Dee's. They had connected with their hearts. They had not yet connected with words. The yearbook photos, after all, were of two "kids". What of today? What should be said? These thoughts, on both of their minds, had yet to find expression.

"Hello! Claire! Charles! Are you there?" Maggie and Dillon were calling through the screen door. It's uncertain if Charlie or Claire were relieved or upset by this interruption of their conversation but they knew very well they had better greet these familiar voices soon.

Carrie, Don, and Dee were right behind and arrived on the porch at the same time Charles and Claire were opening the door for their guests. Once inside the breezy living room, Charles and Claire were told to close their eyes immediately.

"Surprise!"

"Blackberries!" said Claire loudly as she was greeted with two pints of these "black-gold treasures" by Maggie and Dillon. They reached up and gave Charlie two pints also.

"Why thank you so much! How did you know these are my favorite fruit?" Claire bent down to ask Maggie.

"Oh, I think it was an old friend of yours. I won't say who, though." Maggie beamed as she got a hug for her efforts.

When Claire winked at Dee, she could see that twinkle in her eyes was for more than the gratitude she received from this gift.

Dillon, who had run up to Charles to give him his blackberries, couldn't wait to ask him what was most on his mind. "Mr. Charles, Daddy told me you have a metal 'tector. Can I see it?"

"Dillon! Don't bother Charles with that yet. We just got here," Don reacted, once more trying to blunt his son's directness.

"No. No, Don. I not only don't mind. I want to show the kids my detector. It's out in my truck. I put it inside my cab to keep if from rusting in the rain last night. Come, let's go out and I will show you how it works."

With two extensions to his long arms, one a nine year-old girl and one a seven year-old boy, Charles walked out into the sun with a new energy in his step.

"Hmm—seems things are going pretty well, Claire. Am I right?" Dee clearly had a gleam in her eye as she grabbed Claire's hand and walked her into her own kitchen to get the details of this morning's conversation between these long, lost friends.

Don and Carrie found themselves smiling and left alone in the spacious but well-worn living room. It was a warm, comfortable room with a stone fireplace as its centerpiece. They soon realized they were staring at the floor-to-ceiling book shelves of Claire and saw first hand her love of books. They also saw an opened copy of a Hart High School yearbook on a nearby table. *The Hartian. Class of 1942. Home of the Pirates.* "Hey, Carrie, check this out. Here's a picture of Charlie Hargrove and the basketball team. His legs look as tall as the point guard's whole body. I love those short shorts."

"Wait," said Carrie with an agreeing smile, "Turn to the front and see if there are any personal notes from Charlie."

When finding none, just "Best Wishes to you and Charlie and the future," from several girlfriends, Don and Carrie seemed to say, "Duh" at the same time. It hit them that Charlie had already joined the army by the time the yearbook came out. "He probably couldn't get permission from his Japanese captors to sign it while a prisoner in their war camp," said Don sarcastically.

"You will like this metal detector. Listen while I place it by the truck and push this button." The beeping sound grew louder and Maggie was excited to hear the familiar noise. She asked Charles if she could take a turn in using this fun tool. Charles handed it to her with instructions and said, "Yes, but I must tell you that as good as it seems to be in finding things, it didn't find what *you* found with your own detective eyes!"

Maggie smiled broadly as she carefully held this $200 *Bounty Hunter* metal detector and positioned it next to the truck. While it buzzed loudly, Dillon shouted, "Let me try, Maggie!" Maggie obliged but the awkward transfer caused it to drop into a nearby puddle. Charles only laughed as he dried it off. Then he threw some quarters out onto the grass and let Dillon have at it to find the loot for himself. Tool or toy, the three were having a great time. Charles had never felt the joy of being a grandfather but felt now he could get used to it pretty easily.

# Chapter 27

## Lost Treasures Found!

Claire and Dee were like two high school girls in their homeroom class discussing their latest crush. "Dee, Charlie and I haven't said much but—it seems too good to be true. We seem to be in the same place, if you know what I mean. Except, it is obvious he is better off financially than I am. I didn't know what to say when he was telling me he wanted to help fix up the place. I mean, he didn't say anything about us but—."

Carrie and Don didn't know that they had interrupted such serious "girl talk" when they entered the kitchen to grab a cup of coffee to go back and check out more of Claire's great library. Changing gears quickly, the light-hearted Claire said, "There's some cups in the cupboard above the coffee maker."

"Don't worry, Claire, we'll help ourselves. We were just going to back and admire more of your library."

"Oh! My goodness! The books I promised to Maggie and Dillon! Thanks for reminding me."

"Pish! Posh! Claire," said Carrie with a fun mock. "We weren't thinking that. We just love books and wanted to look at yours. You don't need to give our kids any of your valued books."

"Well, Pish! Posh! Back at you! You can see I've had most of them a very long time and it would be my joy and privilege to have your reader-children take some off my hands. In fact, where are the kids? Are they still with Charles? I should have them start selecting their books while Dee and I get some brunch going. Could you call them in?"

Claire "killed two birds with one stone" with that comment. She was able to fulfill her desire to give some books to Maggie and

Dillon—and— she adeptly moved Dee back into the kitchen to glean more of Dee's point of view on what to do with all of this. Dee was her one connection between 1942 and 2009. She valued her Christian insight and genuine concern for her welfare. She felt Dee would tell her the truth. "Was she dumb as a duck to think Charlie had thoughts of marriage or could it be really true," Claire wondered and crafted those direct questions to Dee by the refrigerator.

When Charles saw Dillon enjoying the metal detector as he did, it reminded him of himself as a curious boy growing up around "men toys" and was taught how to use them before most city kids had even learned how to ride a bike.

"Maggie! Dillon! Come on in! Claire wants you to do something for her," Carrie called as she smiled when she saw Dillon holding the metal detector over the outdoor water pump.

That morning was filled with wonderful conversation and the joy of watching these readers select what books they wanted from Claire's prized collection of a lifetime. It was a real challenge. "It was harder," thought Dillon "than going into *'Basket' Robbins* and picking out just one type of ice cream." In fact, Don and Carrie had to lift the two of them up so they could check out the top shelves. "We don't want to miss any book!" they said with big grins.

Dillon had four of his five books selected before Maggie decided on her second. She was thrilled that Claire would let her have her copy of *Eight Cousins* by Louisa May Alcott but the other ten she had placed on the floor were going to be difficult from which to choose. While the adults smiled, no one laughed as they knew Maggie was as intent on this special selection as she was in solving the mystery of the war medals.

Dillon had four of his five books selected before
Maggie decided on her second.

"Let's see—hmm—#2 will be *Little House in the Woods*. I love all of
the Little House series. #3 will be *Cheaper by the Dozen*. It really looks
good." Maggie was so intent on this process she didn't realize she was
speaking out loud until Claire spoke out on her last book selection.

"It is Maggie. You will love it. Dillon will, too," said Claire, as she
sat next to Charles on the davenport. Charles saw her eyes were full of
joy. One would think Maggie was selecting five prized horses from a
large stable the way Claire was watching her.

"#4 has to be *The Secret Garden*. I read it when I got it from the library
but I always wanted one for my own. Is that okay, Mrs. Claire?"

"Yes."

As Maggie was now kneeling on the floor with her double-jointed
long legs behind her, she held a copy of *Sarah, Plain and Tall* in one
hand and a copy of *Watch for a Tall White Sail* in the other. This would
be tough. Both covers intrigued her.

An alarmed Claire said, "Maggie, the *White Sail* book might be a bit beyond you; I read it when it came out when I was even out of high school. In fact, I think I was married. Anyway, it deals with—"

It was too late. Some old, folded stationery with words written in indelible ink and in perfect script handwriting fell out of the book. Claire was frozen and then said, "I'll take those, Maggie." Then, regaining composure with the old letters in her hands, she recommended *Sarah Plain and Tall* to her youthful reading counterpart. The awkward moment was only caught by the adults. But no one wanted to embarrass her by asking what these old letters might be. Maggie didn't realize it but she had discovered some more treasures—this time on the shelf of a farm house library. As Claire told Dee before she left that afternoon and Charles on Sunday night, these were letters she had written to Charles when he was overseas in the army. She could never recall where she had misplaced them. All the envelopes were stamped with "Return to Sender," with post marks of 1942 and 1943 and 1944. It was this book by Margaret Bell that prompted her to wait so long. She wasn't ready to give this particular book up. Not yet.

Up to this point, Charles had been comfortably quiet but he felt the situation called for him to break the awkwardness with redirecting the conversation toward Dillon. "Hey, Dillon, I see you selected *Call of the Wild* and *Where the Red Fern Grows*. Two great dog books. Not sure if it is any encouragement but *Where the Red Fern Grows* was one of my daughter's favorites while she was growing up. She loved dogs. Knowing you do, too, makes me think you will like that book a lot. I personally love *Call of the Wild*, but you might have your Dad or Mom read that one with you or read it a bit later. Good choices though!"

Maggie and Dillon did not need Mom and Dad to prompt them. They gave deep thanks to Claire for her generosity in letting them have some of her "old friends." They promised to take good care of them and to read them all. Claire, for her part, thanked them for all they had done for her. She led them into the kitchen and gave them small boxes in which to carry and protect them.

As Charlie and Claire walked the Burch family and Dee from the porch to the driveway out to their van, they noticed that the puddles were all but dried up. "Looks like it's going to be a scorcher today and it's not yet noon. Have a great time at the Barkleys'. Thank you again for the blackberries!" Charles was talking like he was a well-loved uncle of this family.

"See you in church!" Claire said as she waved to the van, now moving. "I hadn't said that to anyone in a long time," she said as she held Charles' arm and walked back with him to the house. Then she heard Dillon shouting from the open window—"And thank you for letting us have these books and for using the 'tector." It looked like a Norman Rockwell picture with a Winslow Homer brushstroke.

# Chapter 28

## The Treasure of Friends!

Bruce and Ruth Barkley were out monitoring the fruit stand on what was an unusually busy summer Saturday when the Burches and Dee drove up to their home. They saw Ruth motion them toward the driveway as they helped the last customers. Don pulled past the cars parked on the side of the road and into the Barkley's drive. They were greeted quickly by Ashley and Jacob who were barefoot and in swim suits.

"Maggie! Dillon! Hi! Did you bring your swim suits? We are going to the pond after lunch!" The well-meaning Barkley kids found the frowns on Maggie's and Dillon's faces give the answer to their question. Before the sad siblings could answer, a smiling Carrie said, "I can't figure out why but for some reason I packed two items that looked like swim suits in my carry-on bag—and I think they are too small for Daddy and me."

"Yes! Thank you, Mommy! How'd you know?" Not waiting, nor really caring for the answer, the two grabbed their suits and towels from their mother's hands and followed the counterparts to the bedrooms to change.

Bruce Barkley was as ready as the kids for some fun on this pure summer day. "It was a good day of sales. We're getting a lot of traffic. Must be the hot weather or something. Seems everyone is headed out to Silver Lake. Hope it's okay to have Maggie and Dillon join our two at the old pond."

Bruce and Ruth were glad to close down the stand at noon and have some family time with these new friends of theirs. The four carried the unsold fruit and pies to the coolers in the barn. While doing so, they put some pop and fruit into a travel cooler and placed them in the back of Bruce's truck. Ruth went into the kitchen with Carrie and Dee and brought some sandwiches. It was here that Dee said, "If you don't mind me being a party pooper, I think I'd like to take a nap this afternoon while you enjoy the picnic. Hope that is all right with you young people."

"Why of course, Grandmom. I can't fathom how you have kept up all week and not gotten your regular naps."

"Dee, why don't you go into the bedroom. It is the coolest room and, if you turn on the fan, it should be bearable," said Ruth with understanding.

"Carrie, with it so hot and all, we decided to carry out the lunch as a picnic and eat under the trees by the pond. Believe me, it will be a lot cooler than in this place."

The four children—suited up and with towels in hand—joined their parents as if on cue. With Jacob and Ashley climbing up and over the gate into the bed of the truck, Maggie and Dillon did the same. They loved sitting amidst the hay bales, as the truck drove slowly on the worn dirt road back deep into the orchard. Such first-time fun evoked a loud, "Yes!" and a pumped fist from Dillon. He proceeded to quote his Dad, "Yes! That's what I'm talking 'bout."

If one would close his eyes, he'd expect Opie and his Dad, Andy Taylor, to come out of the trees to join them for this picnic and swim. If there was ever a day to take a dip in the cool pond—it was today.

It didn't take much for Jacob to coax Dillon to hold
onto the rope and swing out into the pond.

It didn't take much for Jacob to coax Dillon to hold onto the rope
and swing out into the pond. Maggie and Ashley were almost waist

deep in the cool water already and cheered when the 'Bud' cannon-balled into the pond.

This was that "perfect day." With the "boys", who included Dillon and Jacob as well as Don and Bruce, now swimming, Maggie and Ashley dried off at the water's edge. It was here that two friends had established memberships in the "Friends for Life" club. Ashley showed Maggie how to make a daisy chain and gave it to her for a friendship necklace. "I will always keep this."

Dillon's and Jacob's friendship was sealed when they both did somersaults off the rope on equal dares that the other wouldn't do it. They both did.

≈ ≈ ≈ ≈ ≈ ≈

"Charlie, as you can see from these letters that Maggie unearthed, I had tried to contact you and I *did* wait for you. I sent these five and probably 12 more letters to you over a three year span. What would *you* have done if they were all sent back to you with zero response? Then when we all got news from the paper that you were 'presumed to be dead,' after being a prisoner of war—well—I had to face reality. I assumed you had died in the war, I—."

"Claire. You don't have to explain. You don't have to give a second thought about apologizing. Listen. It's not that I didn't expect you to move on and marry some day. You were too pretty not to. I just held out hope. I have finally come to accept the fact that I could never have done anything to speed my return home any more than you could have done anything to determine I was alive. War does some ugly things." Charles then took Claire's hands and looked directly into her eyes, "Claire, as a result of some real soul searching and meeting with a pastor in Texas, I have made peace with God on these things and—." Charles paused a bit to collect himself once more, "—after last night's events with Dee's wonderful kids, I have also come to see God had a plan in it all. I thought I was searching to find myself and God clued me in—by allowing all of this—that I was searching in all the wrong places. He clearly got my attention and let me know He actually wanted me. Me. He wanted just me. He loves me unconditionally." Charles paused once more. Claire neither said anything nor knew what to say. She listened to every word. "Claire, I have never been good with words. I'm not the reader you are—but—Claire, God has been so good to me to allow me a second chance with Him. I am praying I will have a second chance with you."

With the sun setting at 8:45 and painting the porch orange and purple, the lanky 85 year-old got up off the porch swing, knelt in front of Claire—her face radiant with the sun's *and* the Son's reflection—and asked, "Claire, will you marry me? I so want to take care of you with the years I have left. I love you."

The affirmative response was first given in tears of joy. The "Yes!" came when Charles teased Claire that he hadn't heard "Yes" or "No" yet.

"You crazy fool. I was hoping you wouldn't look at this old, changed girl and walk away again. "Yes! I will marry Charlie Hargrove. I will be glad to finally be MRS. CHARLES J. HARGROVE!"

≈  ≈  ≈  ≈  ≈  ≈

Dee was up and refreshed after a good hour nap. Being like family all these years with Bruce's parents and knowing and loving Ruth so well, Dee took it on her own to do what she does so well—prepare a home cooked supper for the gang of eight. She decided they would be famished. She raided the freezer. Thawed and cut up two chickens. Cooked them. Sliced some vegetables. Prepared her special potato salad. Added to Ruth's cache of lemonade. Raided Ruth's "secret" (*Mrs. Smith's*) apple pie and then—thanked God that she was ready when the motley crew of four kids and four adults—well—two female adults—walked into the kitchen with eyes bigger than the pie she just baked.

"Dee! What have you done? Where did you get your energy? Did Claire come over and help? Just how old are you *really*?" not expecting an answer of course.

Too late. Dillon stated loudly and matter-of-factly, "Grandmom is 82."

All smiled except for Jacob who asked his new friend, "I thought she was your great-grandmother."

True to form, the endearing seven year-old Dillon answered, "Well. she told us we could call her 'grandmother' and we have but, come to think of it, Jake, we *should* call her 'Great-grandmother' because she is a GREATgrandmother. She's the best!"

That brought cheers and "right on's" from all.

Dee was beside herself. She hugged the still wet Dillon and then told everyone to clean up and be at the table in five minutes. "The rolls will be done by then."

With church coming early the next day, the Burch family and Dee excused themselves by 8:45 and left for home. As they cruised slowly during the last vestiges of another Lake Michigan sunset in Mears, they thought about Charles and Claire who were but a half mile away as the crow flies. Dee particularly had hoped and prayed "things" would be turning out well for them. She had no idea how well it actually was!

Maggie and Dillon thought of Charles in a different way. They asked their Dad and Mom and Great-grandmother to help them sing, "God Bless America," With the windows rolled down and the cooler air rolling in, the words began to roll off their lips—

> God bless America
> Land that I love.
> Stand beside her, and guide her
> Thru the night with a light from above.
> From the mountains, to the prairies,
> To the oceans, white with foam
> God bless America, My home sweet home.

# Chapter 29

# Amazing Grace!

Dee asked Don to pull the van over to the side of the road when it arrived at First Baptist. She pointed out the main church sign on Tyler Road and proudly explained how "Doug had helped build it and did all the electrical work for it." She knew this final day would come and although she dreaded it, she was going to savor every memory moment she could from it. One such way was to connect her beloved extended family with her church family. As Dee saw it, it doesn't get much better than that. And as she was approaching church she knew the moment had come.

They almost filled a whole pew. A visitor would assume they were one big family. Dee was proud as ever to walk in with Don and Carrie and the kids and glad she was being seated by Harmon Raga, a long-time friend and usher on duty.

"See that you made it through the week, 'eh, Dee?" Harmon and his wife, Nancy, had heard last week of Dee's week ahead. Although they knew the Burch family a little and were glad they had come to visit Dee, they secretly wondered if Dee would be up for it physically for the whole seven days.

"Yes, it was the best week I've had in I don't know when. I'm tired, yes, but wouldn't trade a day of this week for a month's worth of rest." The she grabbed Harmon's sleeve to bring him closer. "Harmon, when you see Claire—you know, Claire deGroot—come in with a friend, will you seat them with us? We'll save two places for them. That should really fill up this pew."

"I will do just that, Dee. By the way, who are these beautiful children adorning your arms?" "Why, they would be my Maggie and my Dillon. I have been their grandmother this week. That's why I look twenty years younger."

"It's strange you should say that. I was just going to say the same, but I was thinking 25 years younger." They both smiled and Mr. Raga greeted Maggie and Dillon with "low fives."

While the pre-service music was playing, the two detectives were turning their heads often, as they were the self-appointed look outs for Claire and Charles. The places saved for them were not negotiable. They were to sit between Dillon and Maggie. To help make sure they spotted them, they moved to the end of the pew and stood up.

Faces turned when folk saw Claire coming in. She hadn't come to church for weeks. Few knew why, although many could guess. Claire was somewhat self-conscious of this but more concerned what people would think of her coming in with someone who few, if any, would know. She was pleased with the smiles and nods of grace given by most people when her eyes made contact with theirs. She began to beam when a smiling Harmon told her and Charles that they had "requests to sit with that family in the fourth pew in the middle section."

When Charles heard that and then actually saw Maggie face them and Dillon standing in the aisle motioning for them to sit with them, he felt somewhat relieved. The two of them looked like they belonged with this family. Fortunately, Charles had brought some summer dress slacks and shirt that worked for this occasion. Claire found church a perfect occasion to don her yellow cotton dress again.

When Charles saw Maggie face them and Dillon
standing in the aisle—he felt relieved.

The sanctuary was filled this hot August Sunday, as it so often was
in the summer when visitors from the many tourist sites and camps
carve out time to attend church. Perhaps that fact and because the
overhead fans were struggling to move the air, many parishioners
creatively put their bulletins to good use as fans. The heat, however,
didn't seem to deter the joy that this unique "family" in the fourth
pew was experiencing. The highlight for Don and Carrie was when
they caught Maggie looking up from her fan to look at Charles while
he was singing. Charles returned the look and nodded with a smile as
the words to a familiar hymn were being sung.

> Amazing grace, how sweet the sound
> That saved a wretch like me.
> I once was lost but now am found,
> Was blind but now I see.

Carrie checked out the bulletin and the simple single-fold reminded her of her father's churches. She searched for the message and saw the title, "The Answer is Sheep, Coins, and Sons" and the text was to be Luke 15. When the pastor began speaking he soon shared— in Jeopardy game fashion—"And the question is, 'What is lost?'"

Charles had not been in church for some two months, since he stopped going to First Baptist of Hillsboro, Texas. He liked the pastor and the people there. It was just that he felt he didn't belong. He had felt for some time that something was missing and he knew it wasn't the church; it was something inside of him. He felt lost. Today, Pastor Looley's message seemed to be a blur to Charles. Since Claire had given him her Bible, he became glued to the text of the message instead of the message itself. When he got to the last verse, he became almost overwhelmed with emotion.

> But we had to celebrate and be glad, because
> this brother of yours was dead, and is alive again;
> he was lost and is now found.

Although he was in the midst of perhaps 250 people, he felt alone. Even though he fought it, his mind raced back to his years of forced imprisonment. *"This brother of yours was dead."* Charles said to himself. "This is not good; I've got to get myself together." He managed to gain a measure of composure when he recalled the one verse he had memorized from childhood that carried him through many dark nights on Guam. He was but Maggie's age when he would see Isaiah 42:3 on his Dad's shaving mirror:

> A bruised reed he will not break,
> and a smoldering wick he will not snuff out.

Charlie didn't fully understand that as a child, but after suffering many bruises from the butts of the enemy's rifles as a prisoner, he kept telling himself, "I will not break. I will not break. God help me not to break." God was faithful, Charlie now recalls.

Claire, for her part, was feeling the opposite. She was feeling so good—then she looked up at Charles. She saw he was struggling and, instinctively, put her hand on his. A nod and an affirming look from Charles said to her, "I'll be okay."

It was when Claire placed her hand on his that he also realized the "smoldering wick" of their love had not been snuffed out. And most importantly, God's love for Charles never left and He, in His infinite grace, even chose to allow Charles to rekindle an earthly love.

The service flew by it seemed, which was a good thing for Maggie and Dillon as they weren't used to sitting in an adult service. But Claire didn't mind at all when she felt Dillon nodding off to sleep at her side. Dee smiled at the sight and squeezed Claire's hand over Dillon's slumping neck. A return squeeze and smile indicated that all was well for Claire, too. It also sent the message that she thanked Dee strongly for inviting her back to church.

Maggie was anything but asleep. Her mind was in overdrive. The "Kit Kittredge" in her was writing the unusual story of the man sitting next to her in her fertile mind. She just knew the title had to be "Amazing Grace." She also knew that there just seemed something left with his story that was still unfinished. "What could that be?"

After the service, the church narthex was filled with many who had been friends of Claire over the years and they extended words of encouragement as only these dear and real friends could. Charles stood next to her and was pleased to see the response since Claire had indicated to him on Saturday of her reservations of going back to church. Charles thought he had seen a few people he knew from his childhood but he wasn't sure. He was pretty confident that the one door greeter was one of the Gale "boys" who used to pick up eggs and feed from his Dad's farm. There were a few who thought *his* face looked familiar but—"No, it couldn't be. Charlie Hargrove died in the war."

Charles had heard that Hart had become an official city in 1946, almost a year after he had been released from rehab at Walter Reed and he had come back to Hart in hopes of finding Claire still waiting for him. He also noticed that his hometown had changed some. The county fairgrounds were in the same location but sure looked smaller.

The new Hart Dam was the biggest surprise. He also realized that First Baptist itself had moved from downtown to this location. "One thing that had not changed," mused Charlie as he observed the good folk in the lobby from his 6' 4" tower, "the people, the great people!"

# Chapter 30

## The Gift of Honor

While Charles was in deep thought, Maggie and Dillon got his attention as they knew they had to say, "Good-bye." Don and Carrie knew they had a long trip ahead of them and wanted to get around Chicago before dark set in. Knowing that they would be eating lunch at Grandmom's and still needed to get packed, they encouraged the kids to say their "good-byes" to Ashley and Jacob, and Charles and Claire.

"No, you don't! I have something to say and give you before you leave," said Charles as he bent down with a smile to respond to his young friends. He then indicated to Claire what he was doing and she politely excused herself from her friends. They found Dee talking with the Ragas. Charles asked Dee if there was some room or place he could say good-bye to the Burches that was private. "I want to give them something before they all leave."

Nancy Raga overheard him and suggested the library, which she just closed down 15 minutes after church.

Carrie and Don took occasion to thank the Barkleys once more and then saw Dee waving them over to the hallway. Nancy opened the library door and the party of seven entered the much cooler and quieter room. Maggie's eyes were like silver dollars when she saw the books, but when she heard Charles ask for her and Dillon to stand before him while he sat, she did exactly that. He had a smile but looked serious, too. Maggie placed her arm around her brother and the two were indeed like one in listening to their mutual hero.

Maggie placed her arm around her brother and the two
were like one in listening to their mutual hero.

"I know you all must be leaving soon so I will keep this short,"
began their hero-friend. Claire saw Charlie hesitate and she began
praying silently. She knew what he was going to do but she did not
know what he was going to say. Charlie, himself, didn't know exactly
what he was going to say.

"Maggie and Dillon. Today's message by the pastor probably said it better than I will, but I want to tell you something before you leave. I have felt lost for many, many years. As you know, I went off to war and, in so doing, I lost the one I loved like no other. When I was in the POW camp, I felt lost. I knew I was thousands of miles away from everyone I had loved. My parents. My friends. My fellow soldiers—I was even separated from the other 12 prisoners. And, of course, I was separated from my Claire. At times I even felt separated from God. It wasn't true, of course, but I honestly felt it was.

"But I finally praised God when I was found by the American troops that one steamy July day in '44. I thought, Maggie and Dillon, that I would be all right after that. I was 'lost' but then I was 'found.' But, if you can understand this, I realized in rehab that my body was 'found' but I still felt 'lost' on the inside." Maggie walked forward to hug him and Dillon followed. Now with the two but only a foot away, he went on.

"I thought there was hope if I could find Claire and take up from where we left off. Then—well—you know the story." With Claire in the room, standing by Don and Carrie and Dee, he stopped short of saying any more of this so he didn't make Claire feel bad. He knew it was not her fault that he felt lost. "Then I decided to buck up and do something with my life. With the wonderful GI Bill, I was able to go to college and I got a good degree in business from the University of Missouri. I also got married and had a child. I worked very hard, thinking that if I could get financial security I would feel I mattered and not feel so lost. I'm not going to give you my life history—but, please know Maggie and Dillon—God did bless me richly in my real estate business. But then my wife, Harriet, died and I discovered that my daughter wouldn't have anything to do with me after the funeral. I got really depressed and—although it was wrong—I cut myself off from most everybody.

"I finally moved from my home in Creve Coeur, Missouri to retire in a small town like I grew up in, like this city of Hart. So I researched many locations and moved to a town right in the middle of Texas called Hillsboro. To be very honest, it was the harsh Hart winters I wanted to avoid as much as the fact that I really did like Hillsboro. To make a long story short—I am really *am* trying—I decided it was time I went back to church. I did and the pastor at the First Baptist Church there helped me through my self-focused depression and I gave my heart and life to God. I received Jesus Christ as my Savior. I thought that all would be smooth after that, but I still felt I had no purpose for my life and my daughter would still not talk with me."

Maggie was tearing up, but remained quietly patient with Dillon listening very carefully also. "What happened then, Mr. Charles?"

"Maggie and Dillon. That brings me to your Mom and Dad. I told them what I'm going to tell you right now. I asked their permission. You are very special to me. Very. I hope you understand all this. I think you will." Charles took a deep breath, looked squarely from his chair at these friends who were more than 75 years younger than he was. "This past year I was really down on myself and I somehow thought that if I could find the war medals that I had thrown away in anger in your grandmother's orchard—that *they* would somehow make me feel my life had some meaning, that I had done something important with my life. Well," he smiled at them, "I didn't find them—ahh—someone else found them. Thank you.

"This past Friday—when you presented them to me—for the first time in my life—I felt no longer lost. I looked at you two with the medals in your hands and with your proud smile. You made me feel like I was important for more than money or earning some medals or scoring a basket.

"I also recall when you, Maggie, made me feel so accepted that Thursday at the fruit stand. You can never know how down I was that day and you can never know how much your simple act of kindness did to lift me up." Charles paused again when Maggie simply said, "But you *are* important!" That comment triggered Charles to say, "Maggie and Dillon, I still can't believe I used to know your great-grandfather, Doug Howard, so well. He would be so proud of you.

"Back to the medals and my lame promise to keep this short. When you walked up to me to present the medals to me on Friday, I realized that it wasn't my medals that made me feel important and valuable. It was you two, and"—looking up now at Don and Carrie and Dee—"your Dad and Mom and Great-grandmother. All of you made me feel valuable as a person. Then the message today reminded me that it was God all along that says I am valuable to Him and that he proved it by directing me to all of you. HE USED MY SEARCH FOR MEDALS TO LEAD ME TO YOU. HE USED YOU TO LEAD ME BACK

TO GOD. Like the song says, 'I once was lost, but now I am found.' You taught me that by your examples."

The quiet library was kept quiet by Harmon and Nancy who agreed to guard the door "for a bit" but even they could hardly keep a dry eye as they heard this testimony of God's grace in Charles' life. No one knew quite what to say.

Then Charles reached down by his side and took his precious war medals, still in their cases. "Maggie and Dillon. I want to give these medals to you. You have so honored me, I want to honor you. I don't need these medals to tell me I am important. You two have told me that by your actions and attitudes. God has told me so. Claire has. Dee has. Don and Carrie, you have. That's pretty hard to argue against. And, furthermore," seeing Maggie and Dillon drawing back from him and the medals, "I want no arguing from you on this. This is the only way I can think of to thank you for honoring me and for being used by God 'to seek and save the lost'."

The usually verbal siblings could not find words to say nor did they know what to do. They looked back at their parents for some direction. Don and Carrie, knowing what this meant to Charles and seeing Claire's nod of approval, tapped the children on their backs to encourage them to receive these very special gifts.

Finally—Maggie blurted out—"Mr. Charles, I will cherish this forever. Thank you. I love you."

Dillon was overwhelmed and said very simply, "Thank you, Mr. Charles. You are one of my favorite heroes. I can't believe you are giving me this 'Distinguished Service Cross'!" A huge hug followed.

Claire was beside herself. Carrie tried to help her and found a nearby chair for her. Tears flowed. Nancy stepped in and gave her a box of Kleenex.

Charles took over again. He got up off his chair and looked up at Dee. He put his long arm around her weeping friend, Claire, and said, "Dee, we want to thank you for your kind and unconditional friendship and especially for that day you came out to Claire's. That humble act of caring brought Claire back to life. There is nothing more we can say to express our gratitude—but, Dee—Claire and I have one question for you."

Dee was taken by surprise and didn't know whether to cry or smile but finally asked, "And what might that be?"

"Dee, we want to ask you to be Claire's matron of honor at our wedding."

The once quiet library exploded! The ever-vigilant Ragas opened the doors to see what was going on. It sounded like the Hart Pirates just won conference in overtime again over Ravenna High. Dee hugged Claire for what seemed to be minutes. Don and Carrie hugged Charles and happily expressed congratulations. Maggie and Dillon were jumping up and down and one of them kept saying, "I knew it! I knew it!"

After the wonderful hullabaloo, Carrie asked when the big date was. Claire promptly answered, "We don't know yet, but—at our age—it had better be soon! You will all be invited but, if you come, don't come bearing green bananas." The laughter and joy only intensified.

It seemed fitting that they now stood in the center of the library between the fiction and the non-fiction shelves. This story seemed just too good to be true. But it was. A treasure was found in Dee's blackberry cove. And it was no longer the mystery of two long lost World War II medals. Old and young alike discovered that the heavenly treasure Charles discovered in this summer of 2009 was much more valuable than the earthly treasures he had buried in the summer of 1946. It was in this happiest of moments that Don asked the Ragas to join them and they all circled in prayer and gave all praise to God

# Chapter 31

## On the Road Again

After a tearful farewell in the church parking lot, Don and Carrie drove back to New Era along the slower old 31 route. This was their first time to visit this area in awhile and they wanted to celebrate the day at *The Fire Plug*, a unique ice cream shop which Grandma knew to be about half way home in Shelby. Who cared today if dessert came before the meal? Besides, what would taste better than ice cream on a hot day like today? Then Dee said from her perch in the back seat, "And what would be more appropriate than a grandmother spoiling her grandkids at least once this week. I'm paying. No discussion."

After only five minutes eating the cones in the sun, Dee looked at Dillon's shirt and just had to ask, "Are you saving some for later, young man?"

It was apparent to all that no one wanted to go home. But they left Shelby and drove around the slow curve leading to the Village of New Era and on to Dee's home on the hill.

It was but 10 minutes and Carrie could see that Dee was fading fast. "She must be ready for her Sunday afternoon nap," she thought. "*I'm* ready for a Sunday afternoon nap!"

Because the day was extended longer than anyone projected due to Charles' surprise "talk," Don and Carrie convinced Dee to scale down lunch. They also had made some preparations before church, so the packing didn't take long.

They made their last minute searches nevertheless. Carrie found her camera. She put the medals in an old cigar box Dee had given her and walked them personally out to the van and placed them in the glove box. Maggie and Dillon looked three times under their bunk for "anything." When Don was placing his old shirts into a duffel bag, a plastic bag fell out. "The photo of Claire and Charles!" he said out loud. He took it to Dee. She promised to give it to the "lovebirds" Wednesday when she and Claire were getting together to discuss the simple wedding plans. Looking further at it, Dee said, "You know, their basic features had not really changed that much over all these years."

"Oh, no! It is ruined!" Maggie cried as she saw her daisy chain wilted and coming apart. Carrie was nearby and sat her down for a lesson in Botany 101. It didn't help a lot to erase her sadness. So the creative mother secured a Zip Loc bag from Dee and she put the limp daisies in it. "It's the person that counts, Maggie. Remember what Charles said he had learned about that. Also, what matters is that you have a great new friend named Ashley. I don't think she is going to wilt too soon." What turned the frown, however, into a smile was the promise that Maggie could call Ashley when they got back to Elgin.

"Carrie! Where's Dillon?" Don said with some frustration. He found Dillon's bag next to the van, but did not see Dillon.

"I have no idea. Maggie, do you know where your brother is?"

"What? Do you think I'm my brother's—.

"Maggie!"

"Maybe he is in the back yard or down at the barn. He did say he was sad that we had not been able to say good-bye to Ebony."

Don darted out the door and then saw Dillon. He was seated on the lawn chair in the back yard, facing the barn. He walked over and knelt down next to him. "Hey, Bud. Even your detective's eyes won't find Ebony now. Ebony is probably having fun somewhere or getting a cool drink by that creek we crossed on our hike. He is a good dog. I can see why you miss him. He was helpful in us finding Claire's photo and I would bet he is probably telling his buddies down by some fire hydrant right now." Dillon said nothing but simply stared straight ahead. "Besides, this is home for him and—you gotta know, Dillon— you gotta know—look at me—you gotta know we will be coming back to New Era as soon as we are able. I want to. How about you? Then we will look for Ebony first thing, okay?"

"Promise?"

"Promise."

"Maggie! What's in this bag? It feels like a hundred pounds," Carrie said, doing her best to fake frustration.

"Mommy!" Maggie recalled the same conversation when leaving Elgin. Seeing her Mom having a hard time not smiling, she just laughed and took her book bag—*now with five more books*—out to the van. What a difference a week makes. Although no one wanted to go back home, they were all much more relaxed.

Dee did her part to make up some snack packs for each of them. She gave Carrie an extra cooler in which to store four pints of blackberries. It was a much-welcomed gift as she had intended to get some for her mother back in Illinois. "Thank you, Grandmom. I will really miss you. This was absolutely the best vacation we ever had. It was busy, but busy in a relaxing way, if you know what I mean. I put our sheets and towels on the washer in the laundry closet. Hope that is all right with you."

With everyone now outside by the van, Dee thanked each one profusely for her best week in years. "You also gave me back a good friend. You shared my house like my own family. Guess that is because you are. I look forward to the future much more than I have in a long time."

Carrie placed her camera on a step ladder she got from the garage. She then put everyone around Dee by "the tree." She set the timer—found her spot next to Don—all smiled—then—CLICK—a final photo would end her slide show of "OUR VACATION– AUGUST 2009."

CLICK—a final photo would end her slide show
of "OUR VACATION–AUGUST 2009."

The tears of joy were cut off when Don announced it was already
5:00 p.m. and the likelihood of getting around Chicago in daylight was
zero to none. They were so glad to see that their air conditioning was
working. It was still 88 degrees and all were perspiring when they got
into their seats.

"Be sure to call when you get home." *Grandma* Howard hated to
see them go, but *Dee* Howard was also anxious to get on the phone
and call Claire.

On the road again. This time heading south. This time tanned and relaxed. Carrie saw the squeaky sand still on the mats and said, "Guess we are going home, but we will be bringing a lot of Michigan with us." All smiled. Don thought she meant the good memories. Dillon thought she meant the blackberries in the cooler at his feet. Maggie thought she meant the new friends "in her heart" that would go with her forever.

Don was to drive to Holland. Carrie to New Buffalo. Don to that McDonald's at the Des Plaines oasis. Carrie home.

Sometimes even a great and unique week of discovery like the Burches enjoyed doesn't change old habits. On the way home, Don had his CD's playing. Carrie had her water and mental list of things she hoped were in the van. Maggie was quickly into *Eight Cousins*. Dillon—well, Dillon was the exception—instead of checking out cars on the road—he was glued to reading his new book, *Where the Red Fern Grows*. Maybe it was because Mr. Charles recommended it or that he was still missing Ebony. Or very possibly, it was because he was a boy—the book was about a dog—and it was still summer.

"Daddy?" came Maggie's faint request from her seat. She was clearly deep in thought, as she was no longer reading since there was limited light by which to read.

"Yes, Maggie?"

"Do any of your CD's have the song *Amazing Grace* on them?"

The End of One Mystery. Another coming soon

# Epilogue

The reader will be glad to hear Maggie's and Dillon's parents kept their word. The next morning after arriving home, Maggie woke up to discover Ashley's phone number by her cereal bowl. No one was surprised when Maggie took the phone outside under the shade of the secret tree located on the side of their house.

Dillon's wish took longer to be fulfilled. A last minute visit to celebrate Thanksgiving was a surprise to all, but a thrill to Dillon. Upon arrival, his great-grandmother took the family for a walk to the old barn. After Don was asked to open it, a wide-eyed Dillon and Maggie were greeted by none other than the jumping, barking dog named Ebony!

## Coming soon: More adventures with the *Reader Whiz Kids*!

All who enjoyed this *Reader Whiz Kids'* adventure to Michigan in "*The Mysterious Treasure of Blackberry Cove*" will want to be sure to read what happens when they vacation in Wisconsin in "The Startling Mystery of Squirrel Lake Island"! A simple summer canoe trip on the deep blue waters of Squirrel Lake lands Maggie and Dillon in the middle of their biggest caper ever! A secret kept for decades by the Lake's oldest resident is uncovered by a chance discovery in a cabin nestled among the tall pines and white Birch trees of the picturesque Wisconsin north woods!

# APPENDIX A

## Character Traits: Chapter by Chapter

INTRODUCTION:

The reader of *The Mysterious Treasure of Blackberry Cove* will discover a different character trait in each chapter of the book as displayed in the actions of Maggie or Dillon Burch or possibly from another of the key characters in the mystery.

While some of these traits are clearly seen, others are not. It is the desire of this author for the reader to enjoy the mystery story itself of these two sibling adventurers but also to learn from their character as they interact with others. Most of us realize that real character isn't forged just with major tests or events but with the every day challenges that come as being part of a family or school or church or work or sports team and more. We would encourage every parent or the reader himself to reflect on the character traits displayed in each chapter. We hope you utilize this practical study guide to formulate a godly character as you live out the "chapters" in your life with wise character choices.

In other words, this *Appendix on Character Traits* is meant to serve as an interactive discussion guide as you finish each chapter or after you finish the book. There are four essential areas of learning:

1. **The Trait Defined** (with biblical precept defined as its foundation)
2. **The Trait Displayed**
3. **The Trait Discussed**
4. **The Trait Discerned**

***The Trait Defined***: It is one thing to list a character quality and hope someone will learn and live that quality. It is much *better* to define that quality clearly and understandably. That is why each character trait is given first a clear definition and then a given a biblical precept for that definition. A "*precept*" is a commandment given as a rule of action. In this case, we use a scripture verse because in this current world of relative thinking, we want children and young adults to formulate their thinking and character based on God's unchanging truth, the Bible.

**The Trait Displayed**: Jesus used parables in the Gospels to illustrate the truths and character traits He wished to convey to his disciples. We have used the fictional story of Maggie and Dillon Burch and the people that surround them in this story to attempt to do the same.

**The Trait Discussed:** This section is meant to be used as an interactive discussion between the readers and their parents or their teachers by using the very story line to illustrate a particular character trait.

**The Trait Discerned:** This is perhaps the most important discussion section. It is also meant to be used as an interactive discussion between the readers and their parents or teachers. The learning goal in this section is to take the character trait and "bring it home" for everyday application for families.

**The Goal: That every parent and/or teacher and/or disciple-maker may be able to say in the years ahead: "*I have no greater joy than to hear my children walking in the truth.*"**

**III John 4 (NIV)**

# Chapter 1:
# A Vacation Without Books?
## Character Trait: Agreeableness

*The Trait Defined*: Finding a decision, solution, or proposal acceptable enough that I can support and others would not oppose.
*Biblical precept*: "Can two walk together unless they are agreed?" Amos 3:3 NKJV

*The Trait Displayed*: Maggie chooses to be *agreeable* with Dillon after Dillon's joke to her about her bringing so many books on their vacation trip.

*The Trait Discussed*:
    1. What did Dillon say as a joke to provoke Maggie?
    2. Why did Maggie react the way she did? What might you have said?

*The Trait Discerned*:
    1. What does *agreeableness* mean to you?
    2. Why is *agreeableness* a good character trait to have?
    3. Why is it generally better to respond by seeking an *agreeable* solution?
    4. Can you describe a situation in your past where you displayed *agreeableness* with someone or someone chose to be agreeable with you?

# Chapter 2: The Mysterious Light
## Character Trait: Enthusiasm

*The Trait Defined*: Allowing God's energy to be expressed though my mind, will, and emotions.
Biblical precept: "Whatever you do, do your work heartily, as for the Lord, rather than for men." Colossians 3:23 NASB

*The Trait Displayed*: Dillon chooses to obey *enthusiastically* his mother's request to brush his teeth and then get into bed.

*The Trait Discussed*:

1. What did Dillon's mother, Carrie, ask Dillon to do after they arrived at her grandmother's home late at night?
2. How did Dillon respond?
3. How might you have responded in a similar situation?

*The Trait Discerned*:

1. What does *enthusiasm* mean to you?
2. What do you think the Bible verse above means when it tells you to work as if you are working for the Lord and not for men?
3. Can you describe a time when you chose to give your Dad or Mom an *enthusiastic* response to one of their requests? How did they respond when you did?
4. Can you recall an instance when someone gave you an *enthusiastic* response to a request of yours?

# Chapter 3: Daylight in the Swamps!
## Character Trait: Prudence

*The Trait Defined*: Having sufficient information to exercise sound judgment to avoid error and danger and misunderstanding. It means to be discreet or carefully calculate your thinking before you take action. *Biblical precept*: "The mind of the prudent acquires knowledge—(he) sees danger and takes refuge."
Proverbs 13:16; 22:3 NKJV

*The Trait Displayed*: When Great-grandma entered the bedroom, she found Maggie reading, but Dillon was deep in thought on the top bunk as he peered out the window. While he wondered if he really saw a man out his window the night before, "he kept those thoughts to himself, unsure yet if anyone would believe him."

*The Trait Discussed*:

1. Why was Dillon *prudent* in keeping his thoughts about seeing a mysterious man to himself at this time?

2. If you saw what Dillon had seen the night before, would you have kept this sighting to yourself? Why or why not?

*The Trait Discerned*:

1. Looking at the definition, why is *prudence* a valuable trait to have?

2. Can you use the word *prudence* in a sentence to describe an experience in your life?

3. Ask your Mom or Dad to do the same about an experience in her/his life.

# Chapter 4: A Detective's Playground

## Character Trait: Thoroughness

*The Trait Defined*: Being attentive to detail, careful, accurate, and complete.

*Biblical precept*: The Berean Jews "received the word with great eagerness, examining the Scriptures daily to see whether these things were so." Acts 17:11 NASB

*The Trait Displayed*: When trying to figure out the best path to the barn, "Maggie noticed that the weeds and grasses under the old apple trees were shorter than those on the old overgrown path and looked like the best route to get through to the barn."

*The Trait Discussed*:

1. How did Maggie's *thoroughness* display her detective skills?

2. How did her *thorough* observations help her and Dillon in this situation?

*The Trait Discerned*:

1. Can you recall a time when you paid careful attention to detail and it helped you?

2. Can you recall a time when you were not *thorough* and wished you had been?

3. How could you be more *thorough* at home?

4. Ask Mom or Dad how they would answer questions 1 and 2.

# Chapter 5: Where Are the Kids?

## Character Trait: Alertness

*The Trait Defined*: Using my physical and spiritual senses to recognize and respond to dangers.

*Biblical precept*: "Be self-controlled and alert. Your enemy the devil prowls around like a roaring lion looking for someone to devour." I Peter 5:8 NIV

*The Trait Displayed*: After Maggie and Dillon learned that someone had been staying in the barn, they were ready to run out. Then Maggie said, "Wait! I hear someone coming!" Then the two quickly hid behind the old tractor.

*The Trait Discussed:*

1. What do you believe Maggie heard that caused her to warn Dillon and to take leadership to hide behind the Farmall tractor in the barn?

2. All turned out well, but why was it important that Maggie was *alert* and cautious?

*The Trait Discerned:*

1. The above Bible verse suggests that to be *alert* is to also be under control. What do you   think this means? How do these two traits go together? Can you give an example of this?

2. Can you recall a time when you were out of control and were hurt because you were not *alert* to some danger?

3. Can you recall a time when because you were *alert*, you avoided danger?

# Chapter 6: Vagrant or Mystery Guest?

## Character Trait: Sensitivity

*The Trait Defined*: Exercising my senses so that I can understand and respond to the true spirit and emotions of those around me.
*Biblical precept:* "Rejoice with those who rejoice; mourn with those who mourn." Romans 12:15 NIV

*The Trait Displayed*: When Maggie's Great-grandma heard about the vagrant in the barn and seemed to express deep concern, Maggie said, "Sorry, Grandma. We didn't want to scare you with our discovery. Truth is, we didn't actually see someone. We only saw what we thought was some bedding."

*The Trait Discussed*:

1. Read the definition of sensitivity again. How did Maggie show *sensitivity* to her great-grandmother in that situation around the lunch table?

2. To what emotion in her great-grandmother did Maggie show her *sensitivity*?

*The Trait Discerned*:

1. Why is it important to be *sensitive* to other people's emotions and respond accordingly?

2. Have you ever been with a new group of kids and were relieved when one of them showed *sensitivity* to your being new and showed kindness and acceptance to you? How did that make you feel?

3. Can you recall an example when you showed *sensitivity* to someone? Share this story!

# Chapter 7: A Mysterious Photo

## Character Trait: Cautiousness

*The Trait Defined*: Knowing how important right timing is in accomplishing right actions.

*Biblical precept*: "Zeal without knowledge is not good; a person who moves too quickly may go in the wrong way." Proverbs 19:2 NLT

*The Trait Displayed*: When Maggie's and Dillon's Dad was checking out the discovery in the barn, he was surprised and confronted by a growling dog. As the story unfolds, "The dog's growl didn't subside until Don wisely bent down on his knees and put out his hand."

*The Trait Discussed*:

1. How did Don show *cautiousness* when he was confronted by the growling dog?

2. What might have been a wrong move?

3. What other things did Don slowly do to get the dog to calm down?

*The Trait Discerned*:

1. What does *cautiousness* mean to you?

2. Share an example when you were *cautious* and were so glad you had moved slowly.

3. Share an example when you were not *cautious* and moved too quickly.

4. Have your mother or father share an example of *cautiousness* from his or her own experiences.

# Chapter 8: Blackberries!

## Character Trait: Fairness

*The Trait Defined*: Seeking to look at a decision from the viewpoint of each person involved.

*Biblical precept*: "Just as you want men to treat you, treat them in the same way." Luke 6:31 NASB

*The Trait Displayed*: When Dillon finally told his sister about seeing the man and the mysterious light that first night, Maggie at first said, "Dillon, you're pulling my leg." Then Dillon said, "No, I'm serious. I'm telling you the truth." Maggie sensed he was telling the truth and responded, "You are. I can tell. Why didn't you tell me before?"

1. Re-read the Bible verse above. How did Maggie treat Dillon's hard-to-believe story with her words?

2. How did Maggie show *fairness* to him?

*The Trait Discerned:*

1. Can you recall an experience when you felt someone treated you unfairly? What happened? Describe how you felt.

2. Share an experience you recall where someone showed *fairness* to you.

3. How should you respond when it seems you are not being treated *fairly*? Why?

4. Have your Mom or Dad give an example of this character trait in their lives.

# Chapter 9: Is That a Light?

## Character Trait: Courage

*The Trait Defined*: The ability to act on the knowledge that He (God) who is in me is greater than he who is against me.

*Biblical precept*: "You are from God, little children, and have overcome them; because greater is He who is in you than he who is in the world." I John 4:4 NASB

*The Trait Displayed*: When the detective duo snuck out at midnight to the windy, spooky moonlit back lawn that faced the orchard, they came to a point of no return—to go to the edge of the orchard and look for the mysterious light—- or retreat back to the house. To Maggie and Dillon, "...the decision was evident as they looked at each other: Move ahead!"

*The Trait Discussed:*

1. How did Maggie and Dillon display *courage* on that warm but scary night?

2. Were they wise to just stay on the lawn, not far from the back door of the house?

3. How did it help that they were together in this *courageous* moment?

*The Trait Discerned:*

1. Share a time when you showed *courage*?

2. Explain, the best you can, what the Bible verse means about God being greater in you than he who is against you.

3. Ask your Mom or Dad to tell of a time when they chose to be *courageous*.

# Chapter 10:
# What Happened at Midnight?
## Character Trait: Truthfulness

*The Trait Defined*: Earning future trust by accurately reporting past facts.

*Biblical precept*: "Therefore, put away lying, each one speak truth to his neighbor, for we are members of one another." Ephesians 4:25 NKJV

*The Trait Displayed*: When confronted with their disobedience of sneaking out of the house at midnight, Maggie and Dillon "knew very well they had to tell the whole truth to their parents."

*The Trait Discussed*:

1. In this chapter, Maggie and Dillon seemed relieved to have their Mom and Dad completely in the know. What does it mean to completely tell the *truth*?

2. What exactly did both brother and sister have to say to give the "whole" *truth*, even though they thought their Mom and Dad might not believe them?

*The Trait Discerned*:

1. The story also records that "telling the *truth* has a way of bringing peace."

2. How does telling the whole story bring peace?

3. Share a time when you were somewhat afraid to tell your Dad or Mom the *truth* about something you did, but were glad you did in the end.

4. Tell your parent or teacher about this experience.

# Chapter 11: Real Horses

## Character Trait: Kindness

*The Trait Defined*: Exhibiting a pleasant spirit and moral goodness.
*Biblical precept*: "And be kind to one another, tender-hearted, forgiving each other, just as God in Christ also has forgiven you." Ephesians 4:32 NASB

*The Trait Displayed*: On a hot summer day at the fruit stand, a man walked up and just ordered one peach. "As Jacob gave the man a peach, Maggie moved alongside Jacob and kindly asked the older man if he were thirsty."

*The Trait Discussed*:
1. Why and how did Maggie show *kindness* to this older man?
2. What invitation did Maggie give this man when she observed that he was alone?

*The Trait Discerned*:
1. What does *kindness* mean to you?
2. Give an example of someone who showed *kindness* to you?
3. Share a story of how you were able to show *kindness* to someone else.
4. Share a story of how someone was not kind to you. What did he or she do? How did you respond?
5. Ask your parents to give an example of how you have been *kind* recently?
6. Ask your Mom or Dad what *kindness* means to them and to give an example of this meaning from their personal experience.

# Chapter 12: The Fruit Stand Stranger

## Character Trait: Hospitality

*The Trait Defined*: Eagerly sharing my family, home, finances, food, and spiritual refreshment with those God brings into my life.

*Biblical precept*: "Share with God's people who are in need. Practice hospitality." Romans 12:13 NIV

*The Trait Displayed*: When Charles accepted Maggie's invitation to meet her parents and her great-grandmother in the farm house of her new friends, everyone did his or her part in showing this stranger hospitality. Ruth Ackley, the children's mother, offered Charles an iced tea and a chair in the crowded front porch. Don and Carrie joined in warmly greeting this surprise guest. Of course, the indomitable Maggie became the facilitator of this wonderful fellowship that afternoon.

*The Trait Discussed*:

1. Why was Maggie wise and introducing this stranger to her parents and other adults?

2. How did Maggie and the others show their *hospitality* to this man?

*The Trait Discerned*:

1. What does *hospitality* mean to you?

2. Do you remember a time when someone showed *hospitality* to you?

3. Describe a time when your family eagerly shared your home with someone.

# Chapter 13: The Secret Reading Spot

## Character Trait: Gratefulness

*The Trait Defined:* Always make known to God and others how they benefit my life.

*Biblical precept*: "What makes you better than anyone else? What do you have that God hasn't given to you? And if all you have is from God,

why boast as though you have accomplished something on your own?"
I Corinthians 4:7 NIV

*The Trait Displayed*: As usual, Dee woke up early to prepare a full breakfast for her visiting family. She even baked their favorite, cinnamon apple pie. Did you notice that "all four (Dad, Mom, Maggie, Dillon) were up smiling and greeting Grandma with heartfelt gratitude."

*The Trait Discussed*:
   1. How did Maggie's and Dillon's great-grandmother show hospitality to them and how did they respond?
   2. What does "heartfelt *gratitude*" mean?

*The Trait Discerned*:
   1. Give your definition of "*gratefulness.*"
   2. Can you think of something your Dad or Mom has done for you for which you are very *grateful*? What was it and why are you *grateful*?
   3. Talk about an event or occasion in which you showed *gratefulness* to someone else.
   4. Why are you *grateful* to God?

# Chapter 14: Maggie's Big Discoveries
## Character Trait: Discretion

*The Trait Defined*: Avoiding words, actions, and attitudes which could result in undesirable consequences.
*Biblical precept*: "A prudent person foresees the danger ahead and takes precautions; the simpleton goes blindly on and suffers the consequences."
Proverbs 22:3 NLT

*The Trait Displayed*: Although Maggie's main purpose was to go out into the orchard and find a great place to read, her keen eyes and mind saw something else that could lead to danger. She noticed with her ears and then with her eyes a figure she thought might be a man on the other side of the blackberry bushes and made a big decision at that point..

*The Trait Discussed*:

1. Maggie indeed heard a strange sound coming from beyond the nearby wild blackberry bushes. What was that sound?

2. Maggie ran from the tree due her eyes actually seeing something in the area from which she had heard the sound. What did she see? Then what did Maggie do? Do you think she should have stayed longer to get more information about this second observation?

*The Trait Discerned*:

1. Most educators say reading is much preferable to watching TV because a child or adult creates in his or her mind a scene from the very words he or she is reading while the television does the creating *for* that scene or *for* a person. Do you believe this and do you think Maggie's strong reading habits have given her an attention for detail that she would not have if she read little and watched TV a lot?

2. By the definition above, would you consider yourself a *discrete* young person?

3. Can you or one of your parents recall a time when you remembered details of an event or place in which you were called upon to make a very quick and very important decision?

4. Have your parents share an experience in which they were glad they used *discretion*.

# Chapter 15: Treasure in a Tree

## Character Trait: Observation

*The Trait Defined*: Being watchful, giving keen attention to particulars, and adhering to details that please God.

*Biblical precept*: "Observe your leaders, who spoke the word of God to you. Consider (give close attention to) the outcome of their way of life and imitate their faith." Hebrews 13:7 NIV

*The Trait Displayed*: After Maggie took her parents to see her discovery in the tree, it was Carrie, her mother, who used her gifts of *observation*

as an artist and photographer to find the piece of metal buried in the thick "elbow" of the now shady tree.

*The Trait Discussed*:
1. Why does having "rare eyes of *observation*" make Carrie a great photographer?
2. In this scene Carrie saw a "slight reflection" of something in the tree. Why would she decide from that *observation* that there was more in the tree than just bark?

*The Trait Discerned*:
1. Can you think of a time when you *observed* something carefully and were glad you did?
2. Just the opposite: Can you recall a time when you sadly didn't take proper time to *observe* something carefully? Talk about this.
3. Have you ever attempted to do a homework assignment without reading (*observing*) the instructions carefully?

# Chapter 16:
# Grandma's Amazing Story
## Character Trait: Attentiveness

*The Trait Defined*: Acknowledging the worth of a person by giving total concentration to his words. *Biblical precept*: "…We must listen very carefully to the truth we have heard, or we may drift away from it." Hebrews 2:1 NIV

*The Trait Displayed*: Dillon and Maggie were listening to their great-grandmother talk on a rainy evening about her friends, Charles and Claire. When Dee said, "We all heard he (Charles) was sent—like he wanted—to the Asian-Pacific *theatre*—," Dillon frowned, but after he heard his father's answer of what "theatre" meant in this context, said, "You mean our theatre right now is the living room and this afternoon's theatre was the orchard?"

*The Trait Discussed*:

1. Would you have known what a "theatre" in the war meant?

2. What was Dillon's Dad's answer?

3. What comparisons did Dillon make in order to explain what "theatre" meant?

4. How did Dillon's answer reflect he was listening carefully to his great-grandmother?

*The Trait Discerned*

1. Why is it very important to listen carefully while a friend is talking?

2. How does *attentiveness* show honor to a person?

3. When your Dad or Mom is attempting to correct a wrong action of yours by telling you the truth on that issue, why is it important to give "total concentration" to his or her words?

4. How does it make you feel when someone is showing that he or she is being *attentive* to every word you are saying to him or her?

# Chapter 17: Squeaky Sand!

## Character Trait: Initiative

*The Trait Defined*: Recognizing and doing what needs to be done before being asked to do it.

*Biblical precept*: "You yourselves also know, Philippians, that … no church shared with me in the manner of giving and receiving but you alone." Philippians 4:15 NASB

*The Trait Displayed*: After Dee and the Burch family arrived at Lake Michigan for a picnic, Don and the kids ran into the waters of Lake Michigan. Carrie, in the meantime, helped Grandma "commandeer" the one table by the sand dune.

*The Trait Discussed*:

1. Read the above definition of this character trait again and explain how Carrie took *initiative* just after they all arrived at the beach?

2. Did Carrie's grandma ask her to help set up the picnic table?

*The Trait Discerned:*

1. Can you think of an example of a time in which you saw something that needed to be done and went ahead and did it without being asked?

2. Do you have a particular chore you are asked to do each day? What is it? Do you do it without having to be asked or do you only do it *after* being asked?

# Chapter 18: War Medal Found

## Character Trait: Creativity

*The Trait Defined:* Approaching a need, a task, or an idea from a new perspective.

*Biblical precept:* "Intelligent people are always open to new ideas. In fact, they look for them." Proverbs 18:15 NLT

*The Trait Displayed:* When Maggie and Dillon saw their Dad walk up from the blackberry cove with the medal and its ribbon still attached to it, he said to them, "Only thing I can figure is that the sap functioned like a preservative for these medals all these years."

*The Trait Discussed:*

1. What did Don see that made him deduce that sap from the tree was like a preservative? What does "preservative" mean?

2. Why didn't Don and Carrie just use a knife to get the thick sap off the medal? Why do you think *WD-40* was used? What is *WD-40*? Ask your Dad or Mom.

*The Trait Discerned:*

1. Read the definition of *creativity* again. What does it mean to "approach a task or an idea from a new perspective?" Ask your Dad or Mom to help with this answer.

2. Did you know that *WD-40* stands for "Water Displacement, 40th attempt?" It means the inventor tried 40 times with creative thinking to come up with this great product. [Read the interesting history on the website: **www.wd40.com** and click on "history."]

3. When you are faced with a problem, do you look for new, *creative* ways to solve it?

# Chapter 19: Pieces of the Puzzle

## Character Trait: Compassion

*The Trait Defined*: The feelings aroused by the distress or misfortune of others that moves me to meet their needs.
*Biblical precept*: "And Jesus, moved with compassion, put forth his hand, and touched him…." Mark 1:41 NKJV

*The Trait Displayed*: When Charles felt terrible that he hadn't recognized his old friend, Dee Howard, at the Barkleys' farm, Carrie sensed his distress and, with compassion, helped put his lack of memory into perspective by saying, "Don't feel badly, Charles. If it helps you any, I don't think Dee recognized you either. It *has* been a long time."

*The Trait Discussed*:
1. Why did Charles feel so badly?
2. What did Carrie say to help him?
3. Read the definition (above) of *compassion*.
4. Why do you think Carrie chose to show *compassion* at this moment?

*The Trait Discerned*:
1. Can you remember a time when someone showed you *compassion* when you were really hurting?
2. Why did you feel so bad and what did they say or do that helped you?
3. Can you recall a time when you showed *compassion* to someone who was hurting?

# Chapter 20: Two Old Friends Reunited

## Character Trait: Sincerity

*The Trait Defined*: Eagerly saying and doing what is right with transparent motives.

*Biblical precept*: "Have *sincere* love for your brothers, love one another deeply, from the heart." I Peter 1:22 NIV

*The Trait Displayed*: It had been years since Dee had see Claire. When they met that morning on Claire's farm, Dee chose to *sincerely* seek forgiveness for not staying in touch with her as she should have. "Claire, I am sorry—so sorry I haven't visited you after Johanne's death. I won't go into excuses. Please forgive me."

*The Trait Discussed*:

1. How did Dee show "*sincere* love" like the Bible tells us to do with others?

2. What did Dee mean when she said, "I won't go into excuses?" Ask your parent why that displays *sincerity*.

*The Trait Discerned*:

1. Who do *you sincerely* love? Why?

2. In the definition above, what does "transparent motives" mean? Ask your Mom or Dad to explain that and give an example.

3. Who loves you *sincerely*? How do you know?

4. Why does saying AND doing that which is right show genuine *sincerity*?

# Chapter 21: A Mystery Solved

## Character Trait: Appreciation: First Use

*The Trait Defined*: Giving God and others genuine compliments for their importance and value to me.

*Biblical precept*: "Take delight in honoring each other." Romans 12:10 NLT

*The Trait Displayed*: After Don and Carrie explained to Charles that Maggie had discovered his lost war medal, he summarized that Maggie's rare kindness (at the fruit stand)…connected the three of us. Charles wisely pointed out that they could have conceivably eaten at the same restaurant without knowing one another and would never have solved the mystery.

*The Trait Discussed:*
    1. What character trait did Charles point out in Maggie?
    2. Do you remember what Maggie did that connected the "stranger," Mr. Hillsboro (Charles) to her Mom and Dad that hot day at the fruit stand?
    3. Why did Charles *appreciate* this?

*The Trait Discerned:*
    1. Have you ever shown *appreciation* for someone by giving them a compliment? What did he or she do and what did you say?
    2. Have you ever thanked God for someone whom you really *appreciated*? Why? What did that person do that caused you to be thankful?

# Chapter 22:
# Preparing for the Big Evening
## Character Trait: Honor

*The Trait Defined*: Expressing humility and devotion by giving tribute to God-given authority.
*Biblical precepts*: "Honor all men, love the brotherhood." I Peter 2:17. NASB "Let each of you regard one another as more important than himself." Philippians 2:3 NASB

*The Trait Displayed*: While Dee was visiting some friends and the Burches remained at her home, Carrie said, "Maggie, You could honor your great-grandmother by getting her dishes done before she gets back."

Also, when Dee did come back, Dillon ran out and helped her bring in a bag of groceries.

*The Trait Discussed:*

1. How did Carrie explain to Maggie that she could *honor* her great-grandmother?

2. How did Dillon choose on his own initiative to also *honor* his great-grandmother?

*The Trait Discerned:*

1. To what authorities in your life could you show *honor* this very day? How could you do that?

2. Should you show *honor* to these authorities like your parents or teachers even if you don't feel like it? Why?

3. Ask your Mom or Dad for an example of "showing *honor.*"

# Chapter 23: Claire and Charles

## Character Trait: Peacemaker

*The Trait Defined*: One who has made peace with God, leads others to make peace with God, and endeavors to maintain peace with others. *Biblical precept*: "Let the peace of Christ rule in your hearts, since as members of one body you were called to peace. And be thankful." Colossians 3:15 NIV

*The Trait Displayed*: After almost a half-century of assuming Charles had died in WWII, Dee had difficulty now in learning that indeed Charles had not died. However, for him not to have attempted to let his friends—like Doug and Dee Howard—know, just stirred up anger—righteous indignation—in Dee. Charles had already made his peace with God on this and did not find fault with Dee's harsh words, but rather, chose to let Dee express her deep hurt for what she saw as Charles' debt to all of them.

*The Trait Discussed*:

1. How did Charles display this trait of *peacemaking* with his response to Dee's surprising words?

2. Did it work? Was he wise in how he responded to Dee's words?

3. How did Dee respond?

*The Trait Discerned:*

1. How can a person "make *peace* with God"? How does asking for forgiveness from God bring about peace with Him? Look in your Bible at the following verses:

I John 1:9 and Romans 5:1-2 and Romans 10:9-10

2. Read the definition of "*peacemaker*" again. Ask yourself or a parent how you can bring about or maintain peace with another person after you have found *peace* with God first.

3. Have you ever been used of God to bring about *peace* between two people who were upset with each other? Share that experience with your Dad or Mom.

# Chapter 24: The Meeting

## Character Trait: Discernment

*The Trait Defined:* The ability to see people and situations the way they really are, not merely as they appear to be.

*Biblical precept:* "For the Lord does not see as man sees; for man looks at the outward appearance, but the Lord looks at the heart." I Samuel 16:7 NKJV

*The Trait Displayed:* When Charles saw Claire—and when Claire saw Charles— after nearly 60 years, there was dead silence from everyone. Finally, with great discernment, Carrie confirmed what these two lost, aging friends were thinking. Gently, looking at Claire, she said, "Claire. This *is* Charles."

*The Trait Discussed:*

1. Why did Carrie wait awhile before she confirmed to Claire that she was indeed looking at Charles Hargrove?

2. This chapter also records that "Carrie stopped her brief introduction when she saw Charles move toward Claire." Why did this action also show great *discernment*?

*The Trait Discerned*

1. What does it mean to see people "as they really are and not as they appear"?

2. Can you remember an experience when someone thought you did something wrong at first but used *discernment* to "see your heart" and you were so thankful he or she did?

# Chapter 25: The Medal Presentation!

## Character Trait: Appreciation: Second Use

*The Trait Defined*: Giving God and others genuine compliments for their importance and value to me.

*Biblical precept*: "We ought always to thank God for you, brothers, and rightly so, because your faith is growing more and more, and the love every one has for each other is increasing." II Thessalonians 1:3 NIV

*The Trait Displayed*: The time had come to give the long-lost war medals to Charles. While Claire and Dee were hurt by the division "that" war had brought, the family also wanted to show their *appreciation* to this war hero for his duty to his country. Don, using his musical and dramatic skills, chose to not just *give* the medals but to "present" them in military pomp and circumstance!

*The Trait Discussed;*

1. How did Don use music and drama to demonstrate his *appreciation* and honor to
   Charles?

2. How was Charles responding while this heart-warming presentation was going on?

*The Trait Discerned:*

1. Who in your life do you really *appreciate*?
2. How have you shown this person your *appreciation*? How did that person respond?

# Chapter 26: Worth More Than Gold
## Character Trait: Priorities

*The Trait Defined*: Choosing preference to do those things which God values more important than anything else.
*Biblical precept*: "Seek first the kingdom of God and His righteousness, and all these things shall be added to you." Matthew 6:33 NKJV

*The Trait Displayed*: Charles had felt all his adult years that he had blown it as a person and tried to find his medals to make him feel of some worth. Carrie pointed this out when she spoke to Maggie while cleaning up breakfast at Dee's. "Maggie, your reaching out to him at the fruit stand—before you knew anything about him—told him somebody cared for just him—not for his medals or his POW status or the money he has earned."

*The Trait Discussed:*
1. What value did Maggie find most important in people that caused her to be kind to Charles?
2. What had Charles thought would make him feel worthwhile before this?

*The Trait Discerned:*
1. What does God see as most valuable in a person—what he has or who he is? Explain.
2. What do you value most about your family?
3. Why do you think we often prefer to have our friends to be pleased with us even more than to have God pleased with us?
4. Ask your Mom or Dad to explain the biblical precept listed above?

# Chapter 27: Lost Treasures Found!

## Character Trait: Thankfulness

*The Trait Defined*: Choosing to express gratitude, appreciation or acknowledgement for all that we have, knowing that all we have that is of value is from God.

*Biblical precept*: "In everything give thanks; for this is the will of God in Christ Jesus for you."
I Thessalonians 5:18 NKJV

*The Trait Displayed*: When Claire gave Maggie and Dillon a few of the books from her library, they did not need Mom or Dad to prompt them to give profuse thanks to Claire. They deeply thanked her for her generosity to let them actually have some of her "old friends."

*The Trait Discussed:*
    1. Why do you think Maggie and Dillon were so *thankful* to Claire?
    2. What was especially good about them choosing to give Claire *thanks* without the prompting of their Dad and Mom to do so?
    3. Why was Claire *thankful* that these two "kids" wanted her books? Why was it more than all right for Claire to give Maggie and Dillon her "old friends?"

*The Trait Discerned:*
    1. What are you *thankful* for today? Whom are you *thankful* for today? Why?
    2. How can someone be *thankful* "in all circumstances?" Talk to your Mom or Dad about this.

# Chapter 28: The Treasure of Friends

## Character Trait: Decisiveness

*The Trait Defined*: The ability to finalize difficult decisions based on the truth of God's words.

*Biblical precept*: "I have chosen the way of truth; I have set my heart on your laws." Psalm 119:30 NIV

*The Trait Displayed*: Charles told Claire in her home—"through some soul searching and meeting with a pastor in Texas, I have made peace with God." Then he proceeded to trust God to move ahead with a difficult *decision* at his present age: "Claire, will you marry me?"

*The Trait Discussed*:

1. What do you think Charles meant when he said, "God has given me a second chance with Him and with you (Claire)"?

2. Why do you think Charles could be so *decisive* about marrying Claire, even though he had just seen her for less than a week?

*The Trait Discerned*:

1. Can you recall a recent difficult *decision* you had to make? Why was it hard? How did it turn out?

2. How can you trust God when you have a difficult decision to make?

3. Ask Mom or Dad about a difficult but wise decision they have had to make.

4. What is a difficult *decision* you face in the future? Tell your Mom or Dad how they can pray for you about this *decision*.

# Chapter 29: Amazing Grace!

## Character Trait: Confidence

*The Trait Defined*: Relying on the Lord to enable me in every area of my life.
Biblical precept: "I can do all things through [Christ] who strengthens me." Philippians 4:13 NASB

*The Trait Displayed*: While Charles Hargrove was in the prison camp as a POW he felt all alone and was beaten many times. While in the church service, the pastor's message triggered that memory and he recalled a verse his Dad had printed out when he was a child. Similar to the verse above, God used this verse to remind Charlie that God would help him when he felt weak and needed strength.

*The Trait Discussed:*

1. Go back to Chapter 29. What verse was helpful for Charles while in that prison camp?

2. What does "a bruised reed" mean in referring to Charlie in that prison camp setting?

3. What caused Charles to be anxious and feel alone while he was in that church pew?

4. What does Philippians 4:13 mean to you?

*The Trait Discerned:*

1. Have you ever felt weak and needed Christ's strength to help you do something? What was the circumstance? Did trusting Christ give you *confidence* at that time?

2. Ask your parent and/or teacher to relate a time when he or she didn't know what to do and sought to rely on God for help for *confidence* in facing an issue.

3. What do you think happens when we are faced with a difficult situation and try to rely only on our strength to get through it?

4. Share with your Mom or Dad or teacher about some event or circumstance that is coming up in which you want them to pray for God to help you through.

# Chapter 30: Medals Find a Home

## Character Trait: Security

*The Trait Defined:* Structuring my life around what is eternal and cannot be destroyed or taken away.

*Biblical precept:* "But store up for yourselves treasures in heaven, where moth and rust do not destroy and where thieves do break in and steal. For where you treasure is, there will your heart will be also." Matthew 6:20-21 NIV

*The Trait Displayed*: Charles had been looking for his lost "treasures"—his war medals—for a long time. Now, in the church library, he gives the medals to Maggie and Dillon, displaying how he learned what his real treasures were and where he now found his meaning and security in life.

*The Trait Discussed:*

1. Why do you think Charles valued his war medals so much?

2. What did Charles tell Maggie and Dillon he *now* valued as more important than his medals? Also, why do you think he wanted Maggie and Dillon to know that?

*The Trait Discerned:*

1. Read the definition again of the character trait of *security*. What do you think it means when it says to "structure my life around that which is eternal?" How can you do that at your age?

2. Ask a parent or teacher about a lesson they learned in their life that God used to teach them where he or she gets his or her *security*.

# Chapter 31: On the Road Again

## Character Trait: Availability

*The Trait Defined*: Making my own schedule and priorities secondary to the wishes of those I am serving.

*Biblical precept*: "Do nothing out of selfish ambition or vain conceit but in humility consider others better than yourselves. Each of you should look not only to your own interests but also to the interests of others." Philippians 2:3-4 NIV

*The Trait Displayed*: The Sunday the Burches had to leave was a wonderful one but also very draining physically and emotionally. Carrie recognized that for herself but also recognized it was even more so for her grandmother. That is why she encouraged Dee to "scale back the lunch" that she had planned before the Burches long road trip back to Illinois.

*The Trait Discussed:*

1. According to the definition above, how did Carrie make her schedule and needs secondary to those of her grandmother?

2. Why do you think Dee allowed this?

*The Trait Discerned:*

1. Talk about a time when someone put your needs above his or hers and you appreciated it.

2. Share about a time when you put somebody else's needs or wishes over your own.

3. How can you make yourself *"available"* to help someone in your family today?

# APPENDIX B

## "Birches"

## by Robert Frost

When I see birches bend to left and right
Across the lines of straighter darker trees,
I like to think some boy's been swinging them,
But swinging doesn't bring them down to stay.
Ice-storms do that. Often you must have seen them
Loaded with ice a sunny winter morning
After a rain. They click upon themselves
As the breeze rises, and turn many-colored
As the stir cracks and crazes their enamel.
Soon the sun's warmth makes them shed crystal shells
Shattering and avalanching on the snow-crust.
Such heaps of broken glass to sweep away
You'd think the inner dome of heaven had fallen.
They are dragged to the withered bracken by the load,
And they seem not to break; though once they are bowed
So low for long, they never right themselves:

You may see their trunks arching in the woods
Years afterwards, trailing their leaves on the ground
Like girls on hands and knees that throw their hair
Before them over their heads to dry in the sun.
But as I was going to say before truth broke in
With all her matter-of-fact about the ice-storm
I should prefer to have some boy bend them
As he went out and in to fetch the cows—
Some boy too far from town to learn baseball,
Whose only play was what he found himself,
Summer or winter, and could play alone.
One by one he subdued his father's trees
By riding them down over and over again
Until he took the stiffness out of them,
And not one but hung limp, not one was left
For him to conquer. He learned all there was
To learn about not launching out too soon
And so not carrying the tree away
Clear to the ground. He always kept his poise
With the same pain you use to fill a cup
Up to the brim and even close to the brim.
Then he flung outward, feet first, with a swish,
Kicking his feet through the air to the ground.
So was I once myself a swinger of birches.
And so I dream of going back to be.
It's when I am weary of considerations,
And life is too much like a pathless wood
Where your face burns and tickles with the cobwebs
Broken against it, and one eye is weeping
From a twig having lashed across it open.
I'd like to get away from earth awhile
And then come back to it and begin over.
May no fate willfully misunderstand me
And half grant what I wish and snatch me away
Not to return. Earth's the right place for love:
I don't know where it's likely to go better.
I'd like to go by climbing a birch tree,
And climb black branches up a snow-white trunk

*Toward* heaven, till the tree could bear no more,
But dipped its top and set me down again.
That would be good both going and coming back.
One could do worse than be a swinger of birches.

<u>Why include this story</u>: Can you not see Maggie or Dillon climbing one of these birch trees? While Robert Frost no doubt had several themes in mind when writing this poem, one sure theme is that of the joy of an unfettered childhood like the boy in this poem—the boy "whose only play was what he found himself ... and could play alone." Whether your "playground" is in the country or city or in the pages of a great book, use your God-created mind to enjoy His creative universe where God has placed you. Let children be children, for all too soon they will be "weary of considerations." Indeed, "one could do worse than be a swinger of birches."

# APPENDIX C

## The Story of Pearl Harbor

<u>Why include this story</u>: A pivotal part in the life of the character of Charles Hargrove was his decision to join the Armed Services after hearing of the bombing of Pearl Harbor during World War II on December 7, 1941. How this changed his life forever was the true story of thousands of young men and women and America herself. Also, this story was included to honor Maggie's and Dillon's great-grandfather, whom they never met. His name was Brodie I. Burkett who served in the United States Army in WW II and was actually stationed in Hawaii almost exactly two years before it was brutally bombed by the Japanese.

Almost 60 years later—September 11, 2001—the bombing of the World Trade Center towers in New York City by radical Muslim terrorists—has similarly defined Maggie's and Dillon's generation. As a wise man observed, "If we don't learn from history, we are apt to repeat it." This brief recollection of the story of Pearl Harbor is given not only to understand the journey of Mr. Hargrove in *The Mysterious Treasure of Blackberry Cove* but, more importantly, to help the young and old reader alike honor those who fought and sacrificed so much to protect our country and to inspire all for the fight that lies ahead.

The December 7, 1941 Japanese raid on Pearl Harbor (Hawaii) was one of the most important defining moments in U.S. history. A single carefully-planned and well-executed strike on this U.S. army base in the Pacific removed the United States Navy's battleship force as a possible threat to the Japanese Empire's southward expansion into the Second World War as a full combatant. [1]

The United States was completely caught off guard. The devastation was horrible. Some 2400 Americans were dead! We lost outright 188 fighter planes, bombers, and patrol aircraft, out of 402 Army and Navy aircraft. The Japanese brought to bear 360 planes during the attack and lost only 29. We lost 18 fighting ships; Japan lost five midget submarines. It was said by Congress, "the greatest military and naval disaster in our nation's history. [2]

Eighteen months earlier, President Franklin D. Roosevelt had transferred the United States Navy fleet of ships and planes and servicemen to Pearl Harbor to stop such an attack and also to attempt to stop Japanese aggression elsewhere in the Pacific battlefield. Our U.S. officials clearly believed the Japanese would attack in the Indies and Malaya and probably the Philippines. They did not expect that Japan would attack east also.

Japan's aircraft carrier force not only came secretly across the Pacific Ocean toward the U.S Pearl Harbor base, but came with greater aerial striking power than had ever been seen on the world's oceans. These planes hit just before 8 p.m. on December 7 and, within a short time, five of the eight battleships at Pearl Harbor were sunk or sinking with the rest severely damaged. [3]

US Battleships West Virginia and Tennessee after
bombing by Japanese in World War II.

This raid shocked and enraged the previously-divided America into a level of determined unity hardly seen before or since. For the next five months, until the Battle of Coral Sea in early May of 1942, Japan's far-reaching offensives continued almost without opposition. American and Allied morale suffered a lot. Some thought the U.S. would simply yield and surrender this base and Hawaii to the Japanese.

However, the memory of this "sneak attack" on Pearl Harbor fueled a determination to fight on. As with the fictional character of Charles Hargrove, thousands of America's finest men and women enlisted to counter the Japanese aggression. Once the Battle of Midway in early June 1942 had eliminated much of Japan's striking power, the same memory stoked a relentless war to reverse her conquests and remove her and her German and Italian allies, as future threats to World Peace.

CREDIT:
[1] http://en.wikipedia.org/wiki/Pearl Harbor
[2] "Pearl Harbor: Final Judgment." Henry Clausen and Bruce Lee. Crown Publisher, Inc. New York. 1992.
[3] http://www.history.mil/photos/events/wwii-pac/pearlhbr/pearlhbr.htm.

**Interesting true story from a prisoner of war at the Guam Ofuna POW camp** (Note the first name of the soldier): Flyboy Charlie Brown remembered the last day of the war at the Ofuna POW camp: "We had heard from an American prisoner shot down on August seventh that the Americans had dropped a bomb on a Japanese City and wiped it out. We thought he was mentally off. Then on August fourteenth, the guards of our camp lined up in front of the office. We could tell from their demeanor that the war was over. [1] Note: The bomb this soldier referred to was the atomic "H" bomb dropped on Hiroshima, Japan on August 6, 1945 that essentially caused the Japanese to surrender. Can you imagine Charlie Hargrove being there that eventful day?

CREDIT: [1] "Flyboys: A True Story of Courage." James Bradley. Little, Brown, and Company: Boston-New York-London. 2003.

# APPENDIX D

## Songs Used in the Book

### "God Bless America"
### "The Caissons Go Rolling Along"
### "I'll Be with You in Apple Blossom Time"
### "Amazing Grace"

<u>Why include these songs:</u> The reader will recall that Maggie's and Dillon's father, Don, dramatized the giving of Charles' lost war medals in Chapter 23, "The Medal Presentation." In doing so, he chose two songs from some records he found in an old album from Doug Howard's collection. They were, "God Bless America" and "The Caissons Go Rolling Along" (both originating out of World War I and used extensively in World War II). Both epitomized the love and life of Charles Hargrove and many men who fought in those wars. Charles went to battle because he loved America, and his life reflected the words of the second song in that—whether he was in battle or imprisoned or taking on the losses in his life—he kept "rolling along."

"**God Bless America**" could be the theme song for all of our soldiers returning from the horrific battles in both the Atlantic and Pacific theatres. Many of these brave men and women literally kissed American soil as they got off their ships and planes when arriving home. If they didn't sing it before, they certainly wanted to sing "God Bless America" now!

Read carefully the inspiring words of "**The Caisson Song**." Better yet, listen to an audio presentation of it. The spirit of the song was indeed that of Charles Hargrove and the real American soldiers he represented. To make it through his imprisonment by the Japanese, Charles knew he had to trust that his fellow soldiers would possibly find him. For many long and hot summer nights on this small island by the Equator, Charles knew he "would not go home tonight" but he kept, so to speak, "rolling along" day after long day. We would all do well to remember this song when facing personal battles. Winston Churchill, British Prime Minister during WW II, said the same thing in a different way: "Never give up. Never give up."

**"I'll Be with You in Apple Blossom Time"** could be called "Claire's Song" in this story as its words—so popular during World War II—spoke of how Claire, as she represented many girls during those years, waited with the prayerful hope that her soldier would come home.

**"Amazing Grace"** could be called "Charlie's Song" in this story as its well-known and well-loved words spoke to how God gave His grace of love, hope, and salvation to Charlie—and all of us who are recipients of God's saving grace.

Read the words and stories behind these songs that were referred to in the book and the two that were played for Charles' medal presentation. Better yet, find an audio album or go on line to hear the songs played and sung! What do these songs say to you?

# God Bless America

"While the storms clouds gather across the sea,
Let us swear allegiance to a land that's free.
Let us be grateful to a land so fair.
As we raise our voices in a solemn prayer."

God Bless America,
Land that I love.
Stand beside her, and guide her
Thru the night with a light from above.
From the mountains, to the prairies,
To the oceans white with foam
God bless America, my home sweet home. [1]

History of this song: Irving Berlin wrote this song in 1918 while serving in the U.S. Army at Camp Upton in Yaphank, New York, but set it aside. He reintroduced it in 1938 as a "peace song" as he, a Jew and a first-generation immigrant from Europe, saw the rise of Hitler. It was re-introduced on an Armistice Day broadcast and sung by Kate Smith on her radio show. Berlin also changed the song to include the introduction (see above in quotes) and also sung by Kate Smith with a full orchestra. It was an instant hit and was often suggested as a national anthem. [2] In establishing himself as one of America's most beloved songwriters, Berlin wrote more than 1500 songs. Besides the very popular "God Bless America," he also composed "Alexander's Rag Time," "Always," and "White Christmas." [3]

CREDIT: ONLINE:
[1] "Kate Smith: Her Very Best." RCA: United States. Album from the personal collection of Richard Burkett.
[2] http://en.wiki/God_Bless_America
[3] "America: A Celebration!" Martin W. Sandler. A Darling Kindersley:
Book: London-New York-Sydney. 2000.

## The Caissons Go Rolling Along

Over hill, over dale
As we hit the dusty trail,
And the Caissons go rolling along.
In and out, hear them shout.
Counter march and right about,
And the Caissons go rolling along.

Then it's hi! hi! he!
In the field artillery,
Shout out your numbers loud and strong,
For where'er you go,
You will always know
That the Caissons go rolling along.

In the storm, in the night,
Action left or action right
See those Caissons go rolling along
Limber front, limber rear,
Prepare to mount your cannoneer
And those Caissons go rolling along.

(repeat chorus)

Was it high? Was it low?
Where the heck did that one go?
As those Caissons go rolling along
Was it left? Was it right?
Now we won't go home tonight
And those Caissons go rolling along.

(repeat chorus) [1]

## CAISSON:
### FIELD ARTILLERY WAGON
### FOR THE UNITED STATES MILITARY

#### ORIGINALLY USED 1849-1865

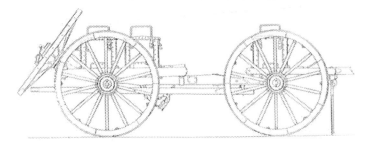

History of this song: Written by General Edmond L. Gruber in 1908, this song was later popularized by John Philip Sousa and played by military and parade bands through the years in America. Gruber wrote this famous artillery song when he was a lieutenant in the Fifth Artillery in the Philippines. In April 1908, the First Battalion came from the States to relieve the Second. Lt. Gruber was asked to write a song that would symbolize the spirit of the reunited regiment. The song was inspired by an incident that occurred during a difficult march across the Zambales Mountains, which was made by the Second Battalion in 1907. Lt. Gruber was sent ahead with a detachment to select the route and repair stream crossings. In the afternoon the battalion was so far behind that he and a scout sergeant went to the top of a high peak in order to see what progress the main body was making. Although he could not see the battalion, they did hear the distant rumble of the caissons (carriages), which was punctuated by the echoing shouts and commands of the drivers as they urged their team along. The sergeant turned to the Lieutenant Gruber and said, "They'll be all right, lieutenant, if they keep 'em rolling." That expression seemed to characterize the spirit of the battalion. History also shows they did indeed "keep 'em rolling" as the battalion made it past the difficult mountain divide. [2]

CREDIT:
[1] "March with The American Legion Band". Conducted by Joe Colling. Decca Records.
Album from personal collection of Richard Burkett.
[2] http://www.gennet.org/usa/mo/county/stlouis/ww1-music/caisson. htm

# "I'll Be with You in Apple Blossom Time"

Lyrics by: Neville Flesson    Music by: Albert Von Tilzer

I'm writing you, my dear,
Just to tell you,
In September, you remember
'Neath the old apple tree
You whispered to me
When it blossomed again, you'd be mine.

I've waited until I could claim you,
I hope I've not waited in vain.
For when it's spring in the valley,
I'm coming, my sweetheart, again!

I'll be with you in apple blossom time,
I'll be with you to change your name to mine.
One day in May
I'll come and say:
"Happy the bride the sun shines on today!"

What a wonderful wedding there will be,
What a wonderful day for you and me!
Church bells will chime
You will be mine
In apple blossom time.

I'll be with you in apple blossom time,
I'll be with you to change your name to mine.
One day in May
I'll come and say:
"Happy the bride the sun shines on today!"

What a wonderful wedding there will be,
What a wonderful day for you and me:
Church bells will chime
You will be mine
In apple blossom time. [1]

History of this song: This song came right out of the heart of America during World War II as it gave our troops hope that they would return and be reunited with their sweethearts back in a stable America. If you read the book and listen to the words of this song, you can readily see how this could have been the theme song for both Charles and Claire during those war years and especially when Charles was a POW. It also is fitting for a couple who grew up in apple blossom country in western Michigan.

"I'll Be with You in Apple Blossom Time" was popularized by the Andrews Sisters during the war and recorded by many groups since: Nat King Cole, Ray Coniff, Bill Haley and His Comets, Harry James and his Orchestra, Steve Lawrence, Mitch Miller, Wayne Newton, Barry Manilow, The Platters, Artie Shaw, Jo Stafford, Fred Waring and his Orchestra, to name a few. Find an audio copy of these lyrics, sit back, and imagine yourself as Claire in the 1940's as she waited for her Charles to return!

CREDIT:

[1] "Fabulous Memories of the Fabulous '40's." Reader's Digest album: Courtesy of

MCA and Capital Records. From the personal collection of Richard Burkett.

[2] "I'll Be with You in Apple Blossom Time." Von Tilzer, Albert. (New York: Broadway Music Corp., © 1920) Duke University Libraries (Music B. 288v) No 96.

# "Amazing Grace"
# John Newton (1725-1807)

Amazing Grace, how sweet the sound,
That saved a wretch like me.
I once was lost but now am found,
Was blind, but now I see.

T'was Grace that taught my heart to fear.
And Grace, my fears relieved.
How precious did that Grace appear
The hour I first believed.

Through many dangers, toils, and snares
I have already come;
"Tis Grace that brought me safe thus far
And Grace will lead me home.

The Lord has promised good to me.
His word my hope secures.
He will my shield and portion be,
As long as life endures.

Yes, when this flesh and heart shall fail,
And mortal life shall cease,
I shall possess within the veil,
A life of joy and peace.

When we've been there ten thousand years
Bright shining as the sun.
We've no less days to sing God's praise
Than when we've first begun.

*Amazing Grace, how sweet the sound,*
*That saved a wretch like me.*
*I once was lost but now am found,*
*Was blind but now I see.* [1]

History of this song: "Amazing Grace" is a Christian hymn written by the poet and Anglican clergyman John Newton. It was published in 1779. It has a wonderful and powerful message that forgiveness and redemption are possible, regardless of the sins people commit. The great words of this song certainly helped to encourage the fictional character Charlie Hargrove that Sunday he As the song states, this is only possible because of God's amazing grace and mercy. "Amazing Grace" is one of the most recognized and beloved hymns of all times. It is found in the hymnals of many denominations.

Newton wrote the words of "Amazing Grace" from personal experience. He "was born in London July 24, 1725, the son of a commander of a merchant ship which sailed the Mediterranean. When John was eleven, he went to sea with his father and made six voyages with him before the elder Newton retired. In 1744 John Newton was impressed into service on a man-of-war, the H.M.S. Harwich. Finding conditions on board intolerable, he deserted but was soon recaptured and publicly flogged and demoted from midshipman to common seaman.

Finally at his own request he was exchanged into service on a slave ship, which took him to the coast of Sierra Leone. He then became the servant of a slave trader and was brutally abused. In 1748 he was rescued by a sea captain who had known John's father. John Newton ultimately became captain of his own ship, one which plied the slave trade. [2]

Newton wrote the words of "Amazing Grace" from personal experience. He grew up without any particular religious conviction but had several near-death experiences, and his life was formed by a variety of twists and coincidences that were often put into motion by his unrepentant disobedience. He was pressed into the English Royal Navy and traded to a slave ship where he began a career in slave trading. One night a terrible storm battered his vessel so severely that he became frightened enough to call out to God for mercy, a moment that marked the beginning of his spiritual conversion. His career in slave trading lasted a few years more until he quit going to sea altogether and began to study theology.

Newton was ordained into the Church of England in 1764 and shortly began to write hymns with poet William Cowper. "Amazing Grace" was written to illustrate a sermon on New Year's Day of 1773. The song debuted in print in 1779 but settled into relative obscurity in England. In the United States, however, "Amazing Grace" was used extensively during the Second Great Awakening in the early 19th century. It has been associated with more than 20 melodies but in 1835 it was joined to a tune named "New Britain" to which it is most frequently sung today.

Author Gilbert Chase writes that "Amazing Grace" is "without a doubt the most famous of all folk hymns." Jonathan Aitken, a Newton biographer, estimates that this song is performed about 10 million times annually. "Amazing Grace" took off again in popularity in the U.S. during the 1960's and has been recorded many times. The list of famous singers who have sung this song would be endless. [3]

For the fictional character Charles Hargrove, the song applied to him and that is why we include this separate appendix of this song. It is the memorable words of this song that Maggie wanted her family to listen to and sing on the ride home after understanding more clearly how a person could be once lost and then "found". Does the song apply to you? Praise God for His grace! The lead singer of the pop group

U2, Bono, told launch.com: "We hear so much of karma and so little of grace. Every religion teaches about karma and what you will receive if you put out. And even Christianity, which is supposed to be about grace, has turned redemption into good manners, or the right accent, or good works, or whatever. I just can't get over grace." [4] How about you? Charles Hargrove sure appreciated God's grace in his life.

CREDIT:
[1] Hymns: America's 28 Favorite Hymns. Word Record: Waco, Texas. From the personal collection of Richard Burkett.
[2] http://www.anointedlinks.com/amazing_grace.html
[3] http://wikepedia.org/wiki/Amazing _Grace
[4] "Amazing Grace: The Story of America's Most Beloved Song. Steve Turner. CCCO. An Imprint of Harper Collins Publications: 2002

# APPENDIX E

## War Medals

As the reader will recall in Chapter 25, "The Medal Presentation", Charles Hargrove earned two medals for his service in World War II. These were the "World War II Victory Medal" and the "Distinguished Service Cross." It is conceivable he would have also earned a third medal—the "Prisoner of War Medal"—when he was in 60's, when the medal was authorized as an official military medal. Although he is a fictional character, Charles represents thousands of brave soldiers who went off to war to protect and win the freedom of the United States of America and—in so doing—set many other countries free from the tyranny of foreign powers.

The author wants these brave men and women never to be forgotten and forever thanked. This deep gratitude includes the author's father, **Brodie I. Burkett,** who served in World War II, the author's brother, **Jerry R. Burkett,** who served in the Viet Nam War, and the author's son's (Derek's) father-in-law, **Denson F. Walker,** who served in World War II and has contributed the Foreword to *The Mysterious Treasure of Blackberry Cove*.

### World War II Victory Medal

The **World War II Victory Medal** is a decoration of the United States military which was created by an act of Congress in 1945. The decoration commemorates military service during World War II and is awarded to any member of the United States Military, including members of the armed forces of the Government of the Philippine Islands, who served on active duty, or as a reservist, between December 7, 1941 and December 31, 1946.

The World War II Victory Medal was first issued as a ribbon, and was referred to simply as the "Victory Ribbon." By 1946, a full medal had been established which was referred to as the "World War II Victory Medal".

The medal's front depicts Nike, the Greek mythological goddess of Victory, standing victorious, holding a broken sword. Nike represents the United States and its allies (Great Britain, France, and the Soviet Union) as victorious over the broken power of the Axis nations (Germany, Italy, and Japan). You will note that Nike also has one foot upon the helmet of Mars, the Roman god of war. Behind Nike is a sunburst, representing the dawn of peace. The reverse side of this medal recalls the "Four Freedoms" speech by President Roosevelt, with a laurel sprig, surrounded by the words "United States of America", and the dates of the conflict, "1941-1945".

The ribbon portrays the multi-colored rainbow ribbon of the Allied World War I Victory Medal as it honors all the allied nations. The wide red center represents the new sacrifice of blood by World War II combatants. The thin red white lines separating the central red band from the outer multi-colored bands represent the rays of new hope, two of them signifying that this was the second global conflict.

To keep with the time-line given in *The Mysterious Treasure of Blackberry Cove*, the fictional character, Charles Hargrove, would most likely have received this medal after he had been released from rehab at Walter Reed Hospital and just before he had come back to try to find Claire.

CREDIT: Wikipedia.org/wiki/World_War_II_Victory_Medal_(United_States)

# The Distinguished Service Cross

The **Distinguished Service Cross** is the second highest military decoration that can be awarded a member of the United States Army It is awarded for extreme gallantry and risk of life in actual combat with an armed enemy force. Actions that merit the Distinguished Service Cross must be of such a high degree—such as extraordinary heroism— to be above those required for all other U.S. combat decorations but not meeting the criteria for the Medal of Honor.

The **Distinguished Service Cross** was first awarded during World War I. In addition, a number of awards were made for actions before World War I. In many cases, these were to soldiers who had received a Certificate of Merit for gallantry which, at the time, was the only other honor besides the **Medal of Honor** the Army could award.

Description of the Medal itself:

It is a cross of bronze, 2 inches in height and 1 13/16 inches in width with an eagle on the center and a scroll below the eagle bearing the inscription "FOR VALOR." On the reverse side, the center of the cross is circled by a wreath with a space for engraving the name of the recipient. Remember in the book how "CHARLES J. HARGOVE" was found engraved in this medal? Also, the ribbon bar (see attached above) is 1 3/8 inches wide and consists of the following stripes:

1. 1/8 inch Old Glory red
2. 1/16 inch White
3. 1 inch Imperial Blue

CREDIT: http://gruntmilitary.com/dsc.shtml

# Prisoner of War Medal

The **Prisoner of War Medal** is an honored military decoration of the United States armed services which was authorized by Congress and signed into law by President Ronald Reagan on November 8, 1985.

Because of this history, it is clear that the fictional character, Charlie Hargrove, could never have received this special medal until long after the war. It could have conceivably been given to him in his 60's, when President Reagan authorized it. We would like to think he did receive it since, in the context of this book, he was indeed a prisoner of war in WW II and since this special medal has even been given to the families of many WW II veterans after the deaths of these veterans.

This special medal may be awarded to any person who was a prisoner of war after April 5, 1917. This date is the day before the entry of the United States into World War I. It is awarded to any person who was taken prisoner or held captive while engaged in action against an enemy of the United States; while engaged in military operations involving conflict with an opposing Armed Force; or while serving with friendly forces engaged in armed conflict against an opposing Armed Force in which the United States is not a belligerent party.

As of an amendment to Title 10 of the United States Code in 1989, the medal is also awarded for captivity by foreign armed forces that are hostile to the United States, under circumstances which the Secretary concerned finds to have been comparable to those under which persons have generally been held captive by enemy armed forces during periods of armed conflict. The person's conduct, while in captivity, must have been honorable. This medal may be awarded after a person's death and given to the surviving next of kin of the recipient.

Description of the medal itself:

On a bronze medal, 1 3/8 inches in diameter, an eagle with wings opened and surrounded by a circle of barbed wire and bayonet points. The reverse side has the inscription "AWARDED TO' around the top and 'FOR HONORABLE SERVICE WHILE A PRISONER OF WAR" across the center in three lines with a space between the two inscriptions for engraving the name of the recipient (as the book describes CHARLES J. HARGROVE). The shield of Coat of Arms of the United States is centered on the lower part of the reverse side with the inscription "UNITED STATES OF AMERICA" around the bottom of the medal. The ribbon is 1 3/8 inches wide and consists of the following stripes: 1/16 inches wide Old Glory Red; 3/32 inch White; 1/16 inch Old Glory Blue; 1/8 inch White; center 11/16 inch black.

CREDIT: http://gruntsmilitary.com/pow.shtml

# Praise for *The Mysterious Treasure of Blackberry Cove*

**From Oklahoma:** *"The Mysterious Treasure of Blackberry Cove* is an exciting story that will make children of many ages a captive audience. The character traits and everyday life principles from God's word are woven skillfully into the story. As a mystery is solved, not only is an earthly treasure found but an eternal one as well." **Connie Faulkner, B.S., Elementary Education. Teacher for 17 years. Pastor's wife. Mother of five and grandmother of 13. (Oklahoma City, OK)**

**From Illinois:** "Developing character does not happen by chance! As a parent and educator, I am always on a quest for a book that combines a good story while developing the reader's character. This book is it! With good storytelling, compelling characters, and delightful illustrations, this adventure will fascinate readers. The strength of the book lies in the interactive parent guide which gives parents that much needed tool to help develop those Bible-based character traits found in the main characters. I look forward to sharing this book with my own children." **Amy Stradtmann, B.S., Elementary Education; M.S. Reading Education. Has served 19 years in education as a teacher, principal, and educational therapist. She is also the mother of two delightful and voracious readers! (Belvidere, IL)**

**From Wisconsin:** *"The Mysterious Treasure of Blackberry Cove* offers something not found in many children's books today. The author includes strong American values, along with character traits based on the Bible, with the intention of teaching young readers (and parents) about how to become better men and women. I recommend the book for inclusion in public and school libraries." **Tim Sweet, a Teacher and Library Media Specialist for 30 years. He currently works for the Clintonville Public School District (Clintonville, WI)**

**From California:** "Refreshing! A creative way of restoring family values and core principles. Add to that the curious, mysterious heart of the 'Hardy Boys/Nancy Drew' books we loved as kids. I can't wait for my children to read this book and this series. Please write more!"

Dave Johnson, Executive Director of Marketing and Program Development, Monte Vista Christian School. He and his wife, Anna, are parents of two young daughters. (Watsonville, CA)

**From Alaska:** "*The Mysterious Treasure of Blackberry Cove* shows the importance of truth, responsibility, and courage for today's children. As an educator, I see clearly how children today need to see the magnitude of these character traits and the benefits of these traits in everyday life. Understanding the significance of history is a constant theme throughout the book. Children must not forget the sacrifices that were given for their freedom." **Jake Reese. B.S. degrees in History and Education. Now in his eighth year as Teacher (7ᵗʰ and 8ᵗʰ grades) in Social Studies for the Anchorage Public School District. (Anchorage, AK)**

**From Minnesota:** "As parents we want our children to become well-mannered, generous and productive adults. The journey begins with well-written literature that has our children ponder, explore, and then understand these traits. Dick Burkett's touching and humorous mystery gives our children a glimpse at everyday heroes and how to develop these qualities within their own lives. Dick's insightful discussion questions about each character trait enables parents and teachers to  guide their children and help them become more Christ-like." **Joan Kenworthy, B.S. degree in Education. Teacher and Missions coordinator for 15 years at Chapel Hill Academy. Pastor's wife. Mother of three adult children and seven grandchildren. (Chanhassen, MN)**

**From Midwest USA:** "As I began Dick's book, I melted into the safe, carefree days of my childhood. The quality character traits woven (not patched) into the story are a needed respite against the busyness and harshness that permeates our society today. The beautiful word pictures leave me longing to step into the scene and be a part of the healthy relationships in this loving, extended family. The sights and sounds and aromas come to life as you drink in this labor of love. *Blackberry Cove* is your coziest chair, your most comfortable pair of jeans, and your most wonderful remembrances from your 'looking up' days. I would highly recommend this book as a beacon of light in a world that has forgotten the innocence of youth." **Steve Lundquist, "MR. STEVE," Midwest**

America's Premier Children and Family Entertainer (20 years). Bachelor degree in Social Science, Trinity University. Youth Director. Husband and Father. (Rockford, IL)

**From Hawaii:** "This is a delightful and heart-warming story for the whole family. On its surface, it is a small town mystery novel much like the Boxcar Children mystery series that any reader will enjoy. Beneath this appealing surface, however, is a story of redemption and forgiveness that is cleverly designed to serve as a basis for classroom or Bible Study discussions of examples of Christian character." **Cheryl L. Olson, B.A., M.A. degrees in Education. An elementary school educator for over 14 years. Cheryl and her husband also have three sons. (Mililani, HI)**

**From Illinois:** "At a time when integrity and virtue seem to be rare in present-day role models for our children, *The Mysterious Treasure of Blackberry Cove* is a refreshing and adventurous must-read. Dick Burkett has written a book that will effectively capture the minds of our youth, and also engage the attention of adults. The interactive questions are a great tool for adult/child discussion and guidance. This book focuses on the Christian character traits that are necessary to grow future, strong leaders of integrity." **Senator Dave Syverson, State Senator since 1993. (Illinois)**

**From Florida:** "Dick Burkett has penned a wonderful story with a powerful message. He gives us a terrific and meaningful reading experience." **Pat Williams, Senior Vice-President of the Orlando Magic and author of "Daily Wisdom." Successful author, speaker. Father of 19 (14 adopted).**

**From Virginia:** "What a wonderful vacation…a heart-warming story that brings two generations together…and a love that spans time. Among the many lessons this book teaches is the one reminding us to always take time to thank our veterans for their services and sacrifices. The author transports you into the hearts and minds of the characters in Blackberry Cove, as well as the lives of World War II veterans. Read this with a handkerchief close by. You won't be able to put this book down." **Colonel John Gessner, U.S. Army combat veteran. Father of three. (Fairfax, VA)**

**From Tennessee:** "This wholesome story of a delightful but very real family living out the character traits woven into the theme of each chapter will appeal to the reader from beginning to end. The scripture passages included with each character trait affords meaningful discussion and teachable moments for parents as they enjoy the story with their children." **Celia Stoneking, B.R.E., Masters of Elementary Education. Educator for 36 years in both public and private education. Named Teacher of the Year (2002-2003) at Chimneyrock Elementary and one of nine finalists for Teacher of the Year for the state of Tennessee (2007-2008). (Cordova, TN)**

**From Wisconsin:** "*The Mysterious Treasure of Blackberry Cove* uses a children's mystery to encourage thirty-one desirable character traits. Along the way, it is a heart-warming story of a multi-generational family, emphasizing the rich rewards possible when children (and adults) appreciate members of other generations. The catchy dialogue will make for a quick read, preferably by parent and child together. An ambitious project!" **Kathy Akey, School Librarian/Media Specialist for 36 years. Masters degrees in English and Library Science. Kohl Fellow and Wisconsin Teacher of the Year 1999-1997. (Clintonville, WI)**

**From New Jersey:** "Engaging, suspenseful with character building themes such as courage, enthusiasm, and sensitivity. Parents and developing readers alike will devour this new book while encouraging a passion for the printed page and growing in wisdom. This new book has everything."
**Darlene Yoder, B.S. degree. Physical therapist turned homeschool mother/ teacher of three for the past 13 years, with two of my "students" now in college. (Cinnaminson, NJ).**

**From Illinois:** "Dick Burkett has given children and families a great treasure in *The Mysterious Treasure of Blackberry Cove*. Parents and grandparents will appreciate their children not only reading a great story, but the positive character traits encouraged in the pages. The interactive question in the Appendix is an extra added bonus that will cause this book to have an even greater impact. A great book for children to enjoy alone or as a joint family experience! Thanks, Dick, for a great book for our kids and grandkids!" **Dr. Bob and Pam MacRae, Professors of Marriage and Family, Moody Bible Institute. (Chicago, IL)**

**From Virginia:** "Dick Burkett has achieved his goal of writing a mystery book for children that they, along with their parents/teachers/ grandparents, will enjoy reading while learning biblical character traits, vocabulary skills, and some important events in our Nation's history." **Ann Pack, B.S. Elementary Education, M. Ed Supervision and Administration. 36 years as a Teacher and Elementary Principal. She has taught Bible Clubs, Sunday School, and more for over 50 years. She presently volunteers for the County Adult Literacy Program. (Forest, VA)**

**From Michigan:** "How often does a children's book come along that not only fascinates the imagination but instructs the reader toward life-giving character? *The Mysterious Treasure of Blackberry Cove* is not merely a good read but an opportunity for children to witness character qualities fleshed out in the characters of Maggie and Dillon. Both parents and educators alike will benefit from the author's added features to assist discussion and enhance meaningful dialogue with children and students." **Patti Damiani, B.A. in Education. Taught K-8 and was Home School Coordinator for Dayton (OH) Christian School. Speaker and Teacher Trainer with churches. Director of Women's Ministry. Pastor's wife. Mother of four adult children and grandmother of 14 grandchildren. (Traverse City, MI)**

**From Pennsylvania:** "The author's style, which is faithful to the Word and builds biblical character, is complemented by vivid sketches, which both captivate and develop a child's imagination. The themes within this book, especially kindness and sensitivity, echo the approach I took while raising my daughters to 'value the preciousness of others.'" **April Lynn Springer, Studied Early Childhood Education in college. Taught K-12 in a Christian School. Taught Sunday School at Children's Hospital (PA). Mother of four daughters. (Lancaster, PA)**

**From Virginia:** "The first installment of the *Reader Whiz Kids* series, *The Mysterious Treasure of Blackberry Cove*, is a welcome and delightful addition to the world of children's literature. Funny and moving, the main characters, Maggie and Dillon, will capture the young reader's heart while at the same time encouraging the development of character traits still valuable and necessary in the world our children live in today. The historical summaries, helpful definitions, and questions in the appendices, will assist parents in family discussion that will transfer these principles from the page to everyday life. This would be a great read for the children's book clubs springing up across the country. I look forward to reading the next installment of the adventures of the *Reader Whiz* kids!." **Dawn Gessner, Speaker and Bible Teacher. Mother of three adult children. (Fairfax, VA).**

**From Illinois:** "As a parent, who does not want the best for their son or daughter? *The Mysterious Treasure of Blackberry Cove* illustrates great character qualities throughout the story and gives opportunity for parents to discuss these qualities with their children. It is a good story with the benefit of seeing these qualities we want most infused in our children, so they may grow 'in wisdom and stature, and in favor with God and men.'" **Dick Miller, Airline Captain, in U.S., Canada, Mexico, and the Caribbean. He and his wife, Ruth Ann, worked with the Wycliffe Bible Translators and the Summer Institute of Linguistics in Papua, New Guinea and Australia for 18 years. Dick served as a Mission Pilot and Ruth Ann as a Nurse. (Aurora, IL).**

**From Illinois:** "*The Mysterious Treasure of Blackberry Cove* is a springboard into hours of exploration, sparked by places, events, and nature in the story itself, then guided by thoughtful conversation outlines, historical tidbits, poetry, and song descriptions. A refreshingly delightful, down-to-earth family story chocked full of lesson of kindness, compassion, wisdom, and the fact that sometimes life is difficult and people experience emotional pain, yet God can and does forgive, heal, and restore." **Susan Colbert, Business owner, teacher, and 19-year veteran homeschooling mom of two sons and a daughter. (Naperville, IL).**

**From Pennsylvania:** "Using family as the main characters in this book will make it a cherished family treasure, but the characters and story have universal appeal to all who desire the development of strong, Bible-based traits in children and adventure in the story. Dick has mastered the writing style and story structures of the early and mid-twentieth century American children's classics. Read this book, and rejoice that God has used Dick to give us this gift for children of the twenty-first century!" **Davina Martin, B.S. Degree (Accounting). Sunday School teacher for 40 years. Youth Pastor's wife. Mother of three adult sons, grandmother of seven. (Perkasie, PA).**

**From Wisconsin:** *"The Mysterious Treasure of Blackberry Cove* is a current day mystery that reflects back to an important time in our American history. Throughout the book, readers will be inspired by character traits intended to lend guidance to today's youth. The appendices provide a structured outline, along with biblical references, for using the book to engage the readers in discussions about the traits portrayed throughout the book. Not only is the book one that could be read by individual readers, but it could also be utilized by classroom teachers for group discussion."
**Shirley Hogston, B.S. in Education, M.A. in Communication Disorders. Currently working as a Speech and Language Therapist in Clintonville Public Schools, where she has taught for the past 29 years. Member of Delta Kappa Gamma. (Clintonville, WI).**

Because of my dad's job, we moved a few times in rural Mississippi when I was a boy. My mother would always agree to the move but with three strong "musts". The town in which we were to move must have (1) a good church, (2) a good library, and (3) a good little league field. I valued from all three.

Author, John Grisham (*The Firm, Pelican Brief, A Painted House, The Testament*), in a rare speech in Waco Hall on the campus of Baylor University. February 25, 2000. [1]

# About the author.................

Dick Burkett, as most friends call him, was as fortunate as John Grisham. He was fortunate to have grown up in the great 1950's when even his hometown of Livonia (near Detroit) had trees to climb, creeks to cross, and ball fields in which to play. He was also fortunate that when it was discovered that there existed a shortage of libraries for students in the first year of the Baby Boomer generation, a wise school board established and sent Bookmobiles (portable libraries) to each of the elementary schools. Fortunate to have a kind librarian who let him reach up to the fifth grade shelves, Dick was able to extend the limited scenery of his neighborhood to the Wild West, the Oregon Trail, the Adirondack Mountains, Michigan's Upper Peninsula, and more. Dick was also fortunate to have a great church and a caring pastor in that neighborhood. Alpha Baptist Church and Pastor Younge and his wife, Lora, took time to impress Christian character in him, especially after his father died when he was fourteen.

Like John Grisham, he was influenced greatly by a wonderful mother. Rearing Dick and his three brothers and sister with very limited finances, Dee Burkett still managed to instill strong character traits in her children. She was always there with words and deeds of encouragement, even after her long hours of working in the kitchens and hallways of public schools.

Today, Dick Burkett is still fortunate. He serves a great God who has blessed him with his wife of 42 years, Darleen. She has served along side him as they have been privileged to pastor in churches in Virginia, Michigan, New Jersey, and Illinois. He also has been blessed with two great kids. Both are now grown with families of their own. He is also indebted to many friends who helped him establish *Restoration Ministries of Rockford, Illinois, Inc.* in 1994, where he continues to serve as its President and as a Marriage and Family Counselor.

The genesis of writing the *Reader Whiz Kids* series was those formative childhood years of reading this great genre of early 20th century children's mystery books. Whether it was the hard-to-put down Hardy Boys series, the great western adventures of the X Bar X Boys, the great mysteries of the Mercer Boys of Woodcrest Military Academy, or any book that took Dick down a wilderness trail, they all had great influences on him. An English major in college, it was a natural for him to pen a children's mystery series of his own—and what better resource material than that of his own grandchildren!

> "I have no greater joy than to hear my children walking in the truth." III John, verse 4

[1] Primary source notes: Author attended this speech while visiting his son, a student at Baylor.